Shoes and Other Stories

Robert Herrmann

BookLocker, St. Petersburg, Florida

Published by BookLocker.com, Inc., St. Petersburg, Florida.

Printed on acid-free paper.

The characters and events in this book are fictitious. Any similarity to real persons, living or dead, is coincidental and not intended by the author.

BookLocker.com, Inc.
2020

First Edition

TO LINDA

Always there. She has given shape to my soul.

In Memory:
*

Robert *Bobby* Brennan
1976 --- 2019
At peace after the storm.

Acknowledgements

I could not have written these stories without the help and support of the following people:

My late father, Robert and my mother, Julia, who filled our home with books, art, music and love. My siblings – Wendy, Laurie and Alan; we played, searched and gathered. And we shared and grew. All three have been teachers (I am in awe!) and at this moment, each one is a talented artist. My daughters, Amy and Katie – through the years, they have patiently listened to my clumsy *life* lessons and now I attentively enjoy the wise eloquence of their own optimistic and enthusiastic observations. My sister-in-law, Sara Herrmann, who edited many of these stories and in her bright and gentle manner, taught me to trust the reader.

Rick Ohler – our friendship has spanned over a half century. He has been steadfast, following a daily discipline, bearing the responsibility of a prize winning columnist. For over three decades Rick has shared his knowledge and expertise as a writers group leader; hundreds have passed through the tender confidence of his tutelage. His love and influence has been invaluable.

The writers group itself. The passion alone is palpable. A place of sharing, not just writing – our fears, hopes, tragedies, successes – we all feel the security of having each other's back. Barb Taylor, a long standing member of the group has been exceptionally supportive. After reading my stories, she stated,

"These shouldn't be hidden away in a drawer. They need to be read."

Glimmer Train, the acclaimed three decades-long literary journal. In one of its seasonal contests, my short story, *Madeleine*, was an honorable mention. I appreciate the kind and encouraging words, a clarion call to push onward.

To the many family and friends who read my work and urged me to continue. And to anyone that I've crossed paths with, who might've said, "Hey, look at that," or "Did you hear about...?"

Table of Contents

Madeleine

It was raining in the morning, a steady downpour that nibbled Roger Grigson's face as he looked down Main Street for the bus. He was three hours late for work, hungover and dressed in the cleanest of his dirty work clothes. Two women stood nearby, close together under an umbrella. They were there before he had arrived and they didn't talk to each other, but assumed the same distant and expecting gaze as Grigson. Perhaps they didn't know each other and the one who owned the umbrella had offered to share it. He imagined there must have been conversation at that point, at least in the offering. It gave him a small measure of good feeling, this act of sharing, but he was glad he hadn't arrived first. He wouldn't have wanted to stand under it with the owner and the idea of refusing it would have been troubling. And even if they were strangers and he had come first and had accepted the small shelter, Grigson thought, he certainly would have surrendered it to the other woman.

These ruminations suddenly struck him as silly and Grigson shook his head as if the motion would help expel them. Generally, there was a pleasure and a happy familiarity in these ponderings about people, but now it felt annoying. Occasionally, one of the women would look at him with the blank, non-committal stare of a city dweller and he would turn away. He scanned the uneven rooflines and lowered his eyes to the throng of traffic, the sizzling of displaced water adding to the chaotic sounds. Grigson noticed flooding around a tree growing out of a square cut into the sidewalk. The small trees were planted as part of a plan to dress up the city. He remembered last summer, the workmen showing up in two trucks. They had taken turns using the jackhammer.

Now there was the neat square and a thin, bare tree emerging. Grigson imagined it choking on the sitting water. When the traffic light changed at the near corner, vehicles lined up and people stared at him. He looked away and focused on the tree again. Grigson wished it was summer instead of March and the tree was laden with green so the people looked at it instead of himself. He felt very low in his shabby work clothes, the collar of the faded jacket wet against his neck and the saturated cap pressing on his head. He wasn't used to feeling this way, ashamed to be going to work late, having overslept and then awoken too nauseous to leave his apartment. He had considered calling in, but he could picture the short-handed crew in the already understaffed warehouse thrown against the overwhelming workload. He had not lived up to his commitment and now they would be hard at it, cursing his name. It was a catch-up game and Grigson had little heart for it as he thought about the previous night. Some of it was lost in dark empty holes, but there were pieces as sharp and clear as shame itself.

It was not so much the play that Grigson had been looking forward to. It had started that way, three years ago as a simple interest in an art form that had always excited him. Years before, he had secretly envied his brother and sister who performed in high school productions. He found it remarkable, the transformation from Tom and Sheila Grigson into Reverend Parris and Abigail Williams in Arthur Miller's *The Crucible* and then back to themselves at the dinner table the next evening. His mother had suggested he try it and he had feigned a scoffing attitude, recognizing a fear too large for him to overcome. But he was always happy to have the opportunity to see a live performance and he had bought season tickets for the local professional theater. A play would usually run four to six weeks. Grigson looked forward to them. Sometimes he would go to the library and read them first, but he wasn't sure if it had any impact on his appreciation of the performances.

The first year he purchased two tickets and had taken his girlfriend, Liz, but she had broken up with him early in the season. There had been a conflict on a Thursday night (their couples' league bowling night) and Grigson wanted badly to see Sam Shepard's, *Fool For Love.* He tried to exchange the tickets for another night, but it was sold out throughout its run. Although Grigson had no intention of forgoing the performance, he attempted to reason with Liz, citing the long bowling season as already excessive. He had never warmed up to the sport and hadn't bowled since he was a child, but Liz's best friend and her husband belonged to the league and had implored her to join. Grigson had been a little curious, having noticed how everyone seemed to be having so much fun at a bowling alley; voices were heightened, faces rounded in open and competitive joy and the hard surface noises of the sport – so loud with the literally rolling suspense. He had realized within an hour of the first night in September that he hated it. The prospect of the long season that stretched into May seemed unbearable. When Liz protested giving up a night of bowling for the play, he had portrayed the weekly event as "brutishly boring," and her friends as "robotically banal."

Liz's head reared from the one-two combinations. She didn't know what 'banal' meant although he could tell she didn't like the sound of it. Stopping to define the word in her mind was akin to turning the knife.

"Why you fucking twerp," she had said. "You really think you're better than everyone else."

"Of course I don't," he said. "I just get bored with the sameness."

"Too *banal* for you?" she had said. "Only an asshole like you would even know a word like that existed."

There was no turning back at that point. Grigson lamented the loss of her although he had always known the relationship wasn't meant for the long haul. He had met her the past summer at Tangos, a neighborhood tavern only a couple blocks from his apartment. The slow-pitch softball team he played for met there after their games, as did Liz's team. Grigson was a marginal player, a third catcher among three catchers on the team and he usually played two or three innings a game. He was actually more scared than eager to play, not being able to erase the possible humiliation of error from his mind. But he had found in this a strange and attractive exhilaration. Liz, on the other hand, was an aggressive athlete, a shortstop and team captain. One night after a game Grigson sat quietly at the bar, having grown tired of the many replays of the game at the team table. Scotty, the bartender placed an empty shot glass upside down in front of him.

"Lady wants to buy you a drink," he said. "But she said you have to smile first."

Scotty nodded toward Liz with an expression on his face that told Grigson he'd be a dumb shit if he didn't smile immediately. He looked up and he felt the smile erupt the minute he saw her. She was simply beautiful and he had long before taken note of her, silently agreeing with a teammate one night as they watched her shoot pool that she had an incredible ass. She told him openly that she was determined to have him. Grigson, who considered himself an average looking guy and far from exciting, wondered about this. Although he felt shallow thinking along these lines and he doubted there was much of a future, the fact was he'd gone berserk with desire. Even though it irked him to see himself as a kind of man he generally detested, somehow he had let that slide. But Grigson was always aware that they were a very different pair. From the beginning she didn't hide the fact she thought him a bit odd, observing how he had his softball jersey pulled off at the end of the game while the rest of the team wore them to Tangos.

"It's like you're embarrassed to wear it," she had said.

He told her he wasn't embarrassed, but he didn't want to be diluted into the sum of the team identity. She also thought it very strange that Grigson didn't own a car.

"I'm an urbanite," he said. "I don't need one."

Liz taught physical education at a local high school. She coached the girls' basketball and softball teams and she seemed to love all sports. She carried this jockish zeal into the bedroom. Liz had been an athletic and vigorous lover, shouting out orders and giving precise directions that had Grigson scrambling and sometimes persevering into what she called "extra innings." One night Grigson had drunk too much and struggled to perform under her demanding tutelage. He finally gave up, flopped heavily on his back and sarcastically called it a "rain out." Liz had been determined not to miss a stroke and shoved him aside with her elbow in the manner of a basketball player clearing under the boards and masturbated to an orgasm while he lay quietly next to her. Watching this had reawakened his libido and he timidly asked her for deliverance. Afterward, Liz chastised him for her "double duty" and fell asleep. Grigson had lain awake and struggled with a taint of shame and smallness. He remembered a phrase his grandfather had used to describe the feeling – *like a penny asking for change.* There was a fair measure of relief at their breakup, but he knew there would be nights when he would miss her.

After the breakup Grigson realized he preferred to go to the theater alone. The three hours he spent were too poignant and demanding for him to share. Once he had taken a theater major to see *Of Mice and Men,* adapted from the Steinbeck novel. Grigson enjoyed the play and was moved to tears a couple times. She thought it was a better movie, explaining that place was very important in Steinbeck's work and the production had suffered without it. She supported her critique with an account of her visit to California and a day spent in Steinbeck's beloved Salinas Valley. "You can feel his presence there," she said. Grigson's travels had the same limited scope as Thoreau's – far and wide in Buffalo, but he had recently re-read the novel. He observed very clearly the lean, but atmospheric narrative and he felt the characters' interaction and the concurrent dialogue was its strength. He kept this to himself, unable to muster the industry and mental stamina required for a debate. He regretted he had asked her along as it whittled away the magic that he derived from the performance.

Grigson requested only one seat for the following season, but he upgraded. He moved into the center section and closer to the stage although the theater was designed for a decent view from any seat. The first night he had been held up at work and he arrived just after the lights flashed and the doors were closed. The usher had given him a frown of disapproval and he whispered an apology and took the playbill. Everyone was settled and the lights went off as Grigson was crossing the row to his seat. He felt a small rounded obstacle underfoot and a muffled cry of pain passed in the darkness. He sat and turned to the face inches away, vaguely illuminated on one side from the stage and looking squarely at him.

"Sorry," he said.

She had turned without reply toward the stage. He could sense the movement of her foot, seeking the capsized shoe and the lifting and dropping of her leg as the foot returned. Grigson struggled through a calming process that at first had him paralyzed. He felt large and oafish. Grigson gripped his upper legs and tried to capture the action on stage, but the actors seemed excessively loud and their words were blunt and solid on his brain. He suffered in this state until they entered into a dialogue that was a string of humorous counterpunches, each line funnier and playing on the preceding line – the audience's laughter building in waves with each quip. By the time he was able to decipher the humor, it had subsided. The laughter died, except the woman next to him expelled a lingering giggle and he heard her whisper on her other side. That she had laughed was enough for him to relax a little.

At intermission Grigson turned her way with the hope of reaffirming his apology, but she was already moving out the other side. He didn't want to follow her, but the man to his left was portly and still sitting. He went up the aisle with her a little ahead and he had to hang back, feeling momentarily like a rock in rushing water as she stopped to talk to someone seated by the aisle. He wanted to avoid engaging her as they shuffled out, feeling the moving crowd not an appropriate place for his imagined conversation and it was too easy to fall prey to eavesdroppers. After she moved on he went to the small bar in the lounge and ordered a scotch and water. Grigson enjoyed this respite. He thought it turned the focus on the watchers. It was one of the few times he could think of that people *en masse* carried themselves with a calm and thoughtful dignity. He thought of them as half in and half out – their minds still subdued and sponge-like, carrying the breezy freight of the play into their little circles, scattered about the lounge and some outside the large glass doors, their voices muffled and cigarette smoke rising above them.

Grigson saw the back of the woman, talking to her companion. Her black hair was swept back and fastened, exposing her ears and dangling silver earrings that shook as she talked. She wore a dark navy suit that contrasted the slice of her white collared blouse and accented the olive tone of her skin. She struck him as "tasteful" although he didn't care much for the word. He had learned it from a tasteful mother and two sisters who seemed to give a certain weight and importance to it. Grigson always thought it too ambiguous, but watching the woman made him wonder. When the lights flashed he quickly returned to his seat. He was leafing through the playbill as she made her way down the aisle. She gave him a nod as she sat down.

"I'm sorry about stepping on your foot," he said.

"Oh, don't worry about it," she replied. "It startled me more than hurt me."

"These clodhoppers of mine can be deadly," he said.

"Really, it was nothing" she said, "Are you enjoying the performance?"

"Very much," he lied. "I like this seat."

Grigson pointed in the direction of his former seats although he recognized it as a silly gesture. The woman turned and nodded and her companion followed her gaze. The woman introduced her friend as Gail and she extended her hand.

"I'm Madeleine," she said.

- - -

Looking back to that introduction, Grigson was upset with himself because he had forgotten her name. He could still hear it in the framework of her voice and the rolling of its brief rhythm, but the name itself dissolved the moment it was presented. Her eyes had an appealing and captivating reach; they were alive in their depth and darkness (a brown almost black) and flooded all his senses. This sort of thing happened quite often to Grigson. His mind would wander in conversation. Something about the person would catch his eye or a random thought would somehow become associated with what was said and he'd be off on his own wayward trip. This usually cost him the person's name and sometimes what was being said. Grigson was aware of the possibility and it was just a matter of being alert to ward it off, but somehow he failed.

Five weeks later he was still searching for her name. It was Thursday night and Grigson was sitting at Tangos, sipping a scotch and water in what the regulars called his "theater duds": the same white shirt, gray tweed sport coat, khaki pants and one of his two neckties. The drink was a ritual on theater night and they found it amusing since he otherwise drank the cheapest draft beer that was offered. They couldn't help commenting among themselves and snickering at this display of ennoblement and they fondly referred to him as "Sir Roger." Grigson was unaware of the title, but he knew they considered him as something apart. He would've been unhappy to know of its elevated nature. A classmate during Grigson's one semester at college had introduced him to Tangos. He was instantly comfortable in the worn and eclectic atmosphere and loved the quality of light that gradually diminished from the large front windows and tunneled to the area of the pool table. This gave the tavern a long and narrow appearance, what he thought of stereotypically as a city bar. During the daytime Tangos was frequented by an older, mostly male crowd – some retired, some unemployable and some workers who came for lunch and a couple of quick ones. A few of these would eventually join the unemployables. At night, especially on a weekend, college students packed the place and the jukebox was turned up. The people seated at the bar were constantly shifting their heads to accommodate the passing of money and drinks to the crowd behind them. He preferred the bar at the end of the day and into the early evening although on this evening not being able to remember the woman's name still troubled him.

The news was on TV and there were small outbursts of opinions. Grigson heard none of it as he again went through the alphabet. His concentration was broken by a slap on the back. Simon Eddy leaned over his shoulder. He was somewhere in his mid-fifties but he looked at least twenty years older. He set his glass down, the contents a whitish syrupy swirl (whiskey and milk to mollify an ulcer) and gripped the bar rail.

"Nose runn'n pisspots," he said.

Grigson knew he was talking about the group of young men at the other end of the bar. Simon had been over there lamenting his baseball career. Everyone knew the story: a quick rise to Triple A and then an abrupt and freakish ending when an inside fastball had caught him in the head. A scar ran up to his hairline from his right eye, lost in the incident and now made of glass. Simon had a habit of running his index finger along it, giving the impression that the injury had just occurred. After three drinks it was all he talked about. Simon turned to Grigson in a half circle of small, shuffling steps.

"Used to knock them out of the park as a lefty," he said. His good eye rode the ceiling. "And I was damn good the other way too. They used to call me Both Way Eddy."

"I heard," Grigson replied.

"Those little bastards down there call me No Way Eddy."

Grigson had heard that too. He looked into the man's eyes, both moist and the one red-rimmed. White hair coiled from under the Yankee cap, contrasted his ruddy face, the brownish nose etched with purple veins. He was usually gone by now, picked up by Loren, his daughter. She drove cab and stopped by after her shift. Normally she'd be there after Simon had only had a couple, but whenever she was late, drink got the better of him. Grigson also knew that she had a thing for him. Simon told him and he'd invited him to their house for dinner a few times. He declined as he thought Loren was a little too young, somewhere in her early twenties. Grigson imagined Simon years before with his life suddenly fractured after the uphill promise. Now he appeared perpetually dazed. Loren, when she arrived, resembled a young mother looking after offspring in a rowdy playground.

"Oh Daddy," she said. "Mom won't be happy."

Simon was allotted only enough money for two drinks. The rest he bummed or borrowed even though Loren repeatedly asked the patrons to refuse him.

"She doesn't have to know," Simon said. His eye moved outward with an offering of conspiracy. He turned a phantom key in front of his mouth.

"Do you think he'll get away with it?" she asked Grigson.

He saw the small twist of her lip – the wryness of the smile.

"Not a chance," he said. "He can't even charm those nit-wits at the end of the bar."

"I know," she said. "But Mom's special. Every day she pays homage to him, gives him a taste of the glory. He won't even remember the shit those assholes throw at him here."

"What do they know?"

"They come here like everyone else," she said. "To fill a dull moment and wait for a great one."

"I guess," Grigson said, glancing at his watch. "Gotta run."

"Play night," she said. "Need a lift?"

"No thanks," he replied. "I get the bus right at the corner."

"It's no trouble," she said. "Dad'll be asleep before I pull away from the curb."

"Naw," he said. "It's part of my ritual."

"Yeah, right," she said. "I didn't mean to intrude."

"No," Grigson said. "It's just something I do…"

"I get it," she said.

Loren hooked her arm under her father's and led him out the front door. Simon called out, "Later, lads" with a wave to the young men clustered at the bar. They didn't respond. Grigson returned to the mystery of the woman's name as he finished his drink.

He arrived at the theater early. In his seat with the playbill in his lap, Grigson replayed the situation of five weeks before when he had met the woman, hoping that it might trigger his memory. A few moments later she approached.

"Hi Rog," she said.

He had always hated the shortening of his name. The one-stroke outburst with the mouth yawning, sometimes too long depending on the speaker and then closing the gate with the quick toss of "ja" was obscene to him. However, somehow she avoided that delivery and the name slid out as a sleek and delicate missile.

"Madeleine," he responded, the name suddenly surfacing and falling from his lips.

"Please," she said. "Call me Maddy."

- - -

Perhaps Grigson had been overly affected by his preoccupation and struggle in recapturing the name, or maybe it was the result of the miraculous moment of recovery, but he found it impossible to comply with her request to use the shortened name. He continued to call her Madeleine in the ensuing three months and she never corrected him. It took that long for him to realize she had unwittingly infiltrated his senses. It was as if his mind had been lent out to someone else and upon its return her existence was added to its contents. Grigson had a way of picturing his mind as a vast storeroom lined with long aisles of stacked shelving. A few years back at his ten-year high school reunion, this idea suddenly blossomed as he was attempting to seduce Jennifer Hewitt, a classmate he had barely known. Grigson explained to her that although their paths had rarely crossed, her presence had made a definite impact. He always thought of her as attractive and desirable and she held a place on a special shelf in his mind. To support this claim he cited a specific party a few years back where they had briefly talked. Jennifer warmed to this vision, partly because of the many glasses of draft beer she had consumed, but also because it seemed to offer more historical substance, deposing the notion of her as something totally new and previously unrecognized. They made love that night and frequently for three weeks afterward, but then it fizzled to an emotional standstill. Talking seemed to be the problem. Luckily, they both recognized the demise with a small degree of disappointment. They were actually apologetic to each other as one would be after recommending a restaurant and the chef had botched the meal. They walked away from each other without any heart tromping or bruised egos and with a pledge of long lasting friendship that naturally failed.

Since then Grigson could sometimes picture his mind as this intricate and accessible structure, but the sudden presence of Madeleine rendered it obsolete. She was simply there and he was surprised and overwhelmed by a hunger he couldn't deny. Each encounter remained bubble-like, as a transparent fortification. Grigson replayed them and there was a nagging anxiety that a detail might somehow escape; he could actually picture them in liquid form, trailing over a ledge and out of sight.

The fourth meeting was the most vivid and revealing although he felt defensive about his livelihood and then foolish for his defensiveness. The play was Tennessee William's *The Glass Menagerie* and Grigson felt self-conscious about some similarities between the character, Tom, and himself. Earlier Madeliene coincidently asked him what he did for a living.

21

"I work in a warehouse," he replied.

"I see," she said.

Grigson knew she had seen nothing at all. He had long regarded it as an invisible occupation. He had fallen into it as a part-timer while he was in college and extended to full-time when he dropped out and his parents would no longer pay for his portion of an apartment he shared with three other students. They hoped the financial strangulation would force him to reconsider, but Grigson enjoyed the taste of freedom and was determined to sustain himself.

He had been raised in a picturesque village, insulated by a twenty-mile stretch of receding suburbs and open farmland. He found the city to be exotic and exciting by comparison. But, he soon found his college roommates, all high school friends, had become boring and obnoxious. They couldn't let go of their former lives, dragging along residual attitudes and prejudices even though they professed to be liberal and open-minded. Grigson found a small, furnished two-room apartment that he could afford. It was basically a kitchen and a living room with a fold out couch and the bathroom wasn't much bigger than a closet. The toilet and shower stall were so close his feet rested inside when he sat on the toilet. He had to shave over the kitchen sink. Grigson fancifully compared his quarters to Vincent van Gogh's, *Vincent's Bedroom* at Arles and he bought a copy of the print and hung it over his couch. The warehouse didn't pay much, but he was usually available for overtime and he was able to afford his simple life.

There were moments when Grigson felt defensive about his work. It troubled him that he felt it in the presence of Madeleine and he told her something that was only slightly less than a lie.

"I'm an artist," he said, feeling instantly gratified with the slight lift of her head and an appealing acceptance in her eyes.

Grigson knew he had little to support this claim, only a sketchbook that he rarely opened and a set of watercolors he purchased after seeing a Winslow Homer exhibit. He struggled with the paints, exercising an unrealistic and naïve optimism that betrayed his lack of discipline and patience. Grigson's pencil drawings were slightly better, but he could never depend on a favorable outcome. Each start became a wild and unpredictable journey marked by a growing tenseness that slowly eroded his intentions, but he felt an instant delight in Madeleine's reaction, ignoring the glaring truth of the thinness and marginal quality of his body of work.

She had asked him about his influences and he became nervous and mentioned van Gogh, Homer and Monet. He would have liked to come up with something more obscure, searching his memory back to a period when he briefly dated an art history major, but nothing emerged.

"Modigliani?" she asked.

"I'm not that familiar with sculpture," he replied, thinking it was the name of a statue by Renior.

"Well, you know he had to give it up," she said. "I think he had TB, but I was referring to his paintings."

"Oh yeah," Grigson said, but he felt the sudden panic of vulnerability, the slippery slope of not knowing exactly what he was talking about. He remembered a similar situation years ago at a party when he told a circle of people that he thought Jethro Tull was an underrated flutist.

"How about you?" he asked, eager to change the subject. "What do you do?"

"I'm in interior design," she said. "Gail and I are partners."

"Oh, nice," he said. "That must be exciting."

"Well yes," she said. "It can be."

Grigson had only a vague idea of interior design. He couldn't understand why anyone would pay to have their home decorated. He considered a person's domestic surroundings an extension of themselves, the atmosphere created by a natural and random accumulation that marked the journey. Grigson thought it strange that someone would give this up to a self-appointed expert's direction. And he couldn't help asking her.

"Well, for the most part," Madeleine replied, "my clients are businesses and organizations."

She explained to Grigson how the nature of the environment could be critical in gaining a specific reaction from a customer or patient.

"Can you imagine Edvard Munch's, *The Scream* in a doctor's or dentist's office?" she said. "Or a Jackson Pollack in a mental hospital?"

Grigson chuckled, his mind drifting to an imagined nude in a nursery school. He remembered a trip to the Albright-Knox Art Gallery as a kid – his brother, sisters and he standing in front of a huge naked female statue, sitting with her legs spread and all of them crowded between her knees and staring into her pubis. His mother had been on the other side of the room, momentarily lost in a colorful Redon still life. She whispered, "Doesn't it remind you of mommy's garden?" The lack of response caused her to wheel around, the quick panic in her eyes turning to embarrassment as she bolted across the room and whisked her tittering brood away.

He asked her how she had become involved in her work and Madeleine told him she started as an art major and eventually received a degree in art history. She spent a semester in Siena, Italy, where she met Gail, who at the time worked summers for an interior decorator in Manhattan. They became fast friends and Gail helped her gain employment in the firm where they both continued after graduation. After a couple of years, the family owned business became too restrictive and they finally broke away and moved to Buffalo to start their own business.

"We found between the two of us a solid bond," she said. "We seemed to be able to combine our strengths." Grigson couldn't help feeling envious of her success. Often he puzzled at the good fortune of others, as if they had unlocked an incredible and elusive secret, well beyond his reach. At the end of the play this feeling festered into a dismal pall of self-loathing, magnified by the comparisons of the character, Tom. Madeleine asked him if he thought the character was realistic. Grigson answered in a self-deprecating manner, giving the impression a warehouse was a form of purgatory and its inhabitants simple and unsophisticated.

"Why the first time I came to the theater," he said, "I went to the lobby and ordered a box of popcorn."

She laughed, but the remark seemed to fade their remaining conversation into stodgy farewells.

- - -

The following week Grigson suffered from a toothache. It had started a couple of months before as a distant and infrequent tingle. In the past week it escalated into a nasty companion to his every breath. He attempted to work at the small table in the kitchen at some pencil sketches, but the pain was too large an obstacle. This shamed him, thinking of the elderly Matisse managing his graceful cutouts from a sickbed and something he read somewhere about Hemingway writing while standing up due to injuries from a plane crash.

He took a bus to his family's dentist, thinking he might stop home afterward. In the waiting room of the dentist Grigson leafed through a copy of *Buffalo Spree* magazine, a monthly publication that included articles on local sights and events and portraits of prominent people in the community – a selective and attractive overview of the area. Expensive and finely photographed advertising showcased varied businesses throughout its pages. He read a short article about a successful television producer in New York City who was a native and a graduate of Buffalo State and turned the page to find Madeleine and Gail in a half page advertisement. The moment of discovery took Grigson's breath away. He closed the magazine with his thumbs between the pages and threw it open again. The glossy image jumped at him. In the photograph, Madeliene and Gail were standing at the far end of a table in front of a large oriental wall hanging. The table was dark and polished, reflecting light coming from somewhere in front of the picture. There was a tall jade vase on the table and to the right a man sat. He was handsome and well-groomed in a gray suit and his black hair glistened. He was looking up at Madeliene who returned his smile with, what struck Grigson as an expression of intimate fondness.

In the dentist's chair while undergoing a root canal, Grigson wondered about the man. He thought he might be an actor or model, based on his comeliness; he was too good looking to be a client, but then reconsidered having observed how a favorable gene pool had a way of accompanying the financially successful. He couldn't imagine less than prosperous companies seeking her services. He fought off a stirring of jealousy amid diggings into his stretched mouth. Grigson pressed his eyes closed and focused on her face in the photograph. Afterward he hurried into the waiting room to find the magazine in the hands of an old woman. Grigson jogged to the drug store to buy it, not sure if it was a recent issue. He was in luck although he turned to the page for reassurance. He decided not to visit his family; he was too excited and he opened and closed the page at least a hundred times on the bus ride into the city.

Grigson cut out the picture and tacked it to the wall above the kitchen table. He carefully sliced the man out, losing a portion of Gail's arm in the process. He knew this created a hint of mystery as Madeleine's gaze was now directed out of the picture. Although Grigson certainly knew the quality of the look wouldn't change, he invented the strange hope that the subject of it could. He took some comfort, remembering the equitable expression – the warmth of her eyes on him as he had proclaimed himself as an artist, but the shadow of deception nullified the effect. The vacancy now outside the picture became a destination and Grigson thought he knew what it would take to get there.

This photograph became the first thing he looked for when he entered the apartment. Sometimes he would march to the table and sit in the chair, his face inches away and his eyes seeking a deeper dimension. He found much in the pose; the upward shift of her right hip created a dark rounded curve and a solid foundation for the flexuous stretching of her upper body. Very casual and candid, he thought. And carefree. The white blouse was loose, but the light from above filtered through and defined her shape. Her facial expression was welcoming with eyes amused and familiar. Grigson gathered, perhaps beyond the picture, a strong sensuousness that sometimes overpowered him and led him into self-pleasuring, but in other moments the passion was more cerebral.

The photograph became the subject of his renewed interest in drawing although the image proved to be far too powerful and elusive for him to capture. He attempted different sketching styles, but nothing worked and the building frustration led him to Tangos. He wanted the tavern to serve as a place of *reentry*, a romantic notion he had read about in an interview of a writer – something he saw clearly as a just reward for the fruits of his labor, but his sense of failure muddied the vision. After two or three drinks the situation seemed more tolerable, but after two or three more he became inflamed with self-abhorrence. Everything around him dropped a notch and bore resemblance to the feeling. Grigson, in creating the strain of truth regarding himself as an artist, had shaken his world. What had been a small and whimsical sideline in his life was thrust to the forefront, as an impatient and demanding mistress. One evening Grigson returned from the tavern and reviewed the drawings he had attempted earlier. He compared them to others from previous days and realized nothing had changed; he was spinning his wheels in the same stagnant mud pit.

The next evening Grigson took the bus to a mall just outside the city line. It had rained an hour earlier and he noticed the varied hues of the colorful signage along the way, reflected in puddles and smeared along the damp road surface. He also noticed how shadows moved and changed shape in relation to light. Grigson was already aware of this, but somehow there was something different in his understanding and appreciation. In the bookstore at the mall he spent an hour in the Art section. Grigson flipped through a book on van Gogh and then Gauguin. He remembered they actually knew each other and had lived together for a short time. He wondered how it was, sharing the same artistic hunger along with the daily routines of living. He recalled there had been strife and they had split, but he imagined there had to be some wonderful moments between them. Grigson felt a shiver of happiness contemplating this kinship and he felt he had entered a new realm of understanding. He bought a smaller sketchbook, pencils, a book on sketching and a backpack. He realized, with an embarrassing sense of over dramatization, a deal had been made, that he was in fact answering a calling.

Grigson experienced an overwhelming anxiety as he opened the new sketchbook. He read the introductory pages, but quickly forgot the author's message; *"...you do not have to feel that anyone is looking over your shoulder, nor that you have anything to prove visually or technically."* His fingers were clammy around the pencil as he attacked the paper. A few moments later he paused and examined the still life of an apple in front of a wine bottle. Grigson couldn't help referencing the book for a comparison. He found there was nothing close enough, but within the search of many examples in a variety of styles and mediums (he thought them all fascinating and attractive) he discovered there was a definite validity in his drawing. He quickly moved on to three more sketches since he wanted to possess a *body of work* opposed to one flimsy representation. He figured if he did three a day, within a week he would have over twenty, which seemed substantial.

At the end of the week Grigson's sketchbook contained twenty-seven drawings, but he found that this statistic was no longer relevant. He had chosen his subjects randomly from inside the apartment and they ranged in size and complexity. Grigson began to carry the sketchbook in his backpack and after a while he overcame an initial self-consciousness that had caused him to cover his work as a grade-schooler fends off a cheater and he freely drew whatever caught his eye. It could be problematic on the bus if he viewed something outside during a short stop, the impulse to capture very strong, creating the frustrating anxiety as it moved away. Grigson developed a way of freezing an image in his mind and scratching a quick likeness; he later recounted outstanding highlights and added them. Sometimes the additions were too complex for the moment and he wrote them as notes in the sketchbook, the words small and enclosed in bubbles like the dialogue of a comic book.

Grigson liked to imagine Madeleine's presence, hidden in the shadows as a tender phantasm that kept a vigil over his progress. He played it as a game – seeing how long and vividly he could conjure up her image, enabled by the reassuring backup of her photograph on the wall. But strangely, the image faded – a crumbling of texture, a withdrawal of light and even the photograph began to lose vivication and a slow panic invaded Grigson and he counted the days until their next meeting at the theater. In December he was excited to see *A Christmas Carol*, but he struggled through the first act when Madeleine and Gail hadn't shown up. During intermission, as Grigson sat gloomily at the bar, he saw her enter the lobby and was overwhelmed with relief. However, he was stymied with a Christmas-wrapped brooch in his sport coat pocket, a gift he had intended to give her – a plan that he felt impossible to accomplish now that the timing had distorted his original vision of the presentation.

In late January Madeleine and Gail were both suntanned, having spent a week in Florida. At intermission Grigson couldn't keep his eyes off her as she and Gail talked with another woman in the lobby. He fought an impulse to tell her of his artistic progress, realizing it would expose him as a novice. He had brought along the brooch, but again the timing didn't feel right.

Grigson welcomed this time of year as it offered a respite from the unavoidable upheaval of the holidays. He pictured it as turning a corner with a sudden fresh view: flat and serene and the vague promise of spring somewhere on the horizon. He fell into a subtle rhythm and continued sketching every day, adding his lunch break at work. Grigson ignored his co-workers' heckling, knowing they'd tire of it after a few days. He moved around the vast building and was amazed at the wealth of subjects and more so, the existence of color – dulled and dusty, but somehow beautiful. This revelation brought a desire to paint, but he approached it diffidently by making simple pen or pencil drawings and adding basic washes. He liked the effect and he was proud of his newfound calm and patience.

Grigson began sitting at one of the small tables at Tangos instead of the bar. He noticed a few raised eyebrows and some curious glances as he sketched, but he didn't care. One night Simon Eddy sat with him and Grigson produced a series of sketches of the old man. Grigson promised him a more colorful rendering in a couple days.

"With my Yankee cap?" he asked.

"Of course," Grigson replied.

"What about my bad eye?'"

"You still won't be able to see out of it,"

Grigson enlarged the portrait, sketching with pen and washing the highlights – the whiteness of his hair, the navy cap and a touch of redness around his cheeks. He carefully charged his eyes with cobalt blue, slightly different in each one. He thought he had captured it. Grigson sandwiched the picture between two pieces of cardboard and wrapped it in old newspaper and carried it into Tangos, but Simon Eddy wasn't there.

"He's in the hospital," Scotty said.

"He okay?"

"I guess so," Scotty said with a shrug. "His ulcer's acting up. Loren stopped in last night and told us."

"Is it serious?"

"I don't think so," he replied. "It's happened before. Loren didn't seem worried."

Later in his apartment, Grigson unwrapped the picture. The idea of keeping it smothered in paper while Simon Eddy recovered was too disconcerting. He felt it was his best work and he tacked it to the kitchen wall with other sketches he favored. The portrait possessed its own vitality, an innate honesty that suggested a substantial life. Grigson was giddy with this realization and he felt nourished even though he was aware of the simplicity of the picture with its slight degree of difficulty. As always he regarded the photograph of Madeleine, glossy and centered among his drawings. It had been a longtime since Grigson attempted to draw the photograph although the inability had haunted him. With renewed confidence he tried, but within minutes he felt as one on a journey without a destination. Again he regarded the photograph, pulling it away from the wall and studying it at close range, hunched under the shade of the table lamp. He stared, his eyes forced wide and searching. Nothing came back and Grigson knew part of it was the pose – her body shifted to one side with her gaze reaching out of the picture. He wanted her front and center, to be able to draw her as he had Simon Eddy.

He searched his memory for a glimpse that would help him, realizing the nature of their relationship would not permit it. It was so rare, he thought, when they had actually faced each other. He had been uncomfortable, feeling intrusive, the few times he turned to look at her with her face so close. However, he was determined and he decided to break down what he saw in the photograph and what he remembered from their encounters. Grigson began a series of sketches from different vantage points, emphasizing different features. The first few were without much detail in pen or pencil, focusing on shape and sometimes color that he added as washes. He didn't fuss with these and looked at them quickly, knowing he was essentially after something beyond reality. He would've felt foolish saying this to anyone, but he understood its truth.

Although Grigson continued his daily sketches of random subjects, he reserved time each evening in his apartment to add to the Madeleine series. He had gone back to the book and studied the variety of sketching styles and he tried some of them. To accommodate this expansion, he bought a set of pastels, a box of crayons and colored pencils. Each effort opened a new frontier and challenged him and soon he had a collection tacked to the opposite wall of different aspects of Madeleine – some of her face, her body (in different poses), eyes, an ear, a hand, some detailed some vague; all were in different mediums and styles. The photograph slowly became ineffectual as he became more dependent upon his imagination. He took liberties, drawing some nudes – projecting his preferences of nipple size, pubic hair density, and the shape of her buttocks. In evaluating this growing body of work, Grigson found something valid in each piece and he found he couldn't discard or even exclude those that didn't measure up. The wall became a celebration of parts, a cluster of images dependent on each other to sum up the whole.

In March Grigson decided to give Madeleine one of his pictures. It was a pencil sketch of her face, slightly turned and exposing one ear with a dangling earring. This and a nude were his favorites and he held them both, but he knew presenting the latter was out of the question so he returned the nude to the wall. The picture was small, the size of an index card and he had first wrapped it in red with a silver ribbon, but he reconsidered because it seemed too formal, opting instead for plain brown bag paper. Grigson was perplexed about the brooch, not wanting to overload the situation so he decided to take it along with the idea of presenting it only if the situation felt right. He fantasized how this might happen, building on the look in her eye when he had proclaimed himself as an artist.

- - -

Grigson, his mind adrift, didn't see the bus approach. It was suddenly there with the hiss of airbrakes and the clamor of the unfolding door. The two women waddled together and stopped at the door where one of them collapsed the umbrella and they ducked inside. Grigson followed and sat in an empty seat against the window. When the bus moved on his mind went back to the previous day. In the warehouse a purchasing error had resulted in an overload of inbound freight. The situation worsened when a co-worker became ill and Grigson had to put in some overtime, but he was able to not stay too long by promising to come in an hour early the next morning.

Grigson had been looking forward to his ritual – a leisurely shower and dinner at Tangos. Instead he rushed through the shower and dressed quickly, although he had been uncertain which tie to wear and he had tried them both on and finally had chosen the first. Then he bungled the knot and had to re-tie it. He ate a peanut butter and jelly sandwich standing in the kitchen and survived a close call of a glob of grape jelly oozing out and falling within inches of his white shirt. On the bus Grigson fingered the wrapped picture in his sport coat pocket and fought off a temptation to open it. The ride downtown was a blur, his usual hunger for observation overwhelmed by a malignant anxiety that took him directly to the bar where he knocked down a fast one.

The bar was empty and the bartenders were making preparations. They were theater majors at Buffalo State and Grigson usually enjoyed talking to them, but he had only offered pleasantries and they sensed his preoccupation and left him alone. As the bar and lounge slowly filled up, he thought it might be better if he gave her the picture before the performance, so he moved to a small table by the large window, hoping to get a glimpse of her as she arrived. Grigson gave up on this strategy, as the gathering crowd obscured his view and he finished his drink and went to his seat. The stage was dark and empty except for a small wilted tree at center stage. A large ball of white light from behind shone through the bare branches, creating a vague halo of gray around the tree. Grigson looked at the playbill, regarding the ghostly cruel and tender face of the playwright, Samuel Beckett. He had read the play, *Waiting For Godot,* during the week, but it had proven to be an ineffectual effort. He recognized distinct possibilities emerging in the dialogue, but he was too distracted to solidify the vagrant drift of ideas.

She surprised him, tapping his left shoulder while he was searching with his head turned toward the back on his right side. Grigson felt suddenly disadvantaged, looking up at her and imagining his dumbfounded expression, as if he had been caught sitting on the toilet. The quick thought passed that he had never perceived her from this vantage point.

"Hey Rog," she said.

"Madeleine," he said.

She smiled and rested her hand on his shoulder causing his head to rear slightly.

"Excuse me," she said.

Madeleine started to move, turning away from him, facing the stage and shuffling sideways. Grigson was slow to respond, the back of her legs against his knees and then he abruptly rose as she continued to move and she brushed against him and he felt the very slight bounce of her buttocks encased in the silky fabric of her dress.

"Sorry," she said, smoothing the dress as she sat.

They faced each other and Grigson felt his face rearrange itself and he saw a hint of redness invade her cheeks, but her eyes were steady. He was aware it was probably the longest time they had really faced each other and he didn't want to turn away. However, a worm of nervousness was stirring within and he felt himself shrinking under her gaze, her face growing larger, losing dimension in the process and leaning toward him as if it might topple over him. Grigson knew a single blink would shatter it, bringing relief, but he was also transfixed by the new image – stretching and flattening and he wished he could move closer.

Madeleine turned her head and Grigson felt it evaporate and he wondered if she had read his mind.

"I have something for you," he said, presenting the thin package.

"What's this?" she said.

"Open it," he said, fighting an urge to say more.

Grigson watched her fingers pry open the seam of paper. The picture emerged with the wrapping falling away into her lap.

"Oh my," she said, holding it at arm's length, causing Grigson to feel self-conscious of those behind him. "Roger, it's beautiful."

Madeleine turned and smiled and he saw in her eyes his just reward. She had turned back to the picture, now held lower and he devoured her profile and reached into his pocket for the brooch. He felt the words forming and brimming just as a dark unfocussed image approached and absorbed the immediate background. Grigson looked up past her into the face of the handsome man from the magazine photograph.

"Look how wonderful," she said to the man.

The man nodded and seemed to measure Grigson, but his eyes softened and he offered his hand. Grigson felt himself dissolving as he released the brooch in the pocket and rose and grasped the soft sturdiness of the handshake against his coarse and calloused hands. He noticed the fine cut of his clothes and the evenness of his voice as they exchanged pleasantries. They sat and Madeliene added to her appreciation of the picture. Both men eyed each other over the flat landscape of her lap and then the lights flashed off and on and quiet settled around the auditorium. Grigson saw her hand rest on the man's and he welcomed the darkness.

- - -

It was a two-act play and Grigson had bolted as the lights went on after the first act, straddling the chubby neighbor to his left and rubbing against knees and pushing past the slow moving herd and into the lights and noises of the street. The motion felt right, as if he was shedding skin and he continued walking at full stride until he began sweating and he finally stopped at a corner and waited for the bus.

They were surprised to see him so early at Tangos and a few wondered aloud why he hadn't stopped before the play.

"Running late," he said to the first couple of inquirers and after that he simply shrugged.

Grigson ordered a White Russian and Scotty asked him if he was sure. He gulped the first two and an hour later he had consumed half a dozen. Around midnight Loren came in and slid onto the stool next to him.

"Looks like my Dad's drink," she said.

"It's a little different," he said. "Tasty little bastards."

"Careful," she said. "They'll sneak up on you."

"So I've been told," he said. "How's old Simon doing?"

Loren told him her father was home and doing fine, driving her mother crazy. Grigson had been lost in his own miserable world and the regulars had sensed it and given him plenty of space. Loren was unaware of his state of mind although she was surprised to see him there so late and drunk. He bought her a beer and she continued telling stories of her father, including his baseball career before she was born and slowly he began to listen. He also seemed to be seeing her for the first time and he began to study her features. Her face was mottled with vague freckles under short, reddish hair sprouting from above the strap of the turned around Yankee cap. Loren's eyes were a younger version of her father's good one, piercing and vibrant and expressive of her feelings that touched Grigson.

After a while she bought a round although Grigson had attempted to override her. Scotty always honored the first one to order a round, a rule he strictly enforced unless a situation arose where a cheapskate had been shamed into buying.

"Dad said you drew some pictures of him,"

"Yes," he said.

"He said you were gifted."

"Gifted?" Grigson said. "Hardly…"

"Dad said you were really good," she said. "He said you were painting a portrait of him."

"Not exactly," he said. "It's more a sketch with some color added."

"So you've finished it?"

"Well, yeah."

"You should give it to him," Loren said. "It might cheer him up."

"I actually did bring it here to give to him," Grigson said. "That's when I heard he was in the hospital."

"I wish I'd known that," she said. "He hated being in the hospital. It might've helped."

It dawned on Grigson how utterly thoughtless he was. He chastised himself for not taking it over, thinking of the minimal effort involved and knowing how much Simon would appreciate it. But the thought had never entered his mind and this was the glaring fact he pondered – realizing how self-absorbed he'd become.

"You could take it tonight," he said.

"Really?" she said. "That would be wonderful."

As they entered his apartment and Grigson had switched on the light, Loren was immediately drawn to the picture of her father, centered among the collection of other drawings. She approached it slowly and sat with her elbows on the kitchen table and examined it closely.

"It's him," she said, stretching back in the chair, teetering on two hind legs. "It's absolutely him."

"I don't know," he said, standing behind her.

"Bullshit," she said. "How could you not? Just look at it."

Loren turned back to the picture and she grasped Grigson's arm and pulled him to a kneeling position next to her. She stared at the picture and squeezed his arm and when she turned toward him, tears welled in her eyes. All this was abrupt and overpowering for Grigson and he slowly rose and stepped back and she had to let go of his arm.

"Beer?"

"Sure," she said, turning back to the picture.

Grigson took beer from the refrigerator and opened them. He turned to find her looking at the series of Madeleine sketches on the other wall.

"Who's this?" she asked.

"Just a model," he said, as offhandedly as he could manage.

"She's very beautiful," Loren said.

Grigson regarded the varied images of her and struggled with a resounding despair. He excused himself and went into the bathroom. He experienced a wave of vertigo and poured his beer down the toilet. Grigson wished he hadn't given Madeleine the picture, knowing it was the best of them. He closed his eyes and saw her hand pressing her companion's hand before the lights went off. It was the last image he had of her.

Loren wasn't at the kitchen table when he came out and Grigson took the opportunity to splash water on his face over the sink. He found her in the living room on the couch, naked and sitting upright on her heels.

"Draw me," she said.

"Oh, Loren," he said. "Not now. It's late. I'm drunk."

"Draw me," she said. "Like you did her."

Grigson sensed a steadfastness that was beyond any objection he could possibly rally. Loren shook her head and fluffed her hair. It was rare to see her without the Yankee cap and unbelievable to have her nude. Grigson pulled a sketchbook from his backpack and sat in a chair across the room. He looked at the blank sheet and felt a shyness that kept him from looking at her.

"Where do I put my hands?"

He studied her and he felt a calmness glaze through him and he thought the lamp on the other side of the couch was offering just enough light to enhance her features and quell the ivory glow of her skin.

"Just set them on top of your legs," he said.

Grigson used a felt tipped pen and drew a few simple sketches, attempting to capture more shape than anything else. She was looking directly at him and after he had twice turned to a new page, she asked him how it was going. He nodded and avoided her eyes and focused on her body. He kept his mind directed this way as best he could, but he suffered moments of disengagement – a pinching - the - skin realization that this young woman was in fact sitting, (*"stark fucking naked,"* his *residual adolescent voice incredulously roared)* before him. But it wasn't until she had changed her pose – stretching the length of the couch, that Grigson fully realized the incredible breadth of her womanhood. He found the horizontal plane of the couch helpful as a lineal complement, especially when he asked her to face away from him, with her left leg bent and under the right, the sole of her foot peeking out and resting below the back of her right knee. The pose, anchored by the slight spread of her buttocks, extended in both directions and seemingly balanced with the back of her head resting on her left shoulder, and the other side with the bottoms of her feet exposed and emphatic as twin rosettes on a door frame.

Grigson stopped and couldn't help admiring what he'd done and Loren rolled over.

"Can I see?" she asked.

Grigson rose and about halfway across the room he felt his arousal and her eyes were directed there and he moved the sketchbook to block the view, a maneuver he hadn't used since junior high school. She sat up and took the sketchbook and flipped through the pages as Grigson pushed his hands in his pockets. Loren dropped the sketchbook on the floor and seized Grigson's necktie and pulled his head down and kissed him. He sat next to her and she helped him out of his clothes. She coaxed him to lie closely and she held him and her breath was light against his ear. They stopped briefly to adhere to the practicality of unfolding the bed and Grigson turned off the lamp and moonlight slanted in the window and spread over them.

He was soothed by her cautious advancement and sexual deftness. The only exception had been a pause where she had looked up at him with a disarmingly wide-eyed expression and said: "You taste soapy," and he remembered the hurried, after work shower. Grigson was drawn, her body warm and solid, but remarkably light against him and her face close – but the image became confusing, flattening out in its proximity as the other image presented herself.

"Let it go," Loren whispered, as if she knew.

Her hands traveled up his flanks and she pushed against his shoulders and her face retreated. Grigson felt the shifting of her buttocks, firming as she sat, the angle pulling at his root. Loren arched her back and he relished her features in the moonlight and he was awash in her motion and he let go.

- - -

The bus pulled into the transfer loop and some passengers left as others came on board. Grigson watched their mechanical movements, drawing inwardly against the cold and drab dampness. Outside, a small group was pressed under a shelter, looking out with the same resigned expression. Raindrops swelled on the window like fat transparent insects, eventually bloating and breaking and trailing downward. Grigson pressed his head against the pane, but the coolness offered no relief. He struggled against an overwhelming feebleness, dreading the resolve he needed to complete the day's journey – seemingly infinite. He wrestled with the events of the previous evening and reviewed his blunders.

Grigson regretted giving the picture to Madeleine and he couldn't help wondering what it meant to her or what she had done with it. He thought of attempting to reproduce it, but the idea struck him as pointless. He pictured her waking in the arms of the man, but the vision he had was false as he imagined bright sunshine flooding her window. This angered him and he reproached himself and squelched the image. He suddenly remembered the sketches of Loren and he pulled the sketchbook from his backpack. Grigson was hesitant to look. Earlier, when he awoke, for a split second all had seemed normal with his body positioned on his side toward the outer edge of the foldout bed. His first conscious breath detected a subtle floral scent and he had looked over his shoulder and there was the curve of Loren's hip under the blanket. Grigson had turned back and seen the clock and the sudden panic and anger converged because he had never set the alarm. He slid out of bed and was besieged by a wave of nausea. He had vomited in the toilet and the headache presented itself in gripping enormity as he raised his head. He returned to the bathroom three times before his stomach felt settled. Grigson dressed quickly and he had taken a last look at Loren asleep before rushing out.

Grigson flipped pages and he didn't recall the first drawing. What struck him were the carefully wrought lines. He had expected a shaky mess, the lineal equivalent to slurring, but given the sparseness of the drawing, he thought a likeness was evident. There were three more – the first two similar to the first with only slight variations of the original pose, but the last was of Loren stretched on the couch, facing away. Here he was smitten, the whole of it absorbing him and pulling him deeper. The drawing offered him enough of a sense of transformation to place him back across the room from her, recalling her scent and the tone of her voice and the fullness of her physical presence.

Grigson wasn't aware the bus had been moving until it slowed and stopped at a corner. Passengers climbed aboard and walked past him. He hardly noticed; everything around was blurred and sound was muffled. The bright yellow of a taxi caught his eye. The vehicle glistened in the rainfall and dredged up an old cloudy childhood memory. Grigson had been in a forest with his grandfather on a wet and gray autumn morning. It was the first visit to his grandfather's farm after his grandmother had died and the old man had taken him for a walk. They had been silent, moving slowly through a light drizzle on the worn path and Grigson felt the depth of helplessness and was on the verge of tears when he felt the old boney fingers tighten. "Look," the old man had said, pointing to a high branch – the bright and delicate spectacle of a yellow warbler. "There she is."

The bus began to move as Grigson remembered the bird's vibrant presence and sweet song amid the gloomy dampness of the overcast day. He saw the taxi that had parked along the curb of the intersecting street. The driver's side door swung open and his heart jumped. The head of a man emerged. He was disappointed even though he knew the image he desired was impossible. Grigson looked at the picture. He closed his eyes and settled back in the seat.

Neglect

They both embraced the silliness. It was more than a mere impulse, but they were glad nobody was around to witness it. Ethan Barnes lifted a kitchen chair from the pickup truck. He set it on the ground and picked up another. As he carried them, the wooden legs rustled against the dry tangle of weeds and wildflowers. Paula dropped the back of the pickup and slid the table to the edge. Ethan returned and they carried the heavy oak table; he was positioned to walk backwards and watched her eyes widen as they approached

."Are we going into the front door?"

"Actually, we're now going through the garage," he said. "We're going up the stairs, into the kitchen," he added, as they continued through the ragged field. He pulled her on a sudden ninety-degree turn. After a few more steps he stopped.

"Where would you like it?"

Paula looked around. She saw the stakes organized in rectangular configurations amid the hardscrabble growth.

"So, this is the kitchen?" she said. "That's where the sliding glass door is, right?"

Ethan nodded. They set the table down. He pointed westward. The field reached toward a distant tree line. The sun was a solid, perfect circle. Below, it seemed to have spilled into a pale yellow smear, spreading behind the tree tops. Paula looked at the landscape while Ethan retrieved the picnic basket. She wandered inside the perimeter of the stakes. He saw her expression change; the visions were accumulating – she mentioned the fireplace. Paula continued to search, compose.

Ethan wanted to keep up with her. His voice wavered and chopped at words not quite adequate. Her eyes lifted. They steadied him, told him she was solidly there. She smiled as an accomplice.

"This is so beautiful," she said.

"It will be," Ethan said. "You'll see."

- - -

They broke ground a few days later. Caprini Concrete showed up to build the foundation. Ethan stopped by after work. Tony Caprini, the owner's nephew, looked up from the trench at his old teammate. Ethan felt the familiar flash of shame. It was a small thread that no longer mattered, but still irrevocably rendered him as beholden. Ethan was no longer the All-State defensive end with the college scholarship and Tony wasn't the second string halfback who had lied to protect him, thus getting himself expelled from the team. The moment passed like a septic whiff. The boney faced lightweight flashed white teeth. A dirty red bandana restrained his long black hair. Dark eyes were cast upward with casual superiority. He squinted when Ethan shifted and a slice of low sunlight struck him.

"You must be getting anxious, big boy," the second stringer said.

- - -

After the foundation was set, Ethan worked on the house every day after work and long days on weekends. He had some experience – five years of carpentry with Dunne Custom Homes, a job he eventually fell into after two years in the army, one of them in Vietnam. He married Paula, his high school sweetheart a few months before he was drafted. Her pregnancy had prompted the marriage and also the loss of a football scholarship to Syracuse. Their daughter Leslie was born before he shipped out to Vietnam. Johnny arrived three years ago. After his discharge Ethan had been uncomfortable living with his in-laws, but moving to the small apartment in the village of Smith slowed the process of saving for a house. He sought advice from his boss, Horace Dunne. The old man understood Ethan's impatience. Horace remembered him playing football. He was in the stands the day his drunken father had shown up and escorted him off the field during a game. He was enraged his son had failed to take out the garbage. The coach followed, citing the responsibilities of commitment. Ethan's father stopped and stepped up to the coach. The brims of their caps touched.

"He is committed to me," he said. "His responsibilities begin with me. At home."

Horace also had been raised by an alcoholic brute. He was moved by Ethan's perseverance and later saddened by the loss of the scholarship. Ethan worshiped Horace. He loved how he spoke of the houses in the female sense, as a sailor speaks of ships. Horace suggested a Cape Cod. The two story design enabled him to complete the first floor with two bedrooms, leaving the upstairs to be completed according to their budget.

Slowly the house took shape. Ethan worked hard at his job. There were days he was exhausted as he pulled in front of the new structure. Within a half hour he forgot about being tired. Some evenings Paula brought dinner. Her enthusiasm was infectious. She loved the smell of freshly cut lumber. Ethan followed her through the skeletal rooms. He saw her dreams unfold in gestures. She spread the meal on plywood, bridging tandem workhorses. They scanned the rafters and chewed on cold chicken legs. Leslie dragged little Johnny in a cardboard box over sawdust coated sub flooring.

They moved in after the first floor was completed. Ethan turned his attention to the yard. He cleared brush and cut down small trees. Horace Dunne showed up on a Saturday with a backhoe. He backfilled around the house and extracted some sizeable stumps. Johnny was excited watching Horace ease the backhoe forward, the overlapped chain's links seizing themselves and tightening; the popping as the roots let go and slid from the earth's grasp. He wiggled his little fingers inside his father's coarse hand.

"It's scratchy, like sandpaper, Daddy," he said and was amazed when Ethan picked up a small piece of two by six and rubbed off the frayed cut edge with his palm.

After the kids were in bed, Ethan and Paula sat in the backyard. They sipped beer and listened into the darkness. Their long silences were treasured as satisfied tributes. Words were uttered sparingly as dreams on the brink. Ethan had finished landscaping. Paula was happy the besiegement of activity ended. The dust had settled and she took a long look at her surroundings. Ethan was less contented. He was troubled by the incompleteness – a plane that doesn't land. At night he climbed the stairs and peeked into the dark emptiness. It reminded him of ascending the narrow, shadowy stairs of various apartments he had lived in as a child. The uppers were usually cheaper. His mother sometimes juggled two or three jobs to make the rent. Ethan hated the idea of Leslie and Johnny sharing a bedroom even though they were perfectly happy. He had dreams. One morning he told Paula the upstairs had spoken to him.

"And what does the upstairs speak of?"

"Neglect," he said.

Paula understood the power of his childhood memories. He told her various scenes of sharing a bedroom with his younger sister, Mary. One acute memory was during early adolescence when he frequently woke up in the morning with an erection. Mary had named it "Mr. Peanut." It became a dreaded nocturnal concern usually followed by the dawning betrayal. His father had an infrequent, but manic influence on the household. His unreasonable anger and terrorism when drunk and his pathetic

47

remorse when sober. Ethan had lived his young life looking over his shoulder.

Paula constantly assured Ethan their situation was temporary. She emphasized the children's compatibility. She told him it was a matter of simple economics. Two years. The projection was beyond his comprehension. Paula's parents offered a loan, but he refused. She wanted to get a job, but he wouldn't hear of it

."Your mother worked," she said. "Mine still does."

"Mine had to or we would've starved," he said. "And it killed her. Yours was simply bored."

The remark annoyed her. Paula breathed deeply.

"They're looking for a bartender at The Corners," she said. "My folks and your sister said they'd be happy to babysit."

"No way," he said. "A barmaid? Are you kidding me?"

"I said, bartender."

"Oh, I see," Ethan said. "Do you think the barflies know the difference?"

"What's important, Ethan, is that I do," she said. "It's the only way if you want the upstairs finished now."

Jed Hartley, the owner of The Corners, had already thrown down a couple *Crown Royal* on the rocks in the early afternoon. Paula walked in the front door for the interview with the sunlight behind her – the outline of her inner thighs showing through the thin fabric of the summer dress.

She worked Tuesday and Friday nights. Tips far exceeded her salary. Within a few weeks Ethan could afford more materials. He framed in the two bedrooms and the bathroom. The electric had slowed him down; book study had never been his strong suit, but he persevered to get it right. He heaved up drywall. A fine film of dust drifted downstairs. Ethan was oblivious. When Paula complained he reacted quizzically, as if she said the car was wet after a rain. Her mother usually came over to babysit the kids. Ethan barely acknowledged her. She had denounced him when Paula first became pregnant. Things were said, as enduring as scripture. She sold real estate, a likely platform to sustain her self-assumed role as arbiter of good taste. When Paula began complaining about Ethan's growing obsession, she was an instant and energetic ally.

His livelihood was increasingly influencing the quality of the house. He was in awe of Kevin O'Malley, Dunne's cabinet maker. Ethan took a look at the downstairs trim work. He had completed it a few months earlier. The flaws were minimal. He saw gaps along the baseboards. Joints not perfectly met. A couple half-moons inflicted above a door. This new inspection carried a deeper scrutiny.

"This ranch style trim has got to go," he told Paula.

"What's wrong with it?"

"It's cheap, ugly," Ethan replied. "It adds nothing to the room."

They were sitting at the kitchen table and Paula looked around.

"I always liked it," she said. "It's practical, easy to clean."

"It's ordinary, simple," he said. "Humdrum."

I always thought that's what we were," she said. "Ordinary. Simple. I don't know about humdrum?"

"As you get better, you expect better," he said.

"He's right, you know," her mother had said. She stretched the word into a revolting connotation: "Raaaannnch."

Ethan returned to the downstairs. He tore out the trim and replaced it with one by four. Paula watched his concentration – a calmness, a glimpse of intimacy with each piece and its careful installation. In the summer he quit softball, then abandoned the long bowling season. Paula was disappointed. She missed the couple's league in the dead of winter. There were other holes developing. Ethan missed family events. He rarely ate dinner at the table. The children were puzzled. Friends and family began to question his absence. Paula hated her own voice – making excuses, doubtful expectations. She thought back to a few months earlier, his dark tan while landscaping. Now there was only paleness and insulated determination. She reminisced the warmth of his body.

Early on Paula tried to reel him back with easy persuasions. He had always been receptive to facts.

"Money's been tight," she said. "You've seen the bills."

"I know."

"And, we hardly ever spend time together anymore."

Ethan peered at her as if the words had been spat at him.

"I'm here aren't I?"

"Well yeah," she replied. "But it's not the same."

"Same as what?"

"Same as doing something, together," she said. "Don't you feel like life is passing you by?"

Ethan let out a long sigh.

"This, all this, as if you hadn't noticed," he said, lifting his arms, stretching, "This is where it is. This is our life."

There were small skirmishes. Some were about nothing – the sound of the other's voice. A reasonable request translated into a harsh order. Ethan trudged on as righteous as a religious crusader. Paula viewed him as something diminishing. Panic set in, as if in the presence of a terminal disease. Ethan had become impatient about anything beyond the realm of the house. Each argument blurred the boundaries of acceptable behavior; Ethan stepped in like a conqueror. He became unapproachable.

One afternoon Paula was scheduled to work, but her mother was unable to watch the kids. Everyone else was unavailable. Ethan arrived from work with his usual impetus – a hiker lost in the romance of his steps, approaching a subsequent climb. He didn't expect to see Paula. His gaze made her feel like a stranger. Johnny's and Leslie's voices carried from the backyard.

"My mom can't make it," Paula said.

"There's nobody else?"

"No," Paula said. "I tried."

"You can't call in?"

"No, Ethan. They're expecting me."

A shriek from Johnny turned Ethan's head. Laughter followed.

"There's leftover stew in the refrigerator," she said. "Just needs to be heated up."

"So I have to babysit?" Ethan said. "Are you fucking kidding me?"

"Well?"

Paula could hardly look at him: A statue, arms poised, one hand on the cold metal of the hammer head in the holster. His face was frozen into a caricature of virtuous stupidity.

"Babysit? Your own children?"

"You know damn well what I mean."

"I don't know anything about you anymore," she said. "Except that you're an asshole and I can't stand it."

- - -

Outside, the morning sounds increase. The coming and going of vehicles. Voices far from the second story apartment: A young couple retrench the evening's drunken argument. A dog's sudden protest. A woman's sweetened response to a pleading child. An old man's impatient rejoinder to his hard of hearing wife. The sounds come with the early sunshine, filtered through sheer curtains. The light inside seems corrupted. The color is a soft blue, but Paula thinks it's gray. The paint's cheap, the application uninspired. Painters' "Holidays" permeate the walls in vague, white freckled clusters. She pictures Ethan in the room, agonizing – his plodding perfectionism. She imagines keeping dinner warm while he wanders the room with the paintbrush, checking and double checking.

A flash of resentment passes through her. The apartment is small. Paula can see into both bedrooms. The twin beds are empty and neatly made. In the other room the bed clothes appear frozen into scalloped waves where passion had kicked them. The tea kettle begins to whistle. Her movements are sluggish as she pours water into the cup. Paula returns to the small table and lights a cigarette. She had recently started again after dabbling and quitting in high school. The taste is meager – *Kents*, the same white filtered brand she used to pilfer from her mother. The box fan in the window is reversed and sucks the smoke out. The kitchen is cramped. At first Paula had insisted they eat at the table. The children fidgeted. There were spills. The following week she bought TV trays at a yard sale.

- - -

Visions from the previous night. They're as startling as a scream; the new truth resonates – Ethan is no longer the only one. The weight of the significance is overwhelming. The situation and the man have come out of nowhere. Returning to the memory of it is irresistible. It's like putting on a shirt you wouldn't normally consider and realizing in a certain light, it suits you.

- - -

Behind the bar Paula had struggled the first couple weeks. The regulars were used to seeing Jed Hartley. They approached with their eyes dropping and widening, as if for the first time seeing the Grand Canyon. She focused on not slopping foam on the bar. Paula was fascinated by the clientele. Some of them showed up each day as if to the demand of a punch clock. She carried more shifts since moving out. Paula knew more than she needed about some and almost nothing about a few. Tony Caprini was one of the few. He drank *Budweiser* and smoked

Old Golds. Paula thought his narrow face had gained a certain seriousness. She found his large, dark eyes impenetrable. In high school they moved in different circles. Paula recalled him on the football team, but not on the field. He became notable by not ratting on Ethan and another teammate when the cops raided a party and caught him.

At the bar Tony was reserved. He projected a determined distance. He didn't speak of the past. Paula was thankful he had come in when he did.

Trixie Fordham had been there for three hours. She was with a man half her age. He fed the juke box. Sinatra. They danced, she at first gracefully, her eyes skimming above the patrons' glances, as if in the grand surround of a ballroom. Later Old Blue Eyes had been replaced by the Rolling Stones. Trixie was falling out of her shoes. The young man was desperate, his arms hovered – as alert as a lumberjack. He steered her close to the wall. Across the bar was another young man. One of many of Trixie's former lovers. She was remembering aloud. There was a scuffle between the two young men. Trixie was delighted. She laughed like a beauty queen. Paula shut them off.

The bar had gone quiet. Trixie was staggered. Her fake eye lashes fluttered, as if there was a sudden, dusty breeze.

"That's too bad," she said. "I was just going to buy the bar a drink."

Paula felt their eyes on her. Trixie looked around. Her bottom lip curled upward – a politicians' knowing smile – counting votes, gaining support.

"You certainly don't want to deny these thirsty, hard working men, do you?" she said.

Paula scanned the group. They stared into their drinks.

"I'm buying this round," Tony Caprini said.

Her movements were braced in self-consciousness as she served the customers. She ignored Tony's money and plodded on throughout the afternoon. The new shadows of the evening were welcome. Faces changed along the bar. Tony had remained.

At two Paula announced last call.

There were only five of them. The young couple had come in less than an hour before. They carried motorcycle helmets, denim jackets were buttoned to the neck. Faces wind burned, smiling. Her hand was tucked into the back pocket of his jeans. They ordered *Rolling Rock* and tapped the green bottle necks together. Their attention to each other was intense; it held secrets, excluded everyone. Two regulars, middle aged men, sat across from them. They were more interested in the couple than each other. Their conversation was drab, self-serving. A variation of a recent conversation, perhaps a few days ago or last week. Each held to the same opinions – loud in declaration, short on comprehension. Kids play-acting. No one had noticed.

The couple finished their beers and pulled on their jackets. They left like explorers, forsaking a sanctuary.

Silence was telling inside as they heard the motorcycle fire up. The gargled idle. Loud acceleration followed and the punctuation of shifting. They more or less shared the same picture: The single headlight reaching into the night. Her arms tight around his waist. The red tail light disappearing in the dark countryside.

The two men looked away from each other and drained their glasses. They stood and gathered their money and eyed each other's generous tip. Their stiff, self-conscious gaits resembled old men as they left.

Tony had sat quietly throughout the evening. His elbows were spread on the bar, a lit cigarette between two fingers.

"You still haven't taken out for that round," he said.

"I'm paying for it," Paula said. "It was my problem."

"It was my round," he said. "Take it. I'll leave it anyway."

"Would you like another beer?"

"A last, last call?"

She smiled and nodded.

"Only if I can buy you one," he said.

At the end of the night there were the usual offers. Some sat there a long time. It was comical how they acted surprised to still be there. Paula refused them as gently as possible. Tony was something else. A blue neon *Labatt* sign remained lit in the front window after she had locked the door and turned off the lights. She drew a beer and offered a silent toast. He pointed to the stool next to him.

"Sit," he said.

A sudden silence distorted their close proximity. She brought up the earlier episode in the bar.

"I don't know what I would've done if you weren't here."

"You were doing okay."

"But she had them," Paula said.

"Trixie."

"What about Trixie?"

"Everyone knows about Trixie."

"I don't, she said. "Tell me."

"She's told," Tony said.

"Told?"

"Everyone knows her act. She gets around."

"But those guys?" she said. "Half her age. Why?"

"Because she can."

"What about you?"

"What about me?" he said.

"Have you been with Trixie?"

"I couldn't say."

Tony's face showed nothing. He drew on his cigarette and flicked it against the ashtray. His eyes were settled on her. The idea of Trixie and him excited her. Paula couldn't help letting in visions. A spark of jealousy. She recognized the absurdity immediately. She felt the path taking her.

"She's at least fifty," Paula said.

"You could call her experienced."

"How about well preserved?"

"You could say that."

"Is her body as well preserved as her face?"

"I couldn't say," Tony said.

Paula smiled. She picked up a cigarette. Tony handed her his lighter.

"I could think of another word to describe her," she said.

"That would be judgmental."

Paula lit her cigarette. The room seemed smaller in the blue darkness. She finished her beer and walked around the bar for another. Tony went to the jukebox.

"May I?" he said.

"Sure."

"Requests?"

"You pick."

Tony pushed buttons. The song suddenly filled the air. A tender ballad. It poured from the shadows. Paula returned to the stool. She watched him peruse the lit up selections. His finger trailed over the glass. The white t-shirt shone above the glare. His arms were lost against the dark paneling. He pushed more buttons. The next song was slower, softer.

"Dance?" he said, reaching for her hand.

- - -

The hot tea causes her to perspire. Paula considers turning the fan around. The benefit from the recent shower dwindles. She loosens the terry cloth robe; the slight movement distills more sweat. Paula slipped it on without toweling off, a habit that had annoyed Ethan. The idea of getting dressed is remote. The urge for another cigarette trumps the desire for the fan. She blows smoke toward the window and watches it snatched from the room. The night comes back to her.

- - -

The refrain of the ballad drew them into an easy collaboration. She didn't absorb the meaning of the words, but the shape of their sounds touched her. His body was warm. Back and shoulder muscles tightened in sleek measure. The contrast of Ethan's bearlike frame, her head tucked under his chin, had passed minutely through her mind. Like a detail under anesthesia. There was a familiar odor on him. She remembered it on Ethan after he started with Dunne. Eventually it seemed to have been stained into him. On Tony there was possibly an additional earthiness. She wasn't sure. Exploring the thought seemed wrong. They danced slower than the music; words hung back like obsolete tools. The ragged drape of his long hair was soft against her face. At first their hands moved cautiously.

- - -

The memory of lovemaking brings a yearning that troubles her. Her gratitude is undeniable. It's also begrudging. The patience of his confidence. His understated arrogance. Paula is surprised she had succumbed to it. She can't take it back, but she's desperate to give it the right perspective.

Upon awakening, she hurried him to leave.

"Ethan's coming with the kids," she said.

"Step aside for the All-American?"

Paula saw a shift in his eyes. He got up and pulled on his clothes. She had been relieved hearing the loose work boots retreating the stairway.

Now in the quiet aftermath, the experience seems fouled by his silent and hasty exit.

Below the screen door slams. Little feet clambering the stairs. Slower, heavier steps follow. Paula crushes the cigarette in the ashtray. A dozen crinkled filters are scattered among the ashes. Some belong to her and the rest are the light brown filters of *Old Golds*. Paula gazes at the open door of the bedroom. There's a trickling of sweat between her breasts. A flash of panic as little hands fumble the doorknob. The heavier steps stop. As the door swings open, Paula leans back in the chair and watches the last wire of smoke escape the kitchen.

The Wind Change

The lake was fixed in its emptiness, bereft of life without the wind. Kevin O'Malley studied the composition from his deck. Instinctively, he searched into the scene – probing for a secret, something beyond the obvious stillness. The sun was low, spreading a sparkling skirt along the horizon. He was drawn forward on the incline of the Adirondack chair, worn silver from years of outside exposure. O'Malley's focus waned when he realized he was already sweating. A half an hour earlier he had walked down the steep stairs to the small plot of beach and taken a swim. The water was refreshing and uncommonly clear, not having been roiled by the normal prevailing wind. He climbed the stairs without toweling off, a strategy that seemed to backfire. The air clung like an inescapable and uncomfortable fabric.

The disc jockey on the transistor radio was discussing the recent hot spell:

"We should take the clothes we wore yesterday and burn them."

O'Malley thought it was amusing, but he soon tired of the jocular commentary and he turned it off and went inside and put on a record. He poured a glass of white wine. The chilled acidity enhanced his hunger. He tore the heel off the loaf of bread he purchased on the way home from work. The kitchen was stifling with the oven on. In the morning he had marinated the chicken in a mixture of olive oil and Dijon mustard with a little garlic, parsley, white wine and lemon juice. He returned to the deck and sat back in the chair. The music, a Mozart piano concerto, drifted from inside the screened door. He closed his eyes. Instead of serenity, O'Malley felt emptiness. He hated the still unreasonable and irrevocable fact that created the difference.

His wife, Susanne had died almost two years ago. It had taken him a year and a half to establish a vague sense of normalcy. Cooking had been an activity they had enjoyed, one of the many things they passionately shared. After her death he found it unbearable, as if he was being purposely condemned as an unnatural survivor, at sixty-one, ten years older than her. Aside from making sandwiches for work and heating up frozen or jarred meals, O'Malley ate dinner at the Sunny Side Diner in the nearby village of Smith. He sat at the counter, against the wall if it was available. He ate in silence, exchanged pleasantries as they occurred, but kept to himself. Sometimes Harold Pratt would join him. Harold, also a widower, owned an apple farm on Route 18 across from O'Malley's property. He was a loud, but pleasant man always dressed in dark green work clothes and smiling below the brim of a squashed John Deere cap.

At first O'Malley didn't welcome sharing his dinner time at the counter, but eventually he began to look forward to his companionship. Harold had been alone for many years. His wife had died in a car accident, leaving two young boys and they had long since grown up and moved away. Harold lived in a large farmhouse that was hidden from the road behind the apple orchard. In the village of Smith he was looked upon as the happy-go-lucky sort, but O'Malley knew he was lonely. He saw it clearly through the loud laughter and the endless stream of jokes. One night they went to O'Malley's house after dinner and ended up sharing a fifth of scotch. As the night wore on the conversation had turned serious. Harold had spoken vividly of his wife and lamented his loss, crying into his handkerchief. The next day at the diner he slid onto the stool next to O'Malley and told him a joke he heard earlier at the hardware store. O'Malley grew tired of the "home-cooked" meals at the diner and also the nightly routine Harold and he had developed – "making the rounds" as Harold called it. After their meals they would wander the local taverns, sitting among the regulars. Harold appeared to thrive on the story and joke telling, the gossiping and buying back and forth of drinks. O'Malley felt uncomfortable and out of place – a quiet observer that after a while, the other bar patrons seemed to resent, especially the women who generally found him attractive. He wanted to ignore this, but Harold seemed to delight in reminding him the next day. He treated it as an agreeable curse that he might capitalize on. O'Malley was embarrassed by what he considered undeserved attention. He sensed an underlying sadness in the regulars' laughter; the gaiety rang false and was charged with an elusive desperation. O'Malley slowly put on weight and began to feel sluggish. He started smoking cigarettes, a habit he had struggled to quit many years ago. For forty years he had been not only proud of his craft as a cabinet maker for Dunne & Son Custom Homes, but he had been impassioned each working day. He never missed work no matter how late he'd been up or how much he drank. But this rigid constitution became a shaky frame for a daily performance without inspiration – a heartless shuffle he could barely endure.

O'Malley had never thought of his home as a *sanctuary* in the dramatic manner he heard from others. He rarely felt as if he were fleeing there from some undesirable place or circumstance. With Susanne, it was an abundant atmosphere, calming and energizing and always nourishing. To O'Malley, her absence had rendered it as a dry and barren garden and he carried his stagnation there. He was well known regionally as an accomplished painter and sculptor, but that part of him had become inactive. Partially formed sculptures and empty canvases stood lifeless, collected dust in the studio behind his house. O'Malley kept the house clean, but he moved around it like an outsider, coming home later in the evenings, turning lights on as he entered rooms and turning them off as he exited. He read by the small light on the table next to his bed, but he retained very little. He followed the words in a dull haze until he heard himself sleeping, lifting his chin off his chest and reaching for the book as it listed over.

The routine eventually became unbearable and O'Malley abruptly stopped making the rounds. He visited the diner only once or twice a week. Harold missed his friend.

"What are you going to do?" he said. "Roll yourself in a carpet and die?"

Harold tried to persuade O'Malley under the guise of self-help; he said it was healthy to socialize and it had been a predominant factor in regaining his life after his wife's tragic death. O'Malley didn't want to hurt his friend's feelings by telling him he was wasting his life away, thus propping a mirror in front of his face. Carefully he explained how he had gotten away from his artwork since Susanne had died. He told him the artwork had been very important to him and because of his grief, he had forgotten about it. As O'Malley continued telling him how his wife's death had left a large emptiness and the lack of creativity had created another one, he could see Harold's eyes go blank. It was the same look one received, after going into great detail about a vacation.

"So you're just going to go home and draw pictures?"

O'Malley merely nodded. It seemed to offer the level of eloquence that Harold understood.

Cooking for himself had been an early step in reclaiming his life. Initially O'Malley found it too poignant, the kitchen alive with memories that he associated with cooking aromas. There were so many wonderful moments with Susanne, sipping wine, listening to music and discussing the events of the day around the island cabinet in the middle of the kitchen. She had taught art history at Niagara University. Susanne loved art although she recognized very young that her talent was minimal. She was simply too moved by those who fully possessed it to frustrate herself with serious intent. They met when she was finishing graduate school after spending a year in Europe. Susanne was a student volunteer for a show in Lockport that O'Malley had entered. He presented three pieces, all wooden sculptures. The piece called *Woman with Flowers* had won first prize. After the show Susanne lingered around the figure, looking from different angles.

"Do you mind if I touch her?" she asked.

"Not at all," he said.

"I hate when galleries have '*Do not touch*' signs on sculpture," she said. "It makes no sense. It's part of the pleasure."

O'Malley nodded and watched her circle the figure.

On the table it stood about three feet tall. The base was roughly textured, became smooth where the roundness of the hips began and curved inward to the waist and then swung upward and expanded out under the bare breasts. The elbows were jutting out, adding a horizontal balance to the figure with the hands joined together at her midriff, the fingers bent and creased and holding a bouquet of flowers. The shoulders, rounded and glossy, reflected light from above and offered an opposing breadth that helped accentuate the perpendicular stretch of her neck – pushing out the angle of the chin below a pursed mouth, her eyes barely opened.

Susanne ran her hand down the nape of the neck under the short crop of hair and traveled between the shoulder blades and diagonally across the swell of the hip and in front up along the slight roundness of her stomach. She cupped a hand under a breast. O'Malley saw her index finger flick like a wiper blade over the protrusion of the nipple. Their eyes met and Susanne blushed and her hand slid down and off the table.

"This is a beautiful piece," she said. "The expression on her face is wonderful – the sense of peace, thankfulness. The flowers must have come from a very special person."

Susanne had looked into his eyes and her smile made him think that the statement was more a question than a suggestion. O'Malley nodded and remained silent. He didn't have an answer, but he was happy the piece gave her pleasure

."Reminds me a little of Marino Marini's work," she said.

"I don't know him," O'Malley replied.

"He's Italian," she said. "I saw his work in Florence and Milan."

Susanne noted some similarities between Marini's and O'Malley's work, all of them positive and she seemed to understand the tricky discretion needed in comparing artwork and she had moved to a broader overview of what she considered a "wealth of talent" from the immediate area. Her description of art was precise and knowledgeable, but O'Malley found her enthusiasm to be overwhelming. He had been captivated by the life in her eyes – how it left as she recounted faraway descriptions and returned, seemingly startled to be back in the present and then focusing on him. He found her details to be incredible stabs of color, taste and smell – offered evenly without pomposity or bravado as a means to connect. She had been telling him about hiking and bicycling in Provence, adding detailed accounts of native wines and delicious meals when he raised his hand.

"Please, you're making me hungry," he said. "Would you have dinner with me?"

They ate in a small Italian restaurant, remaining at the table long after the meal was finished, sipping wine and talking. They walked in gathering darkness along the canal. After sitting so long at the table O'Malley was surprised at her height – her face turning toward him, her soft gray eyes direct and level. Susanne wore her straight red hair shoulder length and it swayed back and forth. Her pale skin shone like ivory under the streetlights. When they returned to her car O'Malley had kissed her and within six months they were married.

- - -

After Susanne's death O'Malley couldn't think about the day they met, but now he raised the vision ceremoniously. His grief had been long and exhausting. It had taken him back to the darkest depths of pain and emptiness and dredged him through the turbid journey of her long illness that had stricken him with an appalling helplessness. Those memories, that for so long seemed imbedded in a pattern of circuitous rewind, had eventually wrung him out and left him. O'Malley began cooking, but found he couldn't divide the ingredients. The result appeared too miniscule so he prepared meals for two as he always had and saved the remaining portion for the next few days. The meals were simple, but he made a point of buying fresh meat and produce if they were available rather than relying on a large-scale weekly shopping trip. He missed the fresh herbs and vegetables from the garden now dormant on the other side of the studio, especially the basil that he had loved to pluck and tear and throw into a marinara sauce Susanne and he had adjusted through the years. As O'Malley resumed the routine of cooking, it offered a reintroduction to the wholeness of his home. He had built the house, thirty years ago with the help of his boss, Horace Dunne and every few years he would add on. It was situated as close to the edge of land overlooking the lake as possible and O'Malley had built it tightly and solidly to withstand the persistent wind and he loved the sound of the wind and the sense of life it carried. Now, it seemed more like a foreign place or a room where all the familiar furniture had been removed.

He rose from the chair with his empty glass and entered the kitchen. He checked the chicken, poured more wine and returned to the deck. The newspaper he'd brought home lay at his feet as flat and motionless as a door mat. The headline stared up at him: *Record Heat Scorches the East.* O'Malley picked it up and scanned the front page. He ignored the latest update on the Watergate scandal and turned to the weather page. The forecast for the following week was spread out horizontally in consecutive squares. In the top of each square was a picture of the sun. Only on Thursday did the sun share its space with the caricature of clouds and slanted lines that designated rainfall. Underneath were projected temperatures, all in the nineties. As he turned the pages he realized how rare it was to be able to read the paper outside on the deck as the wind was generally a forbidding factor. In the regional section he saw a small article:

Body of missing boater found.

Youngstown - The body of Jonathan Case of 113 29ᵗʰ Street, Niagara Falls was found Thursday two days after he and his wife, Martha, had disappeared from their boat on Lake Ontario. The body of Martha Case was discovered on Wednesday. Niagara County Coroner Arthur P. Guess said Case's body was spotted by a boater about 13 miles from shore and the Marine Patrol of the Niagara County Sheriff's Department recovered the body at 3:35 p.m. Officials suspect the couple drowned while swimming. "The two could have become stranded after Case's boat drifted away," theorized B.R. Crawford, Captain of the Niagara County Sheriff's Marine Patrol Unit. "Even with a very gentle breeze, a boat can be pushed along at a rate that even a good swimmer would have a difficult time catching," Crawford said. *"Since there were no eyewitnesses, at this point, it's the best theory we have."Case's boat was found floating close to shore off Six Mile Creek on Tuesday.*

O'Malley shook his head and scanned the lake that was as flat as a concrete slab.

"You sly bastard," he muttered.

He had experienced the many moods of the lake through the years. Before O'Malley met Susanne he had crewed on his boss's boat, a thirty-eight-foot yawl out of Youngstown. He'd been to many harbors on the lake, from Toronto to Rochester and as far as Kingston, Ontario. O'Malley had endured storms with gale force winds, sometimes at night where there was little or no definition outside the boundaries of the craft. He had felt the exhilarating fear that overwhelms the senses from moment to moment, that motivates acute alertness and singles out and demands your mettle. O'Malley understood it as a challenge a boater must be prepared for and he was thankful Horace was a skilled sailor.

But this other thing, O'Malley thought. This deceit and trickery. He couldn't help imagining the couple as Susanne and himself as they swam around the boat in the placid water. O'Malley felt the cool water and the sense of depth underneath and the strange suspension that the small act of treading water brings. The child-like joy of the alien freedom. And who knows how quickly it changed, he thought. He pictured the subtle pocket of air as something probably not visible on a meteorologist's screen – a vague force that didn't stir the water's surface, but strong enough to push against the superstructure of the open boat, like breathing into a paper cup. O'Malley lived the vision as in a trance, felt the helplessness as in a nightmare, watching the boat drift away and grow smaller as they swam after her.

The phone was ringing inside the house. O'Malley thought it might have been ringing for a while, the sound seeming urgent now, prompting him to rush inside. It was his daughter, Abbie.

"I was ready to hang up," she said.

"I was outside."

"Were you working in your studio?"

"No, no," he replied. "Just sitting. Looking at the paper."

"Are you okay, Daddy?"

"Yeah, I'm fine, darling," he said.

O'Malley loved the sound of his only child's voice. He especially loved it when she said "Daddy" and he was savoring the brief rhythm and not listening to what followed.

"Dad!" she said. "Are you there?"

"Yes, darling," he replied. "I'm here."

"Is this a bad time? I can call later."

"No darling," O'Malley said. "I was just day dreaming."

"You sound strange," Abbie said. "You're not getting weird on me?"

"Hard to tell sometimes," he said. "You don't get much feedback when you're alone."

O'Malley was immediately angry with himself for the betrayal.

"So, how is Abigail O'Malley Ernst?"

"I'm fine, Daddy," she said. "I was wondering what day you were coming up next week?"

"Well, I might come up a little earlier than we had planned," he said. "I've got a few things to attend to and then I thought I'd head up on Tuesday. I'm thinking of spending a couple days in the High Peaks, maybe hiking Cascade. I was hoping you could get away for a day or two so we could hike it together."

"I don't know," Abbie replied. "The kids will be out of school next week. I've got exams to grade and reports to write. The store is picking up and John's been busy with his real estate. It seems like every tourist has this dream of owning a place up here. They're mostly tire kickers, but John says, 'You never know.'"

O'Malley had expected this answer, but he was still disappointed. Abbie and her husband had moved to Old Forge, a village about fifty miles north of Utica, three years ago with their two young sons. Abbie taught art at the local high school and John owned a small liquor store and he had recently begun selling real estate. O'Malley understood the attraction to the area. Many years earlier when he had traveled up there with Susanne and young Abbie, he felt the same allure of the dynamic wildness and overwhelming beauty. The three of them had spent many summers and some winters, wandering the length and breadth of the Adirondack Park, favoring the smaller hamlets like Inlet and Long Lake. They discovered hidden gems of large prehistoric-like rocks in dense forests. The lakes were clear and pristine. The mountains offered great vistas and trails teased his expectations around each rising curve and alerted his senses in constant anticipation. O'Malley had never seen so many shades of green and he was in constant wonder of the changing hues of any given color, reacting to the diverse and athletic movement of the sky.

He remembered maneuvering the van along the winding rural roads as he and Susanne looked at property. It had been fun exploring the region, but they gave up that dream, realizing the winters were too long and harsh and the economy was too erratic. O'Malley had seen the blank glaze of monotony and dreariness in the eyes of the locals and he wondered if it was even more difficult to live and work in an area where people came to play.

"How's the store doing?"

"It's better now. April and May were terrible – mostly locals," Abbie said. "But it's been picking up and John's getting used to the ups and downs. He kind of has the rhythm down."

"Well that's good," O'Malley said, but he couldn't imagine his son-in-law feeling a "rhythm" about anything. John Ernst was a stiff and careful man, an unlikely salesman who spoke in a horizontal line with the same measured cadence – like dead wood knocking together. He was of average height, but appeared shorter due to his expansive girth. After meeting him while visiting Abbie at college, Susanne had whispered in O'Malley's ear, "He looks like a bale of hay."

They had never understood the attraction their daughter felt. He was totally opposite of her expressive nature and he was fifteen years older. All O'Malley knew was they had fallen in love and that John was a kind and loving husband and a good father to his grandsons. But he wasn't easy to be around, wrapped up in his world of sales and inventories that never seemed to free him for anything else. John wasn't interested in any of the outside activities the area offered, a fact that baffled O'Malley, knowing his daughter's passion for the outdoors. Washing the car was John's idea of exercise and on a hot day it could be considered his *tour de force.*

Whenever O'Malley visited, he usually stayed in a hotel or cottage although he always brought camping gear. He came every year at this time for the arts and crafts show on Saturday and Sunday, but stayed the following week to visit them and to hike and fish. Abbie had offered their couch, but he knew it would be uncomfortable for everyone and this particular trip he had more time than his usual week long vacation, a fact he would normally welcome if the underlying cause wasn't so troubling. Richard Dunne had stopped that afternoon in the new house where O'Malley had just finished installing the kitchen cabinets. It had taken him two days and Richard was obviously pleased as he inspected the job. He had asked O'Malley what he thought of the cabinets.

"They're okay," he said with a shrug.

"That's what I think," Richard said.

O'Malley was fascinated by the ease that his young boss told him of his decision to switch to the manufactured cabinets. He offered to keep him on as a finish carpenter, but at a reduced salary. O'Malley couldn't imagine Richard's father, Horace, who had been passionate about the physical craft of building, ever making such a decision. There had always been a glaring difference between the two men; since Horace's death the previous year, his son immediately increased production and began cutting corners. O'Malley absorbed the solid punch of this news in silence. He nodded and gathered his tools. On his way out, he told Richard he needed time to consider his proposal and he'd like to add next week to the following week of his scheduled vacation. Richard's face clouded, calculating the impact of O'Malley's absence, but he had agreed.

"If you go to the high peaks, will you be coming through?" Abbie asked.

"Yes," O'Malley said. "I was wondering if I could I drop off my paintings? I've got about twenty canvases, nothing big. In fact, it's pretty much the same paintings I brought last year. Do you have room in the barn?"

"Sure, Daddy," she said. "Have you been working on anything new?"

"Not really," he said. "I'm finishing a portrait and playing with some old stuff."

"Any sculpture?"

"No," he said. "The portrait is of your mother and I'm not sure about it."

"I'm sure it's good," she said.

"Technically, perhaps," he said. "It's different. More realistic."

"Really?" she said.

"Yes," he said. "I haven't painted like this since art school."

"Sounds interesting," Abbie said. "How would you compare it?"

"Perhaps Courbet," he replied. "But more defined. Maybe Manet."

"Oh," she said. "Is it a nude, like *Olympia*?"

"No," he said. "It's actually from a photograph a few years back."

"Really, a photograph?" she said. "This isn't like you, Daddy."

"I know," O'Malley replied, feeling a quiver of impatience race through him. "Anyway, I'd like you to take a look at it."

"Of course," Abbie said.

He regretted his tone, hearing the countenance in her voice, but he didn't want to continue the path of the conversation.

"Are you sure you can't squeeze out a couple days hiking? I'd love it if you could."

"I know," she said. "But it's impossible. We'll be able to get out around here. The boys will love it."

"Okay," O'Malley said. "How are they?"

While Abbie was telling him about the boys, sweat prickled along his hairline. The hot oven intensified the already humid air. When O'Malley hung up, he opened the oven and checked the chicken. Outside he picked up the glass of wine and walked along the edge of lawn overlooking the lake to his studio. He opened the door and flipped a switch on the wall. The overhead tract lights came on. He was greeted by a painting of Susanne on an easel. She was sitting on a sofa, angled slightly to her left – almost a slouch. Her left arm was bent and the forearm sat on a pillow with a glass of wine in her hand. The other arm rested on her crossed legs with her fingers spread over one knee. She wore brown sandals, a short sleeved floral printed blouse with a scooped neck. A khaki skirt rode up toward her hips. Long legs emerged. It was really what you saw first – the long legs with the light coming somewhere from her right side that enhanced their shapeliness and cast a shadow into the skirt opening. Susanne's face was averted a little to her left as if she was listening to someone. There was a small and attentive smile on her face – one eyebrow arched higher than the other, giving the impression she had been intrigued by what was being said to her.

O'Malley painted the picture from a photograph taken many years ago. He thought it was from a party and whoever snapped the picture (he couldn't remember who), had taken it quickly, leaving a dark knee exposed in the bottom right corner. O'Malley found the photograph the past winter in a shoebox. He had many photographs of Susanne, sometimes alone, other times with Abbie or himself and many of all three of them. It was strange how this particular photograph had captured him although the circumstance escaped his memory. At first O'Malley leaned it against the lamp on his nightstand. He loved the way light cascaded on it from within the lampshade. He would interrupt his reading and stare at it for long periods. When he shut off the light he would try to hang onto the image, welcoming the soft textures of remembrance that sometimes carried him to sleep. O'Malley knew that he dreamt of Susanne, the dreams often vividly and intensely in the present. He would awaken, brightly suspended in that happiness for perhaps a full second before he would feel the sudden realization all over again, that she was gone.

For a long time, O'Malley kept the photograph propped against the stem of the lamp. Sometimes, during the day it would tease him. He'd search his memory for precise details.

More than once he had rushed home, directly into his bedroom and turned on the lamp. He found a comforting reassurance in the photograph, but in a mood of self-analysis, he questioned the haunting impact it had on him. On a bright Sunday morning in early March, O'Malley had awakened, looked at the photograph and taken it to his studio. Susanne had been a willing model for many years. O'Malley had painted her, formed sculpture in her likeness and his sketchbooks were filled with quick-study sketches and more detailed portraits. Lately he found some comfort in them and treated them as simple memorials, but the particular photograph stood apart – became a perplexing and compelling force that he couldn't ignore. O'Malley had been taught not to paint from photographs and he had faithfully practiced this purist approach. But now he was beckoned by this representation of a specific moment, a simple photograph that someone had snapped, that stood out from the piles of photographs in his possession; it demanded to be transformed.

When O'Malley took the photograph into his studio and leaned it against a jar on his worktable, he had felt suddenly adrift. His intent was to start immediately on a large canvas, to bring on the image as he felt it in the expressionistic style he had practiced for many years. It simply wasn't there and he knew the impulsive and inspired rush that had driven him from his bedroom to the studio was weightless – as buoyant and telling as the exposed water line on an empty freighter. The emotion brought him back to his early years of self-doubt – the fickle and dramatic stabs at one style or another and the false self-confidence by which they had been delivered and defended. A battle raged inside. O'Malley knew the picture had to be painted. Also, that it demanded a realistic representation, even though it was a style he had forsaken many years ago. The finished product never seemed to satisfy him in relation to the intense effort involved; the emotional release was minimal – a strangled ejaculation.

O'Malley had worked on the painting for the past two and a half months, plodding carefully to reproduce every detail. As he stepped into the studio, he knew from the oily hint of dead humid air, that the picture wasn't quite dry. He had played with it yesterday – a few touches around the eyes. Each time he looked at it there was something that didn't seem quite right. The image affected him like an unreasonable argument, as if he was being fooled by a mischievous twin. O'Malley picked up the photograph, compared it with the canvas and felt the same frustration in the pit of his stomach. Cold and critical rationale told him that it was finished. Whatever was missing came from some intangible place inside, a vague phantasm that he couldn't grasp. As O'Malley placed the photograph against the jar on the worktable he knew it was a moment of finality, a reluctant surrender. He placed a portable fan on a bench, facing the portrait and turned it on. The air quietly pushed against the canvas and O'Malley suppressed the strange yearning to see her hair part from the rush. He stepped back and raised his glass.

"I'm sorry," he whispered and sipped the warm wine.

- - -

On Saturday morning O'Malley emptied tools and equipment from the van. He carefully stacked his canvasses and secured them. The painting of Susanne was dry, but he couldn't decide if he should take it. It troubled him that he wasn't moved by it, but the idea of selling it didn't seem acceptable. Finally, he loaded it, hoping Abbie could give him an honest critique. O'Malley found it difficult to inventory the camping gear as it hadn't been used since Susanne died and he was flooded with memories. The first summer after her death he had been too grief stricken to go and the past year he stayed in a cheap motel around the corner from Abbie's house. He knew the self-imposed solitude of camping was inconceivable and he had actually considered not going, but he wanted to see Abbie and the boys. It was an unsettling week, the area too laden with shared recollections from vivid landmarks for him to enjoy. But he had spent time with Abbie (a hike up Black Bear Mountain where he wept uncontrollably on the summit) and he fished with the boys.

Late in the afternoon, O'Malley finished loading the van. He was sweating and decided on a swim. He descended the stairs to the beach. There was no one around. He stripped and plunged into the water. O'Malley had been floating on his back, his mind vacant with his eyes closed when his name pierced the dead air. Above him Harold Pratt leaned over the railing at the top of the stairs.

"Hey nature boy," he called down. "What's that ugly creature swimming between your legs?"

O'Malley felt a flash of anger as he waded ashore and wrapped himself in a towel while Harold climbed down the stairs.

"You always swim bare-naked?" Harold asked and O'Malley couldn't help smiling at the old, redundant expression.

Harold was excited about a fishing tournament in nearby Olcott the following weekend and he was disappointed when O'Malley told him he'd be away.

"Shit," Harold said. "Lately you've been about as available as a nun in a whorehouse."

O'Malley eased some guilt by offering dinner at the Maple Shade Hotel, a former inn on Main Street in the village of Smith. Now only a tavern, it was known as Slow John's in dubious reference to the old, shaky and bent over proprietor. He seemed to take forever in serving drinks, that at the trembling journey's end, left the glass three quarters full.

"Get shit-faced licking the floor," Harold said, pointing to the splattered trail behind the old man.

They ate cheeseburgers and drank cold, bottled beer (reasonably safe from Slow John's jittery hands) and Harold shared gossip with the other patrons and intermittently commented on the Yankees game on the TV. He ordered another round of beers before O'Malley was finished with his first. He saw the light brightening in his friend's eyes and was thankful he'd insisted on them taking separate vehicles. O'Malley was able to leave a half hour later without too much objection from Harold who was already into the scotch.

- - -

The cottage was situated on a slope about ten yards above the stone wall that separated the lawn from the small beach on Fourth Lake. There were two bedrooms, a living room, bathroom and kitchen. Outside, a covered porch spanned the length of the structure, a feature O'Malley had enjoyed in the past, given the frequent passing rains in June. But there had been no rain and instead of sitting on the porch with his morning coffee, he went to the end of the dock, hoping for a breeze that didn't come. The water was low, showing stain-like absence on the pilings of the dock and the receded shoreline. The sun was behind him, still hidden by the density of the elevated forest and wouldn't break out until later in the morning.

O'Malley had arrived on Sunday afternoon after stopping at Abbie's. It had been wonderful to see her and the boys. Even John seemed unusually animated, having sold his first house the day before, but he was in a hurry to get back to the liquor store. After lunch O'Malley unloaded the canvases into the barn and went grocery shopping. He stopped at John's store where, to his delight, he found a nice selection of French and Italian wines. He selected a mixed case. John had at first refused his money, but when O'Malley insisted, he agreed, feebly offering a "family discount" that was ignored. There were four other cottages on the property, set farther back from the shore and shadowed by tall pines. They were unoccupied, but O'Malley knew they'd be full the following week and for the rest of the summer when the schools let out. He had wanted to take Abbie and the boys for a hike, arguing that Bald Mountain, just a few minutes out of the village, could be accomplished in a mere hour, but Abbie had been steadfast in refusal and reprimanded him after sending the boys upstairs to their rooms. They were supposed to clean their rooms yesterday, but neither had.

"Daddy, it's important I follow through," she said, citing examples of behavioral problems of some of her male students. "They'll be finished with school on Wednesday and hopefully their rooms will be cleaned by then."

After unloading the van and organizing the cottage, O'Malley was stricken with an overwhelming anxiety that seemed to physically shake him. He had rented the cottage a few times before. One summer the weather had been perfect with long sunny days, the air fresh with the rich scent from the dense greenery and the water so clean and pure – he had been giddy and childlike, pulling young Abbie for hours through the shallow water at the beach and tossing her off his shoulders. It was a game they called "shoot-offs" and he remembered her tiny feet grappling his shoulders as he crouched under water and then snapped his legs straight and burst from the water, feeling her fingers let go of his head and her body soaring and blotting out the sun like a passing cloud. So much joy in the small body, suspended in air with her fingers squeezing her nose and the splash and quick emergence – her mouth in muddled competition – gasping, coughing, laughing and yelling, "Do it again, Daddy." Every day they played the game and he was amazed she never grew tired of it. One night toward the end of the week, Abbie had fallen asleep on the couch while O'Malley and Susanne sat on the porch. Later, as O'Malley lifted her to carry her to bed, she had automatically assumed the daytime position – pinching her nose and kicking her feet without waking.

There was another time when the weather had not been so perfect – three solid days of rain; they set a card table on the porch and played a mindless, but addictive board game called, *Sorry*. He recalled Abbie struggling with the conflicting emotions as she sent an opposing piece backward on the board and then her mouth falling open: "Sawwwwwwreeeeee."

And each evening, after Abbie had been tucked in, the wonderful quiet time with Susanne.

O'Malley fled the cottage early the next morning after a sleepless night. It was already hot, the surfacing light a vague promise behind the thick forest. He had made coffee, drank half a cup and was immediately perspiring. O'Malley felt he couldn't escape fast enough, loading essentials into the van, leaving in panic, desperate to stay ahead. After a few miles his heart slowed and he shed the wild tendrils of the spell and welcomed the solid clarity of the winding road. The sky was bright blue, enhanced by the full face of the sun and offering a sharp edged boundary at the top of the wavy tree-line. At certain vantage points, mountains in the distance were well defined and boulders beyond the shoulders of the road seemed to jump forward, offering vivid details – the varied layers – beiges, browns and grays, as a distinct yet cooperative melding; the urgent pull in all directions to see it all.

At Seventh Lake he pulled over on the shoulder before the small bridge spanning an outlet from a creek that fed into the lake. It had always been a favorite place, but O'Malley was suddenly down-hearted as he walked onto the bridge. The smell of decay – a fetid collection of dead fish and rotting plant life floating in the solid green blanket. It stretched on the surface into the stunted landscape that resembled a swamp. It was as if he'd stopped to see a friend and found him bedridden with a terrible disease. On the other side, the surface film diminished until it was gone and sunlight reflected off the flat sheen of the lake, causing him to squint. Exposed tree trunks, the roots dry and Medusa-like were scattered obscenely on the beach, far receded from the normal shoreline around the nearest point of land.

On the road again, the old sound of the van straining uphill and the winging let-go on descent was like a soundtrack accompanying the visions of passing places. They were all familiar, some with specific history and he had enough time between them to sort them chronologically, although he wasn't always sure. He wished Susanne was there to set him straight – this train of thought an ambush that brought sadness and then pissed him off. He spent the afternoon wandering places he had enjoyed, but couldn't shake a deep and unsettling feeling of alienation that rendered everything as unapproachable; he felt as one trying to gain access with fake identification. O'Malley arrived at the campground, down the road from the entrance to the Adirondak Loj with the sun low in the trees. He had planned on sleeping in the van, but the campsite was surrounded by dense foliage so he erected his tent, hoping, but doubting the screened windows would offer a cross breeze. After O'Malley finished setting up camp he drove back to the campground office to purchase firewood. They were out of wood and the proprietor told him where to buy some at a farm down the road, but to ignore the gas station on the way, although there were wrapped bundles stacked in front.

"They get it from this local dude," he said. "He's kind of a half-assed, lazy drip of an outfit if you know what I mean. Two years ago the whole place went up in smoke, some kind of a propane explosion and it all burnt to the ground. It was a pretty nasty fire and there wasn't much left except for the bundles of firewood."

O'Malley drove to the gas station and re-fueled. Farther down, the farm was quiet with nobody attending the fruit stand out front. The buildings were set far back from the road. A wooden box with a slit cut in the top with "$4" carved into the side sat on a table next to bundles of firewood. He dropped a ten-dollar bill into the box and threw two bundles into the van. Back at the campground, he snaked around the dirt roads in the new darkness, exploring the sites. Only a few were occupied and he was annoyed to see one of them was next to his. O'Malley backed into his site and unloaded the firewood. He heard tapping from the back of the next site, but he didn't see anyone. He tore old newspaper and balled up the strips and put them in the fire pit and added a crisscross pattern of twigs that he topped with the larger pieces. He struck a match and lit the paper and watched the fire spread and begin to crackle as it enveloped the kindling. An orange glow danced around the open area and he heard voices of light laughter. Two young girls stood on the other side of a small area of low foliage watching him.

"Ours won't start," one of them said.

The tapping stopped and he heard quick footsteps and a woman appeared behind the girls. O'Malley could feel her eyes scrutinizing him as she gathered the girls.

"Hello," he said.

"Hello," she said. "I hope they're not bothering you."

"Not at all," he replied.

"We can't get a fire started or our tent up," the same girl said.

"Stop, Lindsey," the woman said, her hand reaching over the girl's mouth. "Silly girls want a fire in this heat."

"Well, this silly man is doing the same thing. I can't imagine camping without a fire," he said. "Can I help?"

He opened his hands and smiled, again feeling her scrutiny and realizing under the circumstances that there was nothing he could do to assuage her fears.

"I'm Kevin O'Malley," he said.

"Gail," she said. "Gail Kincaid. This is Lindsey and Celia, my granddaughters and I'm afraid I'll have to accept your assistance."

O'Malley noted the uneasiness that accompanied her admission as he walked over to their site. In the fire pit, black filmy paper of the failed fire sat under four logs, their surfaces slightly licked and oozing sap. He asked her where she got the wood and laughed when she told him. She was offended by his laughter and he told her the story.

"Well, I'll be damned," she said. "Girls, put that wood off to the side. We'll return it tomorrow."

He offered the other bundle of firewood he had purchased, but she refused.

"What about the marshmallows?" Lindsey said.

"Yes," O'Malley said. "What about the marshmallows?"

He looked at Gail and she threw up her arms and nodded. He brought over the other bundle of wood and he waved away the four dollars she offered and finally had to accept it. He let the girls tear up the newspaper and he gathered kindling, thinking it was too dark for them to leave the site. The girls happily pulled up folding chairs after he lit it. The tent was spread out in the back corner and he saw she had been trying to bury the stakes with a rock, but the dried ground was too hard. He retrieved his hammer and set the stakes and Gail helped him attach the poles and they raised it. O'Malley found it strange working closely with the woman, squatting and bending in the darkness, hearing her breathing; it felt conflicted – like a familiar and forbidden intimacy and he was alarmed, but mildly aroused the couple times they bumped into each other.

Gail thanked O'Malley and he stopped by the fire and adjusted the wood with the claw of his hammer. He bid the girls a goodnight and he heard Lindsey ask, "Can't the nice man stay and have marshmallows with us?" as he cut through the foliage to his campsite. His fire was burning well and he added another log and lit the kerosene lamp on the picnic table. He made two sandwiches and packed them in a bag with two apples in the cooler. He opened a bottle of red wine and pushed his folding chair back from the fire. Sitting low, he couldn't see the other camp; there was a slight illumination above their fire and the sky was black without stars. O'Malley thought he saw the slow, filmy movement of clouds. From time to time he heard soft laughter and the deeper rhythm of Gail's soothing voice. After an hour or so, the girls' voices rose in protest, followed by the firm tone from Gail and he knew they were being sent to bed. It became very quiet, except a slight cough and throat clearing every once in a while. O'Malley was tempted to call over to her, but he felt stymied – fearful that he would frighten her and yet he was prodded with a tortuous idea that it was absurd for two people to sit so obviously apart in such close proximity. He became self-conscious about any movements and he was relieved when he heard her retire.

O'Malley had been dreaming of sleeping outside under bright stars in the cockpit of a sailboat. Waking in the dark and confined world of the small tent was alarming although sweating had made sense as the dream was somewhere in the tropics. In the dream Susanne had crawled out of the sleeping bag to go to the restroom, an impossibility that O'Malley had accepted and he watched as she walked away. She was naked and her skin continued to glow in lunar radiance as she diminished into the black distance. Within seconds he was grasping at the remnants of the fleeting dream, down-hearted by her leaving (she had whispered, "I'll be right back" in breath that was warm and smelling of cinnamon) and disturbed by the residual erection that poked through the opening of his shorts. O'Malley pulled on his pants before he crawled out of the tent.

It was 5:30 am and sunlight was low in the trees when he drove out of the campground. His intent had been to make coffee on his Coleman stove, but again he considered his neighbors, so he headed for Lake Placid and had breakfast at a diner.

The parking area was vacant at the trailhead of Cascade Mountain. This pleased him and he quickly pulled on his hiking boots and checked out his day pack. O'Malley was already sweating as he hefted the pack and picked up his hiking stick. He entered the wooded cover of the trail, feeling a mild stiffness in his legs and lower back. Within a half mile the stiffness was gone and he was perspiring heavily. Deer flies were buzzing around his head, forcing him to stop and apply insect repellant. He pulled the canteen from the old army belt and drank. He had stored it overnight in the cooler, but it was warm. He also brought another canteen in his backpack, remembering a lesson learned many years ago when Susanne and he had first started coming to the Adirondacks. They had hiked Rondaxe (Bald) Mountain and Rocky Mountain, both easy with rewarding views, especially Rocky Mountain where from two opposing sides you could follow Route # 28 into the hamlets of Eagle Bay and Inlet. Their next climb was Black Bear Mountain, which originated from the same trailhead as Rocky Mountain and was twice as long, about forty-five minutes. They were delighted at the spacious summit. They planned their trips in early June to avoid crowds and they were happy this wisdom had paid off on Black Bear. After the consistent but not too demanding climb with only one short, steep scramble, they wandered the varied edges of the summit and Susanne chose a small drop – a shelf-like area, secluded, but opened to the refreshing breeze. They peeled off their damp shirts and leaned back against a flat rock, warmed by the sunlight. O'Malley had dozed off and he was awoken by Susanne's finger running down his chest and stomach and prodding into his waistband. She had put on a fresh t-shirt, but her shorts were bunched around one ankle. She turned and situated herself on all fours.

"Easy," she said, smiling over her shoulder. She pointed her chin toward the obvious steepness of the drop below them. "I'd hate to be found at the bottom like this."

Afterward they ate lunch and sat quietly, absorbing the view and O'Malley thought a glass of wine would have been nice. The following June they had ventured farther to Long Lake and nearby Blue Mountain had been suggested as a "pleasant climb" by a local bartender. O'Malley's imagination dictated bringing along a bottle of red wine and a beach towel as Susanne's knees had been scuffed up during their lovemaking on Black Bear. He was happy to see the parking lot to the trailhead empty and his heart swelled with anticipation. But he had stupidly halved their water supply for the wine and the climb had been more grueling with the temperature topping at ninety-two degrees and the air heavy with humidity. The summit was disappointing, the tree line high and obscuring the view all around and obstructing what little breeze existed. There was small relief in the fire tower and they stripped off their sweat soaked t-shirts. Susanne laughed when she opened the beach towel, calling it a "bed spread" and O'Malley's visions of lovemaking were dissolved by the arrival of a group of giggling adolescent girls. Three of them immediately began climbing the fire tower stairs and Susanne and he hurriedly pulled on their fresh t-shirts. O'Malley neglected to mention the bottle of wine that he knew was too warm and it shifted solidly in his pack during the climb down, a constant reminder of his short sightedness and the mocking antithesis to the near empty canteen.

In spite of the oppressive heat, he enjoyed the early going. The trail was remarkably different than the one Susanne and he had hiked five years earlier. He had read that the old trail was replaced with an easier one – more direct from the road and with fewer and shorter steep segments. An hour later, after a constant but not too demanding ascent under wooded cover, O'Malley was suddenly facing an open area of bare rock. A young woman sat, cradling a dog. Her eyes were staring past him. He was doubly surprised, first seeing the woman and then turning to follow her gaze; the view was so immense, it seemed in motion against him and actually forced him to step back. Spread out before him in a vast and airy distance was a panorama of mountains.

"That's Algonquin, Colden and Marcy," the woman said, as if expecting him to ask. "Makes you want to bow, doesn't it?"

O'Malley nodded and turned back to the woman, but her eyes were again beyond him and carried a fervent absorption, as one attending an intense live performance. He released his pack and sat back on the pitch of the rock and looked out into the vast distance of spreading peaks under an ominous sky. The dog yelped. The woman asked if he could spare a little water.

"The streams up here are dried up," she said.

She formed a cup with her hands and O'Malley poured and the dog, an Irish Setter, lapped it up. He offered the canteen to her, but she shook her head and rose and thanked him. The dog, as if responding to some secret signal, started on the trail down the mountain and she followed. O'Malley felt a sudden and profound loneliness. He had expected a welcoming wind in the higher elevations, but there was none. The air was sweltering and seemed to suck the life from him. O'Malley leaned back and closed his eyes. There was nothing but the darkness in his head, the heat around his body and the warm texture of the rock beneath him. He didn't recognize his heartbeat although it had been elevated from the hike and when he did it felt very distant and more in his head than his chest.

After a few minutes, O'Malley reclaimed the trail. He was quickly into a wooded area, but the trees were shorter and the sky closer. Anticipation pulled him. He tried to ignore the burning in his legs, focusing on each completed step as a victory in the incremental process. Soon there was more sky. The passing trees, shoulder height and gnarly. He pushed his hands against the twitching muscles above his knees. Ahead, the rocky summit stretched into the blue sky. He remembered how excited Susanne and he had felt the first time; they had quickly finished the open climb and on the summit wandered around the varied rocky formations with the newness of other higher peaks surrounding them. On that day it had been sunny, but there had been a cool, steady wind and the sky was mottled with white passing clouds, causing slight shadows to dance ghost-like across the surface. The sudden warmth had been remarkable when the sun emerged.

It was all sun now and O'Malley detected a slight breeze that lacked refreshment as he climbed past cairns and arrived at the top. He peeled off his t-shirt and spread it over a rock. He drank from his canteen until it was empty. The views in any direction were dynamic. O'Malley was at first surprised to see a middle-aged couple and a mixed group of seven that he guessed were college students, but he remembered there was at least one other trail. O'Malley went back to where he'd left his pack and he sat down on a flat rock and ate his lunch. Afterward he moved down and sat with his back against the rock. He lit a cigarette and wrote in his journal.

Many years before, O'Malley had begun keeping the journal to store ideas for his artwork, but after he met Susanne he had expanded its purpose after she read entries to him from her own journal that she had maintained during her travels in Europe. He enjoyed her general approach; her voice could be casual and whimsical – describing a couple late at night in an outside café, noting an apparent shyness in the man and the woman "dripping with eagerness to be under him." Descriptions of paintings and sculpture or the listing of ingredients in a recipe were painstakingly entered and he had noticed the script was more upright and formal. O'Malley had adopted a similar approach and he didn't feel compelled to add entries every day. His voice varied according to what he was describing, although he tried to keep deeply emotional thoughts from becoming too involved. After Susanne's death, he found the sphere of his existence could not be accurately expressed, so he gave it up for a while. He picked it up back in March while working on the portrait of Susanne and this was the first time he used it otherwise.

O'Malley wrote quickly in small energetic snatches. He managed a few lines, recounting the hike up the mountain. He lit another cigarette and leaned back against the rock. The taste of tobacco, the exhale – smoke mingling into the air led him back to Susanne and their early relationship. Most of the time she came to his house. They were crazy for each other, making love after a few steps into the door. A shower, dinner preparations in the kitchen – the room filled with herbal aromas and her hair wet and glistening, the taste of wine and her voice clear and uplifting amid the background drift of classical music. He could still remember how insane his happiness was and after dinner they'd go back to his bedroom and make love in the large sleigh bed (Susanne had told him that was the style of the bed and she would sometimes look at him, wink and say, "How about a sleigh ride?").

He treasured the quiet aftermath; dusk filtered through the windows in a pale, bluish haze. They leaned back on stacked pillows and smoked cigarettes with an ashtray between them. All they heard was the wind and the lake washing against the shore and words they uttered came sparingly like shells rolling in with the tide. O'Malley thought of those moments while they were happening as something that he wished could go on forever. Now on the mountain top the irrefutable fact that they wouldn't ever occur again stunned him. This reaction had blind-sided him many times in the last two years and he noted how unbelievably new and devastating each episode was.

More people emerged on the summit and although there was an abundance of room, O'Malley felt crowded, somehow exposed and he stood and pulled on a fresh t-shirt and organized his backpack. By the time he reached the juncture of the trail that veered off to Porter Mountain, he was sweating into his eyes. He stopped to drink from his canteen and tie a bandana around his head. His knees were sore due to the jarring refrain of the descending trail and his toes had been pushing against the front of his boots and he re-tied them. As O'Malley continued downward, carefully shuffling in an area of steep, bare rock and eventually coming upon a large boulder he remembered passing earlier, he heard a familiar voice. Around the curve in the trail they came into view; Lindsey pointed toward him.

"Gramma, it's him," she said. "It's the man from the campground."

The two girls were standing in front of their grandmother who was sitting hunched over on a log. Her forearms were spread over her knees and she looked up at O'Malley and her head dropped. He released his backpack and knelt in front of the woman. He gently raised her head.

"Gail," he said. "Can you hear me?"

"Yes, I can hear you," she said.

Her eyes flickered and her head pitched forward against his open hand.

"Easy now," he said.

He squatted and coaxed her off the log, onto the ground. A slice of sunlight slashed her face and O'Malley helped shift her into the shade. He retrieved his backpack and pulled out the canteen. He supported the back of her head and brought the canteen to her lips. She drank and choked. O'Malley set down the canteen and patted her back.

"Do you feel sick?" he asked.

"She already puked and she had to poop two times in the bushes," Lindsey said and he saw her grandmother's slight frown at the surfacing of this information.

"Are you girls okay?" he asked. "Do you have water?"

"There's some in the backpack," Celia said.

"Gramma wouldn't take any," Lindsey said. "I didn't want to either, but she made us."

O'Malley reached for the backpack and opened it. The two-quart canteen was about half full. There were also three sweatshirts, three caps, a crumpled lunch bag and two bananas. He pulled out two of the smaller caps. He handed the blue and red Buffalo Bills cap to Celia. Lindsey crossed her arms and shook her head when O'Malley offered a green John Deere cap.

"I want the Bills," she said.

"I want the Bills," Celia said, pulling the cap snuggly on her head.

"It's my turn," Lindsey said.

"No," Celia said, tilting her head back as Lindsey took a swipe for it.

"Daddy gave it to me," Lindsey said.

"He did not," Celia said. "You just grabbed it. He was handing it to me."

"Stop it," Gail said. "Take turns. Celia has it today. Lindsey tomorrow."

O'Malley had been uncomfortable holding the green cap. Raising an only child left him ill-prepared for this confrontation and he didn't know what direction to steer it. Lindsey solved the problem snatching it and pulling it down, bending her ears. He pulled another larger cap from the backpack, faded yellow and without signage. O'Malley wiped Gail's forehead and secured the cap. Her face was pale and he sensed her struggle to focus. He felt a bit like an intruder as he studied her features up close, remarkably different than the impression in the fire-lit darkness of the previous night.

"I must be a sight," she said, as if reading his mind.

O'Malley was attracted to her eyes, large and green and almond shaped. Normally he would've said so, but a vague etiquette told him this wasn't the time so he told her she looked fine and offered the canteen. After a few sips he presented a couple salt tablets. Her face tilted – a questioning expression that quickly vanished as she seemed to resign herself to O'Malley's judgment and took the pills. When the color returned to her face, he passed the canteen to the girls. He peeled a banana and broke pieces for all three of them.

"My Dad loves the Buffalo Bills," Lindsey said. "He took me, just me, to a game once."

"I was sick," Celia said. "Mom wouldn't let me."

"Now, that's enough," Gail said. "I don't want to hear anymore."

Lindsey marched off down the trail and Celia followed.

"Lindsey!" Gail said.

"I know," the girl said. "Stay in sight."

Gail breathed deeply and turned to O'Malley.

"Their father and my daughter split up last year," she said. "It's been tough on the girls and real tough on my daughter."

O'Malley nodded and offered his hand when Gail rose from the ground and sat on the log. She asked for her backpack and she took out her sweatshirt and mopped her face. He offered her the canteen and she shook her head, but he pushed it closer and she smiled and drank. Gail told him she was feeling better and she started to get up, but O'Malley rested his hand on her shoulder.

"Not quite yet," he said. "Tell me about the girls."

"I really feel fine," Gail said. "We really should be moving on."

"Just a little longer," O'Malley said, presenting the canteen. "Tell me about the girls."

"Lindsey's ten and Celia's eight." Gail sipped from the canteen and handed it back. O'Malley listened as she told him about the girls and their mother. At first he was more interested in her tone than her content until he was satisfied with the strengthening in her voice.

They came from East Aurora, a village southeast of Buffalo. Their father worked as a sales manager for a nearby building supply distributor and had carried on an affair with a young receptionist for six months. She didn't offer much detail except that the son-in-law had carried on his affair in the early morning, going to work at 5am, playing the role of the hard working provider and attentive family man who was home for dinner every night.

"Since the divorce, my daughter's been working and going to school and raising the girls," Gail said. "Jeanine would never tell me, but she's exhausted. She graduated from college last month and my gift to her was a trip to Tucson, Arizona where my other daughter, Rene lives. They're twins and very close and it's difficult given the distance between them."

"That's a long way," O'Malley said, thinking how little he saw his daughter with the distance small by comparison.

"Oh yes," Gail said. "Rene went to college out there and stayed. She loves it and that makes me happy, but I'm lucky if I see her twice a year. She's still single and there are no grandchildren. I don't think I could bear it if there were."

Her eyes were on the girls, bent over and examining something behind a rock.

"What are you looking at?"

"A pretty white flower," Lindsey said. "Would you like it for your hair?"

"Of course not," Gail said. "What did I tell you?"

"To let nature be," Lindsey said. "But it's behind this rock. Nobody will even see it."

"You did."

"But I was lucky," she replied.

"Yes you were," Gail said. "And maybe someone else will be lucky too."

She turned to O'Malley and her eyes turned downward while her lips parted in a small smile.

"I'm actually terrified that Jeanine will want to move out to Arizona to be with her sister," she said. "Rene has mentioned it to her and I know Jeanine's thinking about it even though she downplays it to me."

O'Malley found himself in the position of responding to the possibility of unfortunate news, but he knew the emptiness had a way of filling in and life has a way of simply going on. He knew he couldn't say this to her; he hated remarks of blanketed optimism, but was spared a response by the girls returning. Lindsey had a triangular flat stone in her palm and asked if it was an arrowhead.

"Could be," Gail said, but O'Malley knew it wasn't, but he refrained from saying, not wanting to add to the girl's disappointment of wearing the least favored cap.

"Do you think you're up to moving?" he asked Gail.

She nodded and O'Malley passed around the canteen and he stuffed Gail's backpack into his own, ignoring her protests. The girls didn't seem to care that they were turning around without reaching the summit. They remained ahead, but in sight as they hiked the descending trail. Gail walked slowly, stabbing the dry ground with O'Malley's stick and accepting his guiding hand on her elbow. As they moved farther down the mountain, more people passed them on the way up. They were all sweating heavily and some asked how much more to the summit. He noted how the downward trek was much more difficult with each passing year, remembering Susanne's constant preaching to him to do stretching exercises. She had faithfully practiced yoga for many years, but O'Malley had been too impatient to follow even the most rudimentary of the teachings. He actually welcomed the slow journey, the extra care taking a measure of violence off each step. The additional effort mustered to guide the woman kept him preoccupied and less focused on the racking pain in his legs and hips.

There were a couple difficult areas that required O'Malley to actually hold her with his arm tight around her and the length of his body close to hers. He felt the slight peeling sensation of their skin against each other, their sweat melding and the back of her head inches away and a vaguely sweet smell from her hair. He sensed this made her uncomfortable and she quickly disengaged him when the treacherous moments passed. Sometimes this created a physical confusion since he was also attempting to disengage with obvious haste and hopefully with a sense of innocence. O'Malley had glanced his hands against her breasts and once he felt the bounce of her buttocks against his leg. He tried to not look closely at her, but he had succumbed a few times; his eyes were drawn to details of her hair coiled up into the cap, a trail of sweat gliding past her ear.

Each time she seemed to have sensed it and turned directly into his face and he was forced to look away.

Eventually the trail leveled to a moderate decline and they were able to walk easily and O'Malley let her lead the way. He was acutely aware this was the closest he had been to a woman in two years, but he was uneasy with the brazenness of the thought. He noticed her stride was stronger. O'Malley tripped on a rock and Gail stopped and turned, watching the frantic stumbling as he struggled to regain his balance.

"Be careful," she said. "It would be a shame to get injured so close to the end."

Twenty minutes later the girls alerted them, pointing ahead.

"There's the parking lot," Celia said.

"We made it," Lindsey added.

At their car, the girls argued about who would sit in front and Gail refereed a compromise, letting Lindsey have it first. O'Malley mentioned he was going up the road to a swimming spot and asked if they wanted to join him.

"We really can't," Gail said. "We're staying at the Sandy Point Motel on Long Lake tonight and the hike has lasted longer than I planned and I'd like to get there..."

"Gramma said there's a beach right there at the motel," Lindsey said. "You could swim with us."

O'Malley declined the girl's invitation, saying he wanted to get some fishing in, even though her Grandmother had offered a polite nod at the suggestion. They both retreated to a formal shyness as O'Malley returned the backpack and they got into the car. After thanking O'Malley and shaking his hand, Gail drove off. He wondered if he would've gone to Long Lake if she had pressed the issue.

- - -

O'Malley backed his van near a small beach on Cascade Lake. He stripped behind the opened van door and pulled on his swimsuit. He waded steadily into the water and plunged below the surface. Hard kicks bulleted against the solid coolness with his arms tight to his sides until he could no longer hold his breath. Low sunlight flashed between trees as he surfaced. He stayed in the water, slowly rotating until he felt his body temperature lower. O'Malley absorbed the view around him. His appreciation of nature's vast range of beauty sometimes thrust him into a creative frenzy. He found it best to temper the stirring; it was a time-tested wisdom concerning the lakes in the Adirondacks. He had painted them many times, but there had been a certain truth absent – a dimension beyond appearance that he felt perhaps only a poet might capture.

After toweling off, he sat in the folding chair in the shade of a tall tree. Even with the sun blocked out, he became warm and prickly and he decided it was too hot to fish. O'Malley swam again and changed. He remembered to purchase more firewood as he drove back to the campground. There were a few more occupied campsites, but there were none on either side of him. He was at first surprised and then he felt silly at his disappointment that Gail and her granddaughters were gone.

Normally while camping, O'Malley enjoyed the ritual of preparing a meal, but he found himself nervous and impatient after starting a fire. He stabbed two hot dogs on a fork and held it over the flames. He was equally impatient to eat and he burnt the inside of his mouth and splattered condiments on his clean, white shirt. O'Malley cleaned up after the meal and sat by the fire and sipped wine, watching the diminishing sunlight through the dense foliage. He was perspiring and sought to be still, but his inner body was hyperactive and felt like it was trying to push outside his skin.

He was forced to his feet and walked away from the confines of the campsite and down the dirt road. O'Malley passed a couple campsites with fires burning and he heard conversations and light laughter. He found a chair in front of the campground office and he sat and lit a cigarette. Darkness brought fireflies (lightning bugs as Susanne had called them) and O'Malley watched their elusive flickering. Beyond the parking lot, across the road, the country was open under a black sky inhabited by a mob of stars. When Abbie was little, Susanne told her the lightning bugs were really stars that became angels and wandered to earth and watched over gardens in the summer. He remembered how Susanne regarded a sky full of stars with total optimism – predicting the following day would be clear and sunny. O'Malley had told her many times of the fallacy of this reasoning – that tomorrow's weather was at that moment probably over the Midwest, but she didn't believe him, selectively citing past days that had turned up pleasant. Through the years it became a silly game between them; she continued her facetious stubbornness under the stars and O'Malley told her each time as if was the first, that tomorrow's weather was right then over Kalamazoo.

Back at camp he brought the fire back to life. He sipped wine and smoked until he felt himself nodding off. O'Malley slept fitfully and entered dreams that were confusing, the images unrelated – people and places that had nothing to do with one another and the activities were determined but ultimately without purpose. He finally crawled out of his tent and found the area layered in fog. All the surfaces were damp and he wiped off the picnic table and benches and fired up the Coleman stove to boil water for coffee. He lit a cigarette and sat with his back against the table and studied the fog. O'Malley realized he had never thought about painting it although at this moment it presented itself as attractive and substantial. He tried to think of paintings from other artists that included fog, but nothing came to mind. What he felt was a cool dampness that was quickly dissipating – a kind of whimsical atmosphere that floated away before the more solid and heated advance of sunlight. Many times he heard the phrase, "the sun burning off the fog" and he had said it himself, but right now he wondered if it was accurate. O'Malley saw the sunlight climbing a tree with dancing shadows from the wind stirred leaves hanging above. There was no remnant of the fog on the tree, but beyond it there lingered the smoky drift and he watched it intently as it dissolved and sunlight peeked between the trees. He felt the promise of another hot day and he finished his coffee and broke camp.

- - -

O'Malley stopped before the bridge on Route 30 that crossed Long Lake and took some photographs. It was still early and the sun was just showing across the lake. The surface was still and the reflection of the shoreline was identical. O'Malley watched a small boat cross the breadth of the shore and saw its wake shatter the image. He drove past the planes tied to the dock across from the Adirondack Hotel and through the hamlet and continued along the southeast shore. He was excited to see Gail's car parked at the Sandy Point Motel and he had slowed the van, but the thought of stopping was ultimately too farfetched. During the early morning drive through Saranac Lake and Tupper Lake he had created a vision based on the simple and what he considered sound rationale that he was stopping to make sure she had fully recovered from yesterday's heat exhaustion. The vision had built with considerable momentum until that very moment in front of the motel when he realized how silly it was to stop by so early in the morning – picturing her roused from sleep to answer the door and her granddaughters awake and questioning his presence. He stomped on the gas pedal, suddenly feeling foolish and not wanting to be seen.

O'Malley continued on the winding road, only slowing as he passed Blue Mountain Lake where he witnessed a lone kayaker slicing the calm water in the shadows below the rising sun. The next few miles the road seemed narrower with tall trees closing in on both sides, a corridor that rose and dropped along it's many curves. He fell into a haphazard pattern of accelerating and braking. As he passed the sign designating Utowana Lake he remembered the many times that Susanne and Abbie had looked at each other and recited simultaneously, "I don't wanna," laughing out loud. Within an hour, O'Malley pulled into the long dusty driveway and through the woods to his cottage. His sweat soaked shirt peeled from the back of the seat as he climbed out of the van. He had left the cottage closed up and the air was stuffy. After he opened the windows and brought in his gear, he changed into his swimsuit and went to the beach. The water was clear and O'Malley swam out past the roped in beach area and rolled onto his back. He treaded water until his body cooled and he swam in and toweled off. O'Malley was anxious to see Abbie and the boys, but he knew they wouldn't be free until later so he sat by the water and sketched. He brought along the sketchbook as an afterthought; the idea struck him after he had locked the house and he was climbing into the van. His first instinct was to nix the idea and he had started the van, entertaining the logic that he had only used the sketchbook recently for some preliminary renderings for the portrait of Susanne. He felt nothing stirring for anything new, but something had prompted him to go back inside and get it.

The first couple sketches were very basic of the boathouse on the property next door. He was beginning the third, an area of phlox growing around a boulder behind the boathouse and he was enjoying the new freedom in his movements when he heard footsteps.

"Hi Daddy."

"Abbie."

O'Malley rose and dropped the sketchbook on a table. He was thrilled to see her. They hugged and he enjoyed the familiar scent of her hair. She sat in the chair on the other side of the table and picked up his sketchbook. Abbie looked over the page he had been working on. She gazed toward the boathouse and nodded.

"So, how are you, Daddy?"

"Good."

"Are you sure?" she asked. "You seem kind of nervous."

"You startled me," he said, pointing to the sketchbook. "I was focusing."

Abbie followed his gaze to the cluster of lavender phlox.

"Aren't they wonderful flowers?" she said. "They seem to know just where to be and they're never overbearing – seem to offer just enough color."

"Yes,' he replied. "But they don't last very long."

"They take their turn," Abbie said emphatically. O'Malley felt the resonance of the phrase as it was passed on from Susanne, who had kept the gardens at their home. She had spent years, strategically organizing the beds to continue flourishing from early spring to late fall. She had been fond of the phlox as they represented the early and promising part of the growing season and she was equally fond of the zinnias for their stubborn longevity against the advance of autumn.

"So, is school officially over?" he asked.

"For the kids," she replied. "I have some reports to finish and then I'm done."

"And the boys?"

"Just a half day."

"Did they clean their rooms?"

"Yes, Dad," she said.

"Can I have them this afternoon?"

"Of course," she said. "What are you planning?"

"I thought a trip to Russian Lake," he said. "We can cook dinner there."

"They'll love it," she replied. "But don't you think it's too hot to canoe?"

"I thought of that," he said. "I'm going to rent a pontoon boat. The hiking part is less than a mile and on level ground, mostly in the trees. We can swim after the hike."

"Well, they haven't been there for a couple years," Abbie said. "I'll make sure they have everything they need in their backpacks."

"Just extra clothes," O'Malley said. "I'll carry the rest."

"Don't overdo it, Daddy," she said. "They're getting pretty big."

"I noticed," he said. "How about some lunch?"

"Sure," Abbie said after looking at her wristwatch.

O'Malley rose and picked up the sketchbook and headed toward the cottage.

"You look pretty stiff," she said. "You sure you can manage this afternoon?"

He stopped and turned. Abbie almost walked into him.

"Of course," he said, his face drawn with feigned indignation and the helpless smile rising in reaction to her face, inches away with her eyes humorous and knowing. He turned and climbed the stairs to the porch, focusing to smooth his gait and slightly pulling on the rail with each step.

They ate lunch on the porch – fried *Spam* sandwiches with sliced onion and mayonnaise that Abbie had requested. It was an old camping favorite although Susanne hadn't shared their enthusiasm for it. The roof over the porch was blocking the sun, but O'Malley was sweating as he told Abbie about his hike on Cascade Mountain. She asked too many questions about Gail, he thought. He blushed when she asked him if she was attractive.

"Dad," she said. "Is there something going on?"

"Of course not," he said, but he had lost control of his face and he felt its betrayal and then tears escaped.

"Daddy," she said. "What is wrong?"

"Nothing, darling," O'Malley said, looking out across the lake.

"Dad, please tell me," she asked. "What's the matter?"

"It's nothing," he said, smiling and feeling foolish. "I miss your mother. It suddenly comes out of the blue sometimes, but really I'm fine."

"But this woman, Gail?" she said. "Were you attracted to her? Daddy, it's been two years. There's nothing wrong with feeling something for someone else."

O'Malley regarded the sensible posture of his daughter's face. Her features were a hodgepodge, as if picked from both parents and thrown into a hat and shaken and then drawn like *Scrabble* letters. The result bore little resemblance to either of them, but there were certain mannerisms and expressions that were perfect imitations and offered a deeper and more profound likeness. He felt the influence of her mother in Abbie's expression and accepted her words as sensible, but the attraction he had felt for Gail was now simply a moment gone, a passing of ships in the night as it were and rehashing it seemed pointless.

"I've been attracted to women all my life," he said. "They're simply beautiful creatures and wonderful to paint or draw or sculpt like gardens and sunsets or whatever. She struck me this way and I guess I'm thinking of her along those lines, like a landscape possibility when you're whizzing by at sixty miles an hour – you know, a missed opportunity."

Abbie nodded and smiled. She rose and began clearing the table. O'Malley knew he was being let off the hook and he was thankful.

- - -

O'Malley enjoyed the afternoon with his grandsons. The weather remained hot and humid and they were forced to make adjustments, slowing their pace and drinking plenty of water. The boys, John Jr. and Bradley, took turns driving the pontoon boat to the east end of Big Moose Lake. O'Malley carried most of their gear in his backpack, letting his grandsons carry only clothing in theirs on the hike to Russian Lake. The trail was mostly under the cover of trees but the shade gave little relief from the heat and deer flies forced them to stop and apply insect repellant. They spent most of the afternoon swimming around the large rock near the only opening to the water on the lake. The rock was much larger due to the shallow water and all around the lake the trees appeared strangely indecent with their roots exposed. There was a lean-to set back from the shore and in front of it a grill. O'Malley had brought in a bag of charcoal and newspaper and after the boys gathered a pile of kindling and the fire was ready, they roasted hotdogs and heated pork and beans in the can.

They returned to the marina in the dark. O'Malley had let the time slip away and he called to reassure Abbie from the marina phone. The boys talked excitedly about the boat ride for the first couple miles on the drive back to Old Forge. They enjoyed the nocturnal visions – water sliding by under the small spectacle of the boat's running lights and above, the sky full of stars. It had been their first experience on a boat at night and O'Malley was telling them about crossing the Gulf Stream many years before on a sailboat; a storm had sprung and it had been a wild ride with the wind from behind and the waves rose and kicked up the stern and drove the bow into the water. He told them of the eeriness of the cresting phosphorescence, "like spitting diamonds" he said, but there was silence; a quick look over his shoulder found them asleep.

Back at his cottage, O'Malley slept restlessly under the whirl of the metal fan. He woke in the stuffy darkness and stared into the ceiling. The moment reminded him of a cabin Susanne and he had rented in Duck on the Outer Banks of North Carolina during their honeymoon. The cabin was smaller than the cottage: a bedroom, another room that served as both a living area and a kitchen and a small bathroom. Outside there was a shower stall against the back wall, an amenity they found to be delightful. There was something wonderful about showering under the open sky.

O'Malley couldn't sleep one evening. He was sweating and very still next to Susanne, his mind reaching for a strong distraction that would settle him. Finally, he rose and pulled on a pair of shorts. On the porch he found no relief. He considered taking a cold shower, but he didn't want to wake Susanne.

The ocean was fairly calm. A small rhythmic reaching onto the beach. Far out there was a distinct pattern of moving lights that he guessed belonged to a passing freighter. The sky was massive with stars. He sat and smoked a cigarette and looked out – the dark emptiness had been pleasing, adding a dimension that was boundless, that he had somehow interpreted as optimistic. O'Malley seemed suddenly energized. He stood and walked toward the ocean. The water was cool around his calves and seashells sparkled in the moonlight on the newly exposed sand in the wake of the retreating tide. He followed the shoreline northward, plowing through the shallow water, his feet gliding the packed floor and he took in the wide range of recently revealed beach that distanced the dunes to his left. To his right, the ocean appeared infinite. O'Malley, on an unexplainable impulse, turned around. He was astonished to see

Susanne, walking toward him. She was naked, her skin radiant; her gait expressed a delicate purpose. O'Malley was mesmerized, frozen where he stood, her eyes devoured him – until she was there. Susanne tugged at his shorts and they lowered to the warm dampness of the sand. They made love and afterward waded out and swam. They walked hand in hand back to the cabin and showered, washing each other. Susanne laughed when he became aroused and she turned the water incrementally to cold. They had watched intently as if they were two students in a science lab and she nodded favorably when he remained erect. Susanne reversed the water to warm and turned away from him and bent forward to bring him along. O'Malley had gripped her thighs and looked up to the stars.

The slap of the screened door woke him.

"Dad," Abbie said. "Are you ready?"

O'Malley rolled on his side. He looked at his wristwatch. He couldn't believe it was ten thirty. The night before he had been insistent they wait until nine to hike Black Bear Mountain since he had kept the boys up so late. "Just be a minute," he said.

They took it slowly up the mountain even though the boys wanted to push ahead. It was hot and the trail was dry and dusty. Both O'Malley and Abbie carried extra water and she had brought along sandwiches, fruit and cookies. Surprisingly, they were alone on the spacious summit. They ate lunch and afterward tried to identify particular areas in the distance based on a map and O'Malley's compass. The afternoon sun became too intense and they hiked down the mountain and passed only a young couple on their way up, asking the usual, "Are we almost there?"

They spent the rest of the day on the beach at O'Malley's cottage. It was a small beach and normally guests weren't allowed since it wasn't fair to the other renters, however the other cottages were unoccupied (with school just out, from the next week to Labor Day they were totally booked) and the owner permitted them to stay. The boys swam and after a couple hours Abbie made them retreat to the cover of the porch and the four of them played board games. Later O'Malley grilled chicken that they ate with potato salad and green beans Abbie had brought. After dinner they sat at the end of the dock and Abbie and O'Malley sipped wine while the boys swam. They stayed an hour into the dark and the boys delighted in the sights of red and green running lights on passing boats, having experienced them, "from the inside" the previous night as Bradley had dramatically exclaimed. Briefly O'Malley regretted that he hadn't pushed harder to rent a boat that evening because the boys had enjoyed it so much, but Abbie had thought it extravagant and she was determined against spoiling her sons. She was equally steadfast against letting them stay overnight with O'Malley although she promised they could help their grandfather set up his booth at the art show the next morning.

- - -

It was still dark when O'Malley climbed out of bed. He made instant coffee and sat on the porch. Another hot one, he thought, but he detected a flimsy breeze and walked to the end of the dock to enjoy what he considered a generous gift. There was actually movement, a slight rustling in the foliage along the shore and rippling along the water's surface. He watched the sun appear and scatter light through the trees and onto the lake.

"There!"

The word as sharp as a snapped branch. O'Malley peered in the direction it seemed to come from. Advancing from the shadows was the vague outline of a small boat. Two figures were standing and casting. O'Malley heard the plunk of cast bait. Slowly, the boat drifted his way and he could make out the faces of the man and a boy. They held to the etiquette of silence that would be absurd in most situations given their proximity although the boy had shaken a slight wave of his hand. The man bent over and started the small trolling motor and they moved away.

O'Malley watched the morning light spread across the lake. He finished his coffee and walked back to his cottage to shower. The village of Old Forge was quiet when he arrived. A doe was wandering down Adams Street where Abbie lived. He found John Jr. and Bradley on the front steps, both of them watching the doe as she scampered away. O'Malley backed the van to the barn door and they loaded the canvases. It was a short drive to the site of the art show, an open area behind the hardware store and overlooking the small public beach. The boys were attentive as O'Malley explained the process of setting up the tent and the tall fence on either side. He noticed their extra care uncovering the canvases, especially Bradley who examined each piece.

It wasn't until after all the canvases were uncovered and hung that O'Malley realized the recent portrait of Susanne was missing. He asked the boys, but neither had seen it. The portrait had either been left in the barn or perhaps Abbie had taken it inside to look at. It was still quiet around the grounds of the show with the morning sun beating on the cluster of organized booths. The afternoon would bring more people now that the schools were out for the summer; they would come *en masse* into the village, a long line of packed cars, trailers and boats parading past the welcoming faces of restaurants and shops. In the past O'Malley had always enjoyed the early part of the opening day. He would wander around and look at the crafts and artwork and visit exhibitors he knew while Susanne settled into their booth. He had been pleased she willingly came with him. She cared a great deal for his artwork and had an easy and introspective manner in discussing it. O'Malley hated talking about his work, feeling the creation of it was enough.

He left the boys to return to Abbie's and retrieve the portrait, but he ended up wandering the exhibits and afterward he went to a nearby bakery. O'Malley bought doughnuts for the boys and a coffee and he walked down to the public beach. Away from the confines of the booths and buildings there was a slight drifting of air, different than recent days; it was refreshing against his skin and it carried a variety of subtle smells from the surrounding landscape that he could only characterize as pure. The lake surface reflected flashing ribbons of sunlight and on the far side he heard the jumpy shrill of a loon. The sky to the west was a vibrant blue and he saw the advance of large clusters of white billowing clouds. Although O'Malley felt a sense of nostalgia with a ghostly companionship that was comforting, there was also another whispering force that was easing into him. It was pleasantly overwhelming and drawing from the outside surroundings and he felt poignantly in the present and welcomed the energetic nourishment.

O'Malley retreated to the grassy area above the beach. He sat and lit a cigarette. Behind, he heard the village coming steadily to life and he considered the boys in the booth. He had instructed them to tell anyone interested in his work to come back in a half hour and he asked Red Searcher, a potter in the next booth, to keep an eye on them. O'Malley figured he had consumed that time already, but he found it difficult to break away. He couldn't shake the urge to pick up the portrait, but there was also a vague obstacle; he felt similar to a procrastinator with the self-delusive override that would hopefully shrink the urge to non-existence. It was a bit of a mystery that Abbie didn't mention the portrait, unless it was still in the barn. He couldn't imagine how it was left behind since all the canvases had been stacked vertically together. This brought an image of the covered portrait alone in the barn which troubled him. It was as if the picture was a captive, even perhaps a hostage in a world of darkness, left in a limbo of sorts.

The boys were fine at the booth. Red Searcher's wife, Mary was with them and she said she'd be happy to remain until he returned. It was a short walk to the house. Abbie was sitting on the front porch.

"What's wrong?" she said and O'Malley knew she meant the boys.

"Mary Searcher's with them," he said. "We don't have the portrait of your mother."

"She's inside," Abbie said.

She rose and O'Malley followed her into the house. In the living room she turned to the north wall and he looked above the fireplace.

"Daddy, she's wonderful," Abbie said.

At first glance it was as if someone else had painted it. O'Malley was drawn into the moment of the picture and it brought a new emotion; he wished he remembered where it was taken and who she was looking at. It carried the same feeling as the sudden attack of an unreasonable jealously at something previous to your involvement with someone. He was puzzled as to why the portrait was acceptable now after he had struggled and actually felt he had failed at getting it right in his studio. O'Malley scanned the room, seeking possible influences of outside light. He knew different parts of the day would have some effect and certainly the artificial lights of the evening would bring another, but he didn't think there would be anything of definable persuasiveness. He fought the impulse to move closer and inspect the work, as if revisiting the intimacy he had already experienced in its creation would be wrong. Instead, he stepped back. Deeply there was a stirring; another power loosened his grasp and simultaneously fed him and his imagination brought him into the picture and more importantly positioned him from Susanne's vantage point. In that instant he felt her general contentment and happiness. O'Malley recollected how it was her constant disposition.

"Mom was so beautiful," Abbie said. "She even makes that old shitty couch of mine look good."

"What's that?" O'Malley said.

"That old ugly couch," she said. "It was in my apartment in Buffalo."

And there it was, rushing into him, the memory present in its totality. The photograph wasn't from a party, but from the day Abbie and John announced their engagement. O'Malley and Susanne had driven down on a Saturday afternoon and met Abbie at the Albright-Knox Art Gallery just a few blocks down Elmwood Avenue from her apartment. They had spent a couple hours at the gallery and on the drive back to Abbie's apartment she asked if John could join them for dinner. O'Malley had been silent as he had not really enjoyed John's company in their few previous meetings. He already pictured just the three of them sitting by the window, overlooking the Niagara River at the restaurant in Jafco Marina. Susanne had piped in quickly that of course John would be welcome.

John had shown up with a bottle of Cotes du Rhone that surprised O'Malley. It was a favorite of his, having been introduced by Susanne and not commonly found at the time in local liquor stores. O'Malley became suspicious when he mentioned its obscurity and he saw a smile pass between his wife and daughter. In the living room of Abbie's small apartment, the four of them drank the wine and chatted. John had been more talkative and O'Malley wondered if he had purchased two bottles of the French wine and consumed one himself. He was comparing O'Malley's painting of Keuka Lake hanging in Abbie's apartment to Cezanne's *L'Estaque on the Gulf of Marseilles* when Abbie had taken the picture. She had gone to the kitchen and returned with the camera.

"Your composition has the same subtle texture and muted brilliance as Cezanne's," he said.

Susanne's eyes had shifted to the man just as Abbie saw the moment and quickly raised the camera.

Five minutes later Abbie told them of their marriage plans. John had nodded slightly toward O'Malley and their eyes met and they both drained their glasses.

"I couldn't remember where the picture was from," O'Malley said.

"At the time I didn't think you were too happy," she said.

O'Malley ignored the remark. He looked at the portrait. Abbie followed his gaze and she came to him and squeezed his arm.

"Do you mind if I keep her?" she said. "It's as if she's here."

"Of course you can," he said. "I can see she belongs here."

As much as O'Malley was intimately aware of every step as he made his way through the village, there was also enough buoyancy sifting throughout his body to make the sidewalk untouchable. He literally arrived back at the booth surprised he was there, as if he was transcending from an intense and action-wrought dream into a morning equally vivacious – within kissing distance of an oncoming train.

"Are you okay?" Sue Searcher asked. "Looks like you have one foot on Mars."

"Yeah," O'Malley said, but his answer held no meaning. He felt he hadn't landed. He did sense an inward scrambling to gain focus, but it felt as if someone else was at the controls, gratuitously spinning dials.

"Did you find the portrait?" she asked.

"Yes," O'Malley said and the vision of it seemed to ground him and everything around him settled.

"You decided not to show it?" Sue said.

"Abbie wants her," O'Malley said.

"That's wonderful," she said.

"I believe it is," O'Malley replied.

It was difficult for O'Malley to remain inside the close confines of the booth. The boys stayed until mid-morning, but then he let them go down to the beach. This had always been a problem for him and he had attempted different diversions through the years to pass the time. Many of his peers would sketch or paint, but he had never been comfortable working in front of an audience. O'Malley had always been an avid reader, but the constant movement of people and accompanying noises was too distracting. To simply sit there made him self-conscious; he felt intrusive watching someone view his work. He decided to catch up in his journal, but he struggled getting started. Ideas that surfaced seemed trite and banal. Anything deeper with more substantial possibilities emerged as coy and elusive. O'Malley became nervous until the blank page represented some sort of ultimate failure and he scribbled in a shaky and hesitant desperation. The act of writing itself created its own power and eventually he was lost in the journey. His mind worked chronologically through the last few days and he enjoyed describing various scenes. He revisited the climb down Cascade Mountain. O'Malley was fixated on the dark ring of sweat on Gail's light green t-shirt and the layers of smells in the damp humidity under the shroud of trees along the trail.

When he looked up and saw her, for a split second, it seemed perfectly normal.

"Kevin," she said. "It's really you."

"Yes," he replied, shaken with the thrust of this new reality and thinking the same thing and wanting also to say it.

"I had no idea," Gail said, her hands open and gesturing toward the artwork.

- - -

The lake continued to roll in the late May evening although the wind had eased to a light and steady breeze. The couple sat on the windward side of the fire in low slung beach chairs with a small table between them. The air was cool behind their backs and they stretched their legs toward the fire. The sun had sunk in the west, but a hint of pinkish light remained. They watched it silently and sipped red wine. As always the man was happy to witness what he considered the daily miracle of the setting sun while he was equally stricken with a reluctance to let the day go. Her hand slid over his on the table. At that moment he thought she had read his mind.

She picked up the wine bottle, tilting it toward him and he nodded. The woman poured for them and set it back down. She asked him if he liked the wine and he told her, "Very much." He knew she was pleased with the find, "It's called Shiraz," she told him earlier, recounting her conversation with the proprietor of the liquor store who told her it was a new grape from Australia. The man had buried the urge to tell her that it really wasn't a new grape, but actually Syrah that had been taken from the Rhone Valley in France and replanted in Australia and given a new name. It was blended with Mouvedre and Grenache in Cotes du Rhone. He knew she would've happily taken in all the information, but somehow it might steal the delicate magic from the moment of her discovery and her excitement in sharing it. Again, he marveled at her overwhelming generosity, the seemingly endless supply of it and the simple grace by which it was presented. They had been together for five years and it had taken almost two for him to shake the dusty scale of comparison that had kept him from moving forward. She had been remarkably patient, even enduring the silly, adolescent moment of being called his deceased wife's name the first time they had made love; she pushed on his shoulders until he was still and she had reached over and turned on the light. "There," she said, her smile suddenly vivid in the glow from under the lampshade. "That should end any further confusion."

It had been a weekend relationship in the beginning and they took turns at each other's homes. She lived in the same house in the village that she had shared with her husband, an alcoholic and unfaithful man, until she had thrown him out. The husband had lost his six figures a year job and lived in an apartment above an automotive supply store with a waitress who one day found him dead in the bathroom "Elvis style" as she liked to tell it. There were the twin daughters to raise and the woman got a job as a finance clerk for a company in the nearby township of Elma. She had a strong attachment to the village and she had been unwilling to give it up until her daughter had moved with her granddaughters to be with her sister in Arizona. The departure of her daughter had left her adrift and she considered following except she had been falling in love with the man. He had been willing to visit every other weekend, a pattern they fell into without discussion, but she knew he missed being by the lake and gradually after spending time there and returning to her empty house, she preferred the lake and the man.

They had decided against marriage without any hard conviction – "Why bother?" they seemed to say. They were both retired, although he took on an occasional side job and she worked for an accounting firm during tax season. His hands began to swell with arthritis, forcing him to only accept small jobs and he gave up sculpture except crude whittlings he passed on to his and her grandchildren. His painting had taken on a more dramatic quality with his slightly altered grip. They walked the beach almost every day and collected driftwood, seashells, stones and sea glass. She began to create assemblages from these materials, adding wine corks she had saved and pieces of tile a contractor friend saved for her. She had been surprised to discover this interest and the abundant satisfaction it brought. She tried to spend a few hours each day on the assemblages, a process that required a combination of whimsicality and structural practicality. She added the assemblages to his artwork at an art festival in nearby Lewiston where she sold three pieces. They bought a small RV and traveled south in the winter favoring the North Carolina coast and the Florida Keys although they had enjoyed Asheville as it reminded them of the Adirondacks. From there they headed west and settled for a month in Tubac, Arizona where they wandered the countryside and enjoyed her family. They went often to Old Forge and he was delighted how his daughter had taken to the woman.

The silence was suddenly obvious as was the darkness on the horizon – the gradual surprise, like aging, he thought. The breeze was dying and the coals were less vibrant and coolness wrapped around him.

"I'd like to add a Russian sage to the garden," she said. "I thought it would be a nice neighbor to the aster."

He asked for a description of the flower and she told him and specified where in the garden it would be planted. He tried to visualize the garden, but it was elusive even though it had been a recurring spectacle every spring for many years. His late wife had started it and each year she added to it and she sometimes cut back certain aggressive flowers. It was always exciting to see the perennials return and equally exciting to add their favorite annuals and watch the garden change through the growing season. The woman had deftly added to the garden and detracted nothing. He felt her hand again and found himself looking forward to the morning and the garden that was at this moment taking nourishment from the soft moonlight.

Zigzag

I had gone in early, because I couldn't sleep. I never was a great sleeper; a wake up to pee became a precursor to review my troubles. It was the unwanted invitation that was impossible to refuse. At that time, my struggling business was the biggest contributor, so it seemed reasonable (if there is such a thing as reasonable thought in the middle of the night) to get up and head to the store instead of creating darker than black phantasms of fear, dread and remorse on my bedroom ceiling. I slid from bed, a careful and reluctant retreat from my wife's warm aura. I carried my clothes into the bathroom. A quick shower and I tip-toed past my children's bedrooms, downstairs and immediately out the side door. It was dark, mid-April; dawn was an hour and a half away. I drove the three blocks to Main Street. Across the street I saw the 24-OPEN employee checking the gas pumps. Every few months there seemed to be a new one. As I pulled in, I was surprised to see a cigarette between his lips. I parked next to the building and walked toward the front door.

"Doesn't seem like a great place to smoke," I said.

He had a clipboard in one hand, a pen in the other – I saw annoyance twist his lips. He withdrew the cigarette.

"That's overkill," he said. "It's to keep imbeciles from lighting up at the pumps."

I wondered what cousin to the word, "imbecile" he was related to?

"Getting coffee?" he said.

"A large one and a paper."

"Coffee's on me," he said. "Just leave for the paper."

I poured coffee, grabbed a newspaper and left money for both. The young man came in as I was leaving.

"I told you I had the coffee."

"I didn't think it was yours to give."

As a small business owner, I was a little sensitive.

The wine shop fronted Main Street, where the street dipped to allow ample clearance for the railroad viaduct. The road surface covering the dip was brick; I thought of it as kind of nifty, like the cobblestones on Nantucket. There was a front door and a wide sidewalk, but not much foot traffic. The substantial commercial area of the village was half a block east. It was mostly quiet, only the occasional vibration slightly echoed from the partial grasp of tires going under. Then the smooth chorus of breakaway as the tires gripped the pavement and continued. The parking lot was empty behind the store and I parked as far as possible away from it. I unlocked the back door and entered into a stuffy coolness. I flipped on the lights; two rows of florescent tubes hummed to life along the ceiling tiles. A short hallway past the closed door (behind it a bathroom and small storage area) led into the open expanse of the shop. It was a modest rectangle – fifteen by twenty-five, the walls were lined with shelves, except the front, a large bay window over a two-foot-high sill next to a glass door. Double-sided, three and a half foot tall wine racks filled the floor. I set the coffee and newspaper on the counter next to the cash register.

I had closed the night before. The cash register was all set. The books were up to date. A pile of unpaid bills were a threatening Goliath, stacked neatly under the counter, next to yesterday's meager "take"; it was hardly a David. Not worth a trip to the bank. I almost pulled up the bills to peruse again, but I had just spent a couple hours in my bedroom, doing just that. An approaching train, my anticipation automatic and fulfilled as the metal wheels rattled above the store – inside the chiming as bottles shook against each other and then gone. The silence emphatic. I pulled the stool forward and sat. I picked up the newspaper. Words of all sizes flipped past. None of them called to me. I folded it and pushed it aside. The coffee was still hot. It seemed to distill inside and radiate throughout my head. I decided to open the doors. Back door first, pushed out, into the parking lot. I kicked a wooden wedge under it. When I opened the front door, the slight cross breeze was immediately at my back; the room was transformed into something alive – aromas of springtime.

The rising sun reflected dully off the drab gray viaduct. A small shred of light struck cubist refractions into the wine bottles, a limited section representing France. The illumination was momentary; the sun was on the move. It was enough to ignite the names – the exotic sounds – *Corbieres, Cotes du Rhone, Ventoux* that reflected the places that produced the flavors. My mind gathered snapshots from the many colorful pages of the trade magazines. The sometimes outlandish descriptions that promised to play like a symphony on the palate: "bouquet of cherries, strawberries, spice and dried flowers" and the wonderful word, *terroir*, that gave credence to their environment. I loved this romance of the business. It was a thrill to fall into an inspired chat about a particular wine. I found it akin to discussing a good book, a favorite movie, an eye-popping work of art. My enthusiasm, however, had a way of overpowering the information – a multi-layered splattering of color where a simple black and white diagram would've sufficed. Me standing there, holding the bottle as the customer made a vague promise of a possible future purchase. What I didn't like was the business of the business. It was a hard thing to realize, after the fact. I felt helpless watching the hole get deeper, my shovel seemingly smaller; sometimes I wondered how long my whimsical outlook would survive the bluntness of this reality.

My reverie of a shimmering morning glow in the countryside of Provence was shattered by a familiar dry cough. A puff of cigarette smoke preceded Arnie Slater into the store. I pictured the cigarette left smoldering on the parking lot.

"S'up?" Arnie said.

His shoes thudded against the counter. He moved a thick, waxy strand of hair off his forehead. Someone once said he combed it with a porkchop. Arnie pulled out a pocket – a mishmash of crumpled bills, wrappers, a lighter, coins and lint spilled onto the countertop. He pointed to the shelf behind me.

"Little one," he said.

I selected the half-pint of vodka and set it down. His hands trembled like a pianist as I picked through the rubble and rang it up. Arnie collected the remains (minus the lint) into his pocket and left. Past the doorway, I saw him bend over to pick up the burning cigarette. The cough stung him again. I knew a few steps around the corner he'd be guzzling the half-pint to stir up his day.

This was another aspect of the business that I hated. When I first opened the store, I had been strongly advised to carry a few spirits along with wine. I expressed my dislike to sustaining the addicts to one of my distributor's representatives. I told him I felt like a drug dealer.

"If not you, then they go down the street," he said. "Usually they alternate between the three stores in the village."

"It seems so wrong," I had said. "I don't know if I can do it."

"Who are you to decide?" he said. "If this was a grocery store, would you not serve pastries to fat people? How can you decide, who or who not?"

He followed with the optimistic hope of a corresponding purchase. Perhaps a chardonnay – a little something for "the wife." I was doubtful.

In moments like this I like to reach into my feeble toolbox of supportive quotes and mantras; I remember an idea by Saint Thomas Aquinas (from an introduction to philosophy course that I barely passed) about doing good simply for the sake of goodness. I loved the purity of the idea, but in my own way, I had narrowed the view. Why was it so easy for me to overlook some well-dressed lawyer drinking a couple bottles of *Chateauneuf-du-Pape* for dinner and then treating his wife like shit? A girlfriend from a nearby, but less affluent town once told me that my friends were as big as assholes as anywhere else; they just used better grammar and possessed a keener fashion sense. It's fascinating how a simple sale (or lack of) can create such emotional havoc.

I sat down and picked up an issue of *Wine Spectator*. Yesterday, I had started reading an article about the late French winemaker, Didier Dagueneau. He had been known as "the wild man of Pouilly" – a motorcycle racer, a renegade purist who used a horse-drawn plow to turn the soil between his vines. His appearance was an apt reflection of his attitude – a surfeit of tangled, shoulder-length hair, his face lost in an equally consuming beard. I was in a full hero-worshiping trance, scanning the bold, colorful photographs, when something so very slight perked up my ears. It was like perceiving the stealthy movement of an errant mosquito in a dark room. I waited, frozen. The dull thud of my heart, a slight distraction. As I gently guided the page downward, I heard it again.

A tinkling.

It was gentle, I thought self-conscious. As it continued, I realized there was a steady yet erratic pattern. It was coming closer. I went to the front doorway and stepped outside. To the left, about thirty feet away, an old man approached. His appearance struck me as strangely serendipitous; the resemblance was uncanny – a full curtain of twisted white hair along a ruddy face covered in a churlish beard. An older version of the French winemaker in the magazine. He shuffled toward me, poking forward a walking stick. The tinkling followed; two small bells dangled from slender straps tied under the hand grip. Within a few steps of me, he stopped. The tinkling continued, a slightly slower cadence; I noticed the small quiver of his hand. Age related, I thought, perhaps a neurological disorder. What impressed me were his eyes. Bright blue, piercing. They contradicted his apparent feebleness. The drabness of the gray sweatshirt and wrinkled khaki pants. Black socks under brown sandals.

"Good morning, young man," he said.

The voice was strong, purposeful; it came from beneath an overflowing mustache, uneven and partially stained yellow. I guessed unfiltered cigarettes. His teeth were a different hue of the same color. He centered the stick in front of him and wrapped both hands around it. Above his grip, the last four inches was a smoothly carved naked woman, from hips to head. I returned his greeting and told him I admired the walking stick.

"She's from Switzerland," he said.

Both of his hands, in turn, climbed and caressed the figure. He smiled and gazed over my shoulder. I assumed he was looking over the ocean into the past

."Nineteen fifty-four," he said. "I was with a French prostitute. Her name was Nicole."

I was a little taken aback by the offering of this information. He probably saw the flicker of fascination in my eyes.

"We were in a little shop, a shop of pretty things," he said. "I had pulled it from a barrel of assorted walking sticks. I loved how it looked. I loved how it felt. Then her hand slid along my wrist over my hand. 'Let me,' she whispered; I dropped mine and she moved her hand over the top and ran her thumb along the front of the figure. 'It is nice, like a memory, yes?' she said. Her smile came from deep inside. She wanted to buy it for me. I laughed and she frowned, as deeply as her smile. I told her I didn't think it would come to good use. 'A memory?' she said. 'With a song,' she added and jiggled the bells. I had to let her buy it. Can you blame me?"

I imagined her hand, slender, red finger-nail polish, floating. He told me his name was William; I lost the last name immediately. I asked him why he was in Switzerland.

"Actually, I was in Marseille on leave," he said. "I was in the navy. That's where I met Nicole."

The name, "Nicole," the way he said it – how the second syllable seemed to dissolve. I couldn't help a surge of desire – "Nicole from Marseille."

"I was at the bar, in the hotel where I was staying," William said. "I had just arrived. My room wasn't ready. I ordered a beer. I remember I had rested my duffel bag against my left leg. I took a swig and lit a cigarette and she was there."

This man, William, his eyes widened. I'm sure he saw my interest in his story. I felt his self-awareness, confidence in the dramatic pause.

"She was something," he continued. "She slid onto the stool to my right and hooked a finger on my pinky. 'Hey sailor boy', she said. 'Zigzag?'"

William shifted the walking stick back and forth as if to mimic the word.

"Zigzag," he repeated. "I had no idea. Never heard it and I thought I'd been around a bit."

His face unfolded like an opened gift box.

"Nicole was a very beautiful woman. We had drinks. She was delightful, engaging – I sensed a fairly extensive education. The concierge informed me that my room was ready. 'Perhaps I might assist you with your unpacking?' she said."

William lifted a bushy eyebrow. I felt somehow initiated.

"Later, we lingered in my room. I remember the light changing, shadows emerging; there was a bluish cast to it. Like a Picasso," he said. "We were sipping a local rosé and picking from a *chartcuterie* platter. I told her I was on leave for four days. She suggested Switzerland."

"'Geneva,' she said. 'It is beautiful. I have a car.'

"She spoke slowly in English – her French accent was like little dollops of frosting on a cookie. I was nineteen. A young little piggy, full of piss and vinegar. Up until then, I had ravaged in alleys and on torn back seats of outdated vehicles. I had never experienced anything like her. It was four days of heaven."

I noticed he was blushing. A vibrant contrast against the cottony whiteness surrounding his face. There was more traffic echoing under the viaduct. A couple friendly horns. I waved. It struck me that I had never seen this man before. Could it be our paths had simply never crossed? Did he recently move here? Was he just visiting?

"Did you keep in touch with her?" I asked.

His blue eyes seemed to pulse, suddenly rounder. Like someone stabbed. He shook his head.

"Years later, I saw her on TV," he said. "I was still in the navy, sitting in a taverna in Athens. It looked like some sort of scandal, I believe in Paris. The news was in Greek. I didn't understand, but there she was. It was unbelievable. She was a little older, but still beautiful. And then she was gone."

William looked at me. Regret? Finality? Longing? Like setting down a great book after the last word has passed through your mind. But then, he seemed to shake himself into the present; I stepped aside as he moved forward, turning into my doorway.

"Let's see what you have in here," he said.

I followed his slow gait, the tinkling as he made his way between the wine racks. He didn't really look around. I was poised to explain the basic layout, offer suggestions, but it became clear he was headed to the counter. As I moved behind it, he nodded toward the shelf.

"Vodka," William said. "A little one, please."

He handed me a five and I made change. He stuffed the bottle into a front trouser pocket.

"It's been a pleasure, young man," he said.

William appeared suddenly shy, wanting to leave more quickly than he was able. Upon turning, he noticed the opening to the rear doorway. The bells wrangled during a clumsy pivot as he changed course. After he left, the bells continued until I didn't think I heard them anymore.

The Blanket

I remember that July afternoon; I was thinking about the lyrics, "the heat was hot" while I stretched my legs across the cockpit. Flies zigzagged and nibbled behind my knees. A sudden bite inside the opening of my khaki shorts. I picked up the folded newspaper and swatted. The flies ducked between the teak grates of the cockpit floor. Above, the mainsail luffed. The boom swung, listless. The jib slithered like a wash cloth across the main mast. Uncle Clay's voice barked before his head appeared.

"What the hell?"

"I'm on it," I said.

I turned the wheel. The vessel settled like stubborn disobedience.

"Let the sheet out," Uncle Clay said. "Then follow her as you feel it."

I stood and loosened it. I waited, hoping beyond my understanding. I didn't want Uncle Clay to have to come up. The boom moved back to the port side and the jib filled. I carefully adjusted the sheet. Slowly, the vessel found meager purpose. Uncle Clay nodded as the thirty-foot sloop fell back on course.

"Try to keep her that way," he said and stepped down into the cabin.

I sat and pulled my legs from the cockpit. The flies had instantly returned. The sailboat was barely moving in the slight wind. There was no relief from the heat and humidity. The sun was a hot white circle in an empty blue sky. I still couldn't believe my uncle's refusal to turn on the auxiliary engine.

"Twice as fast," I had told him that morning. "And a breeze to at least keep the flies off."

"No," Uncle Clay said. "That's not how your old man would want it."

"Yeah Wes, Unc's right," Lee, my older brother said. "Dad wouldn't want us wimping out."

I just shook my head. It was the second day of the dead humid air. Yesterday it had been the same slow meander under sail until we ran aground going into Sodus Bay. It was subtle and a surprise, the exasperating motion into standstill as the vessel slid into the muck. Uncle Clay was standing at the helm. He barely stumbled, but looked immediately aloft.

"Wes, Lee," he called out.

"Yeah?" I said.

I stood in the cabin by the open hatchway. The sensation was trivial, like walking off an escalator. Uncle Clay loosened the jib sheet and was stepping onto the cabin roof to drop the mainsail.

"Take the jib in," he said. "Lee," he yelled. "We need you."

Lee had been napping below in the forward v-berth. I saw his head appear. He bent to gather the massive pile of fabric that flopped onto the cabin top and invaded like a landslide into the cockpit. I knelt onto the deck and tugged the foresail down and gathered and secured it between the forestay and the bow rail. Uncle Clay handed Lee a bunch of nylon gaskets. He followed him aft along the boom, tying as his uncle organized the sail a few feet at a time.

"I don't get it," Uncle Clay said. "Should be in plenty of water."

He held up the folded chart as if providing evidence. The sailboat was fairly upright. The feeble, humid wind seemed to more mock than threaten our situation. Uncle Clay walked forward and looked over the bow.

"Well, we're in it," he said. "Luckily there isn't much wind. Could've torn the sails to shreds. Supposed to be eight feet deep. Looks more like three." He glanced at the chart again and shook his head. "We're drawing about four, but I think we can back her out."

Uncle Clay told us to stand on the stern. He started the engine.

"Hold tight," he said.

We grasped the backstay as he put her in reverse. Below the transom, the water bubbled up brown and foamed hysterically as the power was increased. The craft didn't budge. Uncle Clay looked into the cabin at the depth sounder.

"Yep," he said. "Three goddamned feet."

He directed us amidships to the port side onto the small width of deck next to the cabin.

"Let's try a little side-to-side."

He instructed us to move together across the cabin to the starboard side deck and continue the back and forth, hoping to free up the keel from each side.

"Just stay together," he said. "Grab the shrouds and lean out. Keep it going."

At eighteen, Lee weighed about one sixty, twenty pounds more than I was, two years younger. We quickly worked ourselves into a sweat without creating much movement. Another try in reverse was fruitless. Uncle Clay looked into the sun and then out onto the waterway. On the other side, the shore was perhaps a quarter mile.

"Let's get the anchors out."

Uncle Clay hooked up the swim ladder. Lee and I lowered into the warm water. Uncle Clay handed down the anchors. He pointed off the stern in diagonally opposing directions. We were in, up to our waists. My feet sank ankle deep at each step. We continued until we were up to our chests. The anchor was hard and heavy against my leg.

"Right there, boys," Uncle Clay said. "Push the blades into the bottom."

Lee bent forward, his head under, raising his hips as he drove the double points of the Danforth anchor into the muck. I did the same and Uncle Clay waved us back. By the time we climbed aboard, he had the anchor lines a couple turns around the winches.

"Tail these on the cleats," he said. "Maybe we can pull 'er off."

I wasn't sure what we were doing. Luckily he started with Lee on the port side. Uncle Clay fitted the handle into the top center of the winch. He cranked clockwise. The line rose out of the water and tightened. Behind him, Lee pulled what was given and took a turn around the cleat. On the starboard side he duplicated the process. All three of us were sweating heavily. Uncle Clay alternated cranking the winches until the port side anchor tore off the bottom and the line went limp.

"Well, fuck all," he said. "How in the hell can we be so hard in? We were barely moving."

Lee and I went back in to retrieve the anchors. After we passed them up to Uncle Clay, he let the boom out perpendicular to the boat. He had tied a line that dangled off the end.

"Both of you pull all your weight on it," he said.

We tried the starboard side first. Uncle Clay put her into reverse. Nothing. We tried with the same result on the other side. We climbed back aboard. Uncle Clay shook the winch handle toward the open water. He turned almost full circle, cursing.

"Unc," Lee said, pointing toward land on the port side. "Someone's coming this way."

A motorboat was heading toward us. The bow was riding high. A wake fanned out like sparkling plumage and sunlight flashed off the windshield. Uncle Clay trained his binoculars on her.

"Looks like some sort of working boat," he said. "About twenty two feet. Twin screws. Loaded for bear."

I didn't know what he meant until the boat slowed behind us and turned. Centered on the back deck was a thick stanchion affixed with a large cleat. Both exhausts were deeply voiced. Two men stood behind the windshield inside the small superstructure. In the muggy heat of that day, I was amazed – they were buttoned to their necks in dark green long-sleeved work shirts, matching trousers and caps. The boat backed up within two feet of us. One of them held the stern off with a long pole.

"Somebody fall asleep at the wheel?" he said.

Pulling off the sailboat was easy. The hard part was watching Uncle Clay eating his pride; from his compromised smile responding to the man's sarcasm to the expression on his face when the tow price he offered at fifty dollars was refused and ended up doubled. I could imagine my dad's response to his younger brother, "So, Clay, did he kiss you before he fucked you?"

Yeah, Dad had been a tough one, mentally and physically. Emotionally, I'm not so sure. He was more legend than real. Of course Mom knew the difference and suffered it. After four years she'd had enough. I was surprised she supported my uncle's plan, a promise to take his ashes on *Aphrodite* to this special place, where the Niagara River flowed into Lake Ontario. That's where he wanted them scattered. It was a strangely sentimental back reach for my dad. A distant boyhood memory with my grandparents. Uncle Clay was taken by surprise at the request, but he had shared the very root of it. He could close his eyes and be there as my father had. That's how Mom explained it:

"Always, with your dad, his real passion was the sea," she said. "And his real love was *Aphrodite*."

The name adorned the stern of my dad's sailboat.

"Your Gramma Lowell used to say that your father sailed into life under the bright bloom of a full spinnaker."

Mom's mouth twisted a little, as if biting into a cake of unexpected richness. She raised her hand and seemed to be smoothing the air. I took it as an act of self-policing.

"As boys, your dad and Uncle Clay sailed pretty much every weekend with Gramma and Grampa out of Niagara-on-the-Lake. And apparently many times late in the season, after a full day, many hours under a cooler, stronger wind, as they approached the shore, there would be this sudden, steady waft of warm air. It was explained as an off-shore breeze. Basically it was the same wind experienced farther out in the lake, but because as you got closer, the wind gliding along close to the radiated ground offered this warm, welcoming change – like something you slid under. They named it 'the blanket' and Uncle Clay told me how your dad and he would go up forward and sit against the front of the cabin and wait for it. He said, there was a wonderful smell from the land of vineyards and apple orchards."

My mom, for years, had barely spoken about my dad, good or bad. Their split-up was as decisive as the drop of an axe. She was awarded custody of us. He was required to pay child support and alimony. Dad walked directly out of the courthouse into a waiting taxi, to the airport. Within six hours he was aboard *Aphrodite* at the city marina in Fort Meyers. That had been his escape, and from then on, his home. He was a sales rep for a major aluminum manufacturer and was able to change his territory to the southeast. Eventually he quit and took his marketing expertise to yacht sales. As the saying goes, he worked hard and played hard. Dad was dutiful in seeing us – a day or two during holidays, birthdays. I could probably count on both hands, the total days he spent here in any given year. As we got older, Dad would invite us down there. Mom didn't let that happen until Lee turned twelve.

We flew down with Grampa Lowell during Easter vacation. Dad had been excited when he picked us up at the airport.

"Three generations of Lowell men," he said. "It'll be an epic voyage."

Dad seemed to be glowing from within his walnut colored skin and bright white teeth. His blue eyes sparkled, exuding pleasure and pride in both sides of his lineage. I felt a tender strength in his fingers as he grasped my shoulder and turned me and we headed across the tarmac. It was my first whiff of a tropical breeze and original glimpse of palm trees, swaying in the distance. The trip expanded on these introductory sensations as we sailed around the area – Sanibel island, Captiva Island into Port Charlotte and farther north to Sarasota. The weather had been agreeable – warm, steady winds carried us to marinas, anchorages and amazing beaches. Dad knew every cove, reef and sandbar along the west coast. He also seemed to know mostly everyone wherever we made landfall.

"Hey Cap," he was greeted.

I saw the pleasure the nickname brought. He preferred it to Duane, only spoken by Grampa (Duane Sr.) and Gramma. And it was evident he deserved it, based on his seafaring reputation. In the bars, restaurants and yacht clubs, usually someone was hailing him, anxious to share a story or anecdote, springing for drinks. Both men and women seemed excited to see him, spend time with him. And I observed the pride and maybe a little envy in Grampa's eyes. I didn't understand it then – the passing of time, the subsequent losses and gains. I also witnessed a resurfacing of competition between them. It started as small matters – the length of an anchor line, the influence of current on a specific compass course. At first, Dad ignored him, simply proceeded as he wished without response. Grampa stood there, his mouth still open after the unheeded words drifted away.

"Cut from the same cloth," I remember overhearing – a gin slurred tone from Mom's brother, Daniel. "One is just more worn, faded."

It was the first time I heard the phrase. Such condescension from Uncle Dan didn't seem fitting. Even as a very young boy I sensed a certain instability about him. Loud, overbearing – a man who answered his own questions. He seemed to delight in his expansion of the metaphor, like he had bulls-eyed a shot at brilliance. I guess it was memorable enough, because it came to mind on the sailboat, as these differences began to kindle. Did my grandfather not see where my dad's determination came from? Didn't my dad see what his father was desperately holding onto? And I pictured this massive cloth as I witnessed the identical rigid setting of a jaw, the same aggressive pitch of voice and exhausting efforts not to show weakness. My observations seem *cliché,* but nonetheless as valid as my wind bag of an uncle, or "Unc-Ass" as Lee called him. My older brother was passionate in his dislike; he didn't exercise the same restraint as I did toward Mom's only brother. And, likewise Lee's feelings about Dad and Grampa went far beyond my careful admiration. He worshipped them.

That first trip had thrust my eyes open. I was certainly dazzled by the scenery – the immense breadth of the Gulf of Mexico. The multiple personalities of weather – sometimes clear and calm, the abrupt storm or stealthy fog, soupy with heavy humidity. Closer to shore, the briny over-ripe aromas and everywhere, the colorful variety of creatures. To actually experience beyond what you've seen on TV, in childhood picture books, the exotic boldness of the *National Geographic*. To be able to knowingly nod at a gathering as my dad waves his arm like an orchestra conductor, sips from a glass in the other and doles out adventure tales: yes, I see myself on the bow, standing forward on the pulpit, perched over the high crest in the rushing wind. Dolphins gliding on each side like playmates in wondrous stride. Or the more subtle discovery – slipping along with an easy breeze, out into the vast openness, behind land becoming a mere line, then gone. Eyes naturally drawn forward – the fantastic repetition, like the pleasing chorus of a favorite song. And it's there, a small rounded island, bobbing in and out of sight. In the binoculars as we approached, the sudden disbelief – the silly gesture of dropping the binoculars for a better look, only to pick them up urgently.

"Sea turtle," Dad said. "All of seven feet."

"I'd say five feet," Grampa said. "Six at the most."

It wasn't so much the contradiction as Grampa's expression. A slight shake of his head. Eyes thrown askance as if confronting some form of deceit. Dad ignored him, steering as close as possible to the sea turtle.

"It's seven for sure," he said

."Better get your Ray Bans, son," Grampa said. "Those baby blues are getting burned out down here."

There was a certain finesse to their back and forth – sarcasm and innuendo; they each gloried in their mental alertness. Lee seemed to enjoy the sparring. He was inspired – developed his own version to challenge me. I wasn't interested. His approach was predictable – a playground maverick hefting a bag of marbles. I waited him out, like watching a leaky tire deflate. He gave up on me, but continued to try to fulfill Dad's and Grampa's every whim. Both were even competitive in offering praise to my overachieving brother. Lee hopped around the sailboat in response to their sometimes conflicting orders. On one occasion both yelled for him to secure two different lines during a difficult docking. The overlapping mess brought to a head, who's really in charge? The answer aboard *Aphrodite* was Dad, as it should have been. I was surprised at Grampa's stubbornness. I tried to distance myself from future conflicts as best as I could, recognizing a similar peril as a boxing referee in the confine of the ring with two aggressive heavyweights.

In retrospect, it was a good trip. The overall experience dominated the minor eruptions. The next spring we returned for a more ambitious voyage that would take us to Florida's east coast and across to the Abacos islands in the Bahamas. Only this time Uncle Clay came instead of Grampa. In some ways I found this a more pleasant combination. The age difference between Dad and his brother was pretty much the same as Lee and me. Also, the difference in our dispositions seemed to mirror each other. Like my dad, Lee became fiercely competitive. He played any organized sport available in season. On the field, on the court, Lee was a natural. He possessed all the stuff – strength, agility, instinct and a full understanding of the game at hand. He was usually the captain, the high scorer, always leading the charge. I wasn't a bad athlete, just not too committed. I was told that early, before I fully realized it. In Little League while Lee was sweeping up hard grounders in the infield dust, I was standing dreamily in right field, gazing at wandering butterflies. On offense I rarely got on base.

One time I had made it to third. I led off. Suddenly, I was wacked in the ribs.

"You're out, dumbass," the third baseman said.

He waved the mitt. The ball was imbedded like a pearl. I was stunned, oblivious. My coach was incredulous; the fact that I was thrown out by the catcher. That we were down by one run with the bases loaded, two outs in the bottom of the last inning, with Lee at bat. It was a slow walk back in, teammates quiet with backs turned, heads shaking.

In the parking lot Uncle Clay was waiting at the car.

"Oops," he said.

I thought Uncle Clay's lack of competitiveness would make for a less stressful voyage. He was a knowledgeable sailor. He followed orders. If he observed something that he thought was relevant, it was presented as an observation or question instead of an opinion. He understood shipboard life and knew his place on *Aphrodite*. Around my father, I witnessed an inherent lack of confidence, a sense of impending physical failure. The strong possibility of humiliation seemed to plague him. The smallest task could throw him into an awkward, cautious approach. And instead of careful adjustment, many times he'd go haywire, unravel like a broken spring-propelled toy. A notable example is when we were slowly motoring into Cannonsport Marina in West Palm Beach. It was after two and a half days crossing the Okeechobee Waterway. Dad was at the helm. We had arranged the fenders along the port side. He told me to handle the stern line. Lee was amidships, prepared to secure the spring line. Uncle Clay went forward with the two bow lines. A man stood on the dock, watching us approach.

"Hey there, Cap," he said. "How they hanging?"

"Hanging loose," Dad replied.

"Must be nice," he said. "Enough crew for the Queen Mary."

"My brother and my sons."

"Seems like a crowd after watching you usually come in solo."

The man nodded to Uncle Clay. His arms slightly opened, like an invitation to play catch. It was a perfect throw, the nylon rope high in the air, uncoiling and stretching over the man's shoulder so he could grasp it and secure it to the dock. The line kept coming, all of it. The man was surprised as the spliced loop bounced off his chest and flopped on the dock."

"A generous throw," he said. "Perhaps a little too generous."

The mistake had no impact on the docking. Dad brought her in straight; his delicate touch, the slight shift to reverse to stop the forward motion. Lee stepped off the craft and circled the spring line around the piling. He held fast as the fenders kissed the dock. My job was simple, dropping the lasso over the piling off the stern. I looked at Dad and he nodded and I tied it. He turned off the engine. The man handed the fugitive end of the line back to Uncle Clay. He slipped it through the port side chock and cleated it. In turn he dropped another loop on the cleat and passed it through the starboard side chock to the man.

"Ah, so we're friends again," he said, securing the line.

Uncle Clay nodded. He thanked the man. He turned to see Dad's wry smile, like a coach after a bad play, saved by a penalty.

"This is Scotty," he said. "And this guy, so anxious to throw away my stuff, is Clay."

Afterward Dad adjusted the dock lines to anticipate the changing tides. Uncle Clay rinsed off the boat. Lee and I straightened up below. We showered and walked (a bobbling sort of gait that was commonly known as "sea legs") down the road to a seaside restaurant. I ordered seafood chowder and wahoo steak broiled in lemon butter. It was quite a stretch from the fish sticks and tuna casserole that we called "seafood" at home. Dad and Uncle Clay ordered martinis. I thought they were attractive little beverages, but skimpy next to my tall lemonade. I was surprised how quickly Dad emptied his and ordered another. He seemed suddenly enlivened. I didn't know then it could be like pouring rocket fuel into a biplane. He was rejoiceful to have reached the openness of the West Palm Beach area after the slow motoring through the sometimes swampish canal. It was over a hundred and fifty miles of mostly backwoods and some open pasturelands. It was obvious Dad regarded it as an unpleasant necessity, probably like a tractor-trailer driver thinks about certain stretches across the Midwest.

"But, weren't those horses magnificent?" Uncle Clay said. "So close to the canal. I was dumbstruck."

"I guess that explains your deck performance," Dad said.

Uncle Clay's chin dropped. He knew there was nothing to say. I also knew that silence, even the peaceful stoicism of Gandhi wouldn't suffice. Dad dropped both fists on the table.

"What if we were in a heavy wind?" he said. "What if…"

Uncle Clay gulped his martini. The swallow took the wrong route and he began to cough. His attempt to suppress it backfired and escalated into a fit.

"Christ," Dad said. "Get a grip."

"Sorry."

The word slipped out in an uneven tumble. His eyes watered. Nostrils bubbled. Uncle Clay clutched the table edge and continued to cough. I pushed a glass of water in front of him. He tried to thank me. His lips puckered and twisted. He picked up his napkin and slobbered into it. Dad drew back his chair. He crossed his forearms in front of his face; false drama: A vampire at dawn.

"Grab hold of yourself!"

The dining room had grown quiet. Dad looked at Lee.

"I'm sure glad you're onboard," he said.

The next evening we cleared the Cannonsport Marina at 9:10 PM and had raised the jib and mainsail at 9:35 PM. Dad placed me at the helm, steering by compass, one hundred twenty degrees (ESE). West End, Bahamas was around fifty-six miles into the Gulf Stream. The wind was behind us at six and a half knots. I felt the constant tug on the wheel. Dad was just inside the companionway, reviewing the chart, a quick look aloft and then he peered around the cabin opening at the compass. Lee and Uncle Clay sat forward of me in the cockpit. Dad climbed up and took the wheel. The compass needle moved to one hundred twenty three degrees.

"One twenty three," he said.

I grabbed the wheel. Within the next hour, lights from the shoreline receded. The moon was full, it's reflection stabbing randomly at the building waves. The wind from the west was slowly shifting to the northwest. What was originally lively, became more rambunctious. My actions seemed to be misunderstood. Suddenly it was like something falling from my hand. I turned the wheel, felt the resistance again. I turned the other way, into nothing. The empty gesture brought instant response from the compass needle, away from the course.

"You're falling off," Dad said.

There was a pause, like the cartoon coyote suspended after running off the cliff. A large wave followed; it swept beneath the stern and drove the bow downward. Then it rose. Shards of water caught in the moonlight. Dad was back at the helm. I slid next to Lee.

"Wow," I said.

He looked at me and shook his head.

In another hour the wind increased to fifteen knots. The moon had disappeared. Three of us sat in the cockpit. We were dressed in bright yellow foul-weather gear. Dad stood at the helm with his hand tight on the wheel. His eyes like a fugitive, constantly in motion. He uttered small sentences, phrases, an occasional word. Most of it was lost. The heavy, confused seas followed, waves capping seven or more feet. There was a sensation of surfing on the crests, speeds sometimes over seven knots. Then the drop into the trough; the bow shoveling into the retreating wave while behind us, a wall of water, taller than us, raced liked crazed vengeance. Huge splashes of phosphorescence – an eerie light show; fascination amidst my fear. I kept an eye on the compass; a jittery course somewhere between one hundred thirty and one hundred forty degrees. To compensate, a controlled jibe to one hundred ten. It went on for hours with erratic gusts to twenty knots. Dad mentioned that the original course of one hundred twenty three was a good one, also taking into account the Gulf Stream current. But he explained it was impossible to hold it, thus the two different bearings. Another sailboat, *Mistress*, originally from Bar Harbor, Maine, had left just behind us and maintained radio contact. For a long time, she was the only sign of lights we saw (erratically) in what seemed an otherwise empty and angry ocean.

Around 4:30 AM the wind dropped to around twelve knots. Another call from *Mistress*. Dad waved Lee to take the wheel while he descended into the cabin. There was the crackling sound of the radio – a freighter was spotted, somewhere ahead. Dad stuck his head up and looked forward, elbows spread over the companionway. He saw a distant pattern of lights and stepped back down and talked into the radio and hung up. The freighter was far off the port bow. Even though the radar reflector was up, Dad had plugged in the large flashlight and fixed it against the mainsail. The beam shone like an abstract expressionistic billboard.

"Always good to be seen," he said.

Mistress had been in contact with the freighter. She advised Dad a course change to ninety degrees from the freighter's present position. An hour later we changed our course. The wind was slowly dropping down. The waves continued, but seemed more rhythmic and manageable without the constant scrambling between the wind and current. A little before six, we saw the West End tower light. A few minutes later, a pinkish dawn began to stretch below it on the horizon.

"Figures we'd see the light just as the sun comes up," I said.

"I'm just happy to see the new day," Uncle Clay said.

At 7:10 we saw the West End tower. Dad directed Lee to change course to eighty degrees, heading toward Settlement Point. The wind diminished and the seas began to level out.

"We should make the marina by nine or so," Dad said. "Clay, do you think you can straighten up below?"

Uncle Clay nodded and stepped down into the cabin. He was back up a few minutes later. His face was drained of color.

"You left your Florida tan down there," Dad said.

The smile Uncle Clay attempted, became a mask of futility. He stepped toward the stern, but Dad pointed otherwise.

"Not into the wind," he said.

Uncle Clay turned and scrambled on all fours along the deck. At amidships he flattened with his head bent over the side. He gripped the gunwale. His body looked like it was trying to throw itself over the side. When the retching stopped, he rolled on his back. Eyes closed. His lips were rounded, breathing deeply. Dad opened the locker in the cockpit and pulled out a long-handled rag mop.

"Hand this to your uncle," he told me.

- - -

Point Breeze. Not yet dawn. The idling of the diesel seemed unruly in the quiet marina. Lee untied the bow lines and tossed them to me. He then walked along the dock and released the spring line and dropped it on the deck. Uncle Clay pulled off the stern line. He stepped down into the cockpit and put her in reverse. Lee walked the sailboat back and hopped aboard. The water roiled behind the stern as Uncle Clay shifted to forward – the subtle, mechanical change of voice, vibrating beneath us. Out of the marina, between the breakwaters. Beyond, Lake

Ontario and the black sky, three flashing lights pierced from the outermost breakwater. That last barrier ran parallel to the coast, ensuring the safety and comfort we were leaving. I coiled the bow lines and carried them aft. Uncle Clay was standing, one hand on the wheel. His eyes in a methodical whorl as we approached the wide openness.

"Looks like we'll be beating all day," he said.

A warm wind from the southwest as we left the protected area. Small waves rolling along the hull. I could barely make out a few, scattered white caps – thin curly lines of white, like insincere smiles. Uncle Clay told me to steer three hundred degrees (WNW). He disappeared down below. A few minutes later he came out of the head. The dimness and the distance into the cabin tricked me momentarily; the resemblance to my dad was uncanny. The slight angle of a head turn, the lips tight against his teeth as he pondered the chart under a small galley light. This quick view. The fact of death; the sullen reminder of his ashes molded inside the vase. So strange at that moment in the midst of the seafaring vivacity that had been his life. It was hard for me to grasp, that he was alive at the onset of this voyage. Just he and Uncle Clay. Over a thousand miles from Fort Meyers to Virginia Beach. It was there the disease and his stubbornness overwhelmed him. Dad had told no one, until he confided to Uncle Clay that he was sick.

"On the river of no return," he told him.

"He really stuck it to him," Mom said. "The arrogance, knowing how hopeless it was, but as always his brother would be there, no matter what."

She had been speaking to Lee and me the day after Dad's funeral service. Uncle Clay left the boat in Virginia and flew with his ashes and the promise. He considered leaving them on *Aphrodite*, but he wasn't sure about Mom's reaction. She agreed with Gramma Lowell, "Half in the ground here with us and the other half out there." She threw her hand as if there was something stuck on it. Uncle Clay had written a eulogy for the service, but within speaking two lines had slumped into a tremulous bundle. The minister looked to Lee, but he too folded into his grief. He either passed me over due to my age or my own stricken face. Mom shook her head. The minister picked up the paper and started over. Famous for his feistiness and hurling dogma to the four corners of the church, his delivery was like a brick flung after a kite. Uncle Clay was stricken. He quickly rose and wiped away his tears.

"My brother," he said, reaching for the paper. "My words."

Those first two lines, again. The gentle resolve; the key sliding in after fumbling in the dark. From there its own dazzling voyage, perfectly trimmed and Uncle Clay held the course. Mom was forever plagued by Uncle Clay's dedication to Dad. She had wept during the eulogy. But I knew it was more her brother-in-law's words than the fact of Dad's death.

The decision at hand was if Lee could accompany Uncle Clay in bringing *Aphrodite* back? They figured roughly a month. Lee graduated from high school the previous spring. He was working part time at a local gym and a few hours each week with a Uncle Clay, learning carpentry. There had been some talk about moving south, learning the ropes of yacht sales from Dad. My brother continued to spend spring vacations with him and any other vacation that Mom would allow him. I quit going after the Bahama trip and Uncle Clay stopped the following year. We didn't discuss it and I'm not sure about my uncle, but I hated the confinement. It wasn't easy to choose. There was no denying the adventure and excitement. I discovered, that for me, a little goes a long way. I would suddenly feel trapped, almost suffocated. And more so, I absolutely needed a period of solitude to balance it out, to digest. And to recharge. Lee was all in, anytime. He worked well with Dad; they galloped (in retrospect I carry the image of them, leaning in with hair lifted in the wind) through whatever situation was presented. Lee had the right attitude; he accepted sarcasm and bullying as a rite of passage. Of course, he received a tempered dose based on his inherent skills.

Mom tried to talk Uncle Clay out of fulfilling his promise. She witnessed the bruising of his heart, again. It was only a year since Grampa Lowell died of a massive heart attack. Uncle Clay stepped up immediately. He made the arrangements. He soothed Gramma, a difficult task; for months she had been slipping into the uneven and unpredictable landscape of dementia. Dad had flown up. He approached as always, a blustering wind, but found out quickly he didn't have a clue. To see Gramma coming full circle back toward childhood was unfathomable.

"She's fucking batshit," he said to Uncle Clay. "Why isn't she in a nursing home?"

It was difficult for Uncle Clay to explain; the first impression after a long absence was indeed, shocking. Every day was different and demanded a loving alertness and agility, a kind of chess match on a moving, shape-changing board. Also, a brother and sister lived nearby and offered substantial support. She was still able to remain at home. She was happy there. So Dad had returned to Florida, to his own decline and death. Mom threw in Gramma's illness to support her argument against Uncle Clay honoring the promise, but my aunt and uncle were adamant that they could "hold the fort." Finally Mom gave in. Uncle Clay had arranged his work schedule. He lined up quite a few good jobs that Lee could help him with when they returned. The gym would also welcome him back.

It troubled me that I felt a little forsaken when they left. The trip seemed much more attractive without Dad being there. Guilt after grief. Odd, what we are compelled to lock inside after realizing the enlightenment and pain the heart offers if you are honest. They flew to Virginia and had cast off on June 3rd. Uncle Clay called Mom every few days from various landfalls as they sailed northward. Some bad weather. They held up at Chesapeake City an extra day and a week later, two nights anchored off Atlantic City. Lee sent me a postcard, a photograph of a high-kicking chorus line dancer, "Misty" scratched in pen under the upper leg. On the back: *"Bad weather, my good fortune. Won $200. Spent it on Misty."* After the trip, Lee carried on about Misty. I didn't really believe him, but just the proximity was enough to rankle me. Of course I couldn't divulge my own private adventures with the high-kicking Misty postcard.

After the weather calmed down, they sailed into New York City Harbor. Again, my brother sent a postcard. This one not as titillating as Misty, but that crowned woman hovering three hundred feet over Upper New York Bay; it was a postcard tipped sideways, the arm stretched and strong, holding the torch. I was envious – *"Sailed into this giant curtain of skyscrapers! I have a date with Lady Liberty. A real mind blower,"* he wrote. From there, they entered the Hudson River, still under sail. Mom told me they sailed sixty-four miles to Nyack that day. A severe thunderstorm welcomed them. The marina was closed, all moorings outside full, so they anchored. A break in the rain, Uncle Clay took the Zodiac into the marina, hoping for a pay phone. An old man on the porch asked for a $15 anchorage fee. All Uncle Clay had was a twenty. The next day, the marina manager told him the old guy was a con man. There was no anchorage fee. He apologized and offered a discount on the charts that Uncle Clay purchased.

"Can you believe your uncle was actually upset that your dad was judging him from the afterlife for being swindled?" Mom said.

Aphrodite continued into the heart of the Hudson Valley. In Catskill the mast was un-stepped at the Riverview Marine Services. I finally finished school and met them in Albany. An odd sight – the mast traversed the length of the sailboat, overhanging five feet at either end. The rigging was labeled with tape and tightly strapped like arteries on a limb. On deck (the widest point amidships was nine feet) it took some getting used to. It was also strange not to have Dad there – a recipe without the major ingredient. Stranger was seeing Lee wearing his sailing hat. It was a black wool Greek fisherman cap that Dad bought while sailing in the Cyclades many years ago. Lee must've seen it lying in a drawer and put it on. I always liked the cap. I was surprised it wasn't included when Dad was cremated. We cast off as soon as my gear was stored. Uncle Clay was anxious to push on. Within three hours we were tied up at a marina in Cohoes. It had been pleasant, moving into the onboard routine, although I was just feeling my way in. After dinner we lingered in the cockpit. Tall trees around the marina offered a dark insulation below a starry sky. Fireflies sprinkled along the shoreline. I was just a few hours wedged into this long voyage; there had been two different trips, each around a month long. I could feel a special bond had developed between my uncle and brother. After all day every day together, it made sense. However, I couldn't help the ambush of envy, the unreasonable grip of it.

Four days later we motored into Oswego. It was enough time for me to regain a confidence of belonging, although I never lost that sense of the one, always in the back seat, looking over shoulders. I also saw the difference between their personalities. There was no question Uncle Clay was the skipper, but his orders were generally presented as suggestions with a deferring look toward Lee. It was a thrill to see the openness of Lake Ontario after the monotonous crawl (only a twenty one mile break crossing Oneida Lake) through the canal. I later learned that the name of the port was derived from an Iroquois word, osh-we-geh. It means, "pouring out place." The air was still and humid. Luckily the marina could step the mast immediately. We spent the afternoon reattaching sails and rigging. Afterward, I sat at the end of the dock, reading. The sun suspended above. The heat was stifling. Uncle Clay continued to fuss with the rigging. He purchased Lake Ontario charts that morning at the marine store. He studied the charts in the cockpit. Lee sat with him. I watched them, fingers trailing the chart, their eyes scanning the lake, the sky. Heads nodding, shaking – like generals.

Two days later, coming out of Point Breeze, I held the course as a vague glow appeared to the east. We continued diagonally away from land into a puny west wind. The knowledge that it was the last day, albeit a long one, had escaped my thoughts. The act of sailing, the persistence of motion (even barely), has a way of overwhelming other concerns. After a while, Uncle Clay told me to come about to two hundred twenty degrees (WSW). We were only doing a couple knots. Steering was difficult; the light wind with a tendency to whimper. An hour later, the sun was high enough to offer more than a hint of the oncoming heat. There was nothing else in the sky. I could still see Point Breeze behind. On this tack, the compass was a quick reference. Uncle Clay pointed to a distant rooftop, one story taller than its neighbors.

"Try to keep her nose to the right," he said.

As we moved closer to land, we'd eventually come about and pick up a compass course around three hundred degrees. Around noon, Uncle Clay took over the helm. Lee went below. A little while later, he passed up sandwiches and cans of cola. All three of us sat quietly, sweating as we ate. The wind remained a constant whisper from the west. *Aphrodite* continued to tack into the afternoon. I continued to swat flies.

"Looks like the Olcott lighthouse," Uncle Clay said, pointing off the port bow. His voice shocked me. I'd been daydreaming, almost lulled to sleep. "Gramma and Grampa used to take your dad and me there."

We were very close to Olcott Beach. A few people spread out on blankets, under umbrellas. A few in the water. A couple boys standing on the old, crumbled pier, waving. Seagulls scattered about like twitching debris.

"There was an amusement park," Uncle Clay continued. "Sometimes Grampa snuck off to that corner gin mill for a couple *Corbys*. Then Gramma would drive home while Grampa told stories about when he was in the merchant marine. He told the same three or four stories, over and over. If he didn't, your dad would ask him to. He never got tired of hearing them."

"But you did?" Lee said.

"Well yeah," Uncle Clay said. "After a while, well they just got boring, even though the seas got higher, the winds stronger, the men tougher with each telling."

"Why did Dad like them so much?" Lee said.

"I don't know. In some way, maybe he could picture himself in the stories."

"And you couldn't?"

Uncle Clay seemed rattled with the question. He smiled nervously at Lee, who stared back at him.

"I guess your dad and I were just different."

Uncle Clay brought *Aphrodite* about. I exchanged sides with him. He pointed back at Olcott and chuckled.

"One time we were there, a hot day like this. We were at a picnic table under one of those tall oaks. Even in the shade it was miserable. Gramma took us to the amusement park. We rode the Ferris wheel, the bumper cars and played some games.

It was terribly hot walking on the pavement. We came upon a guy selling 'Cool Caps.'"

"What's a Cool Cap?" Lee said.

"They were so ugly," Uncle Clay said. "The brightest pastel colors imaginable, made of foam, those sporty caps with snap-button lids. You could soak them in cold water, wring them out and they'd keep you cool. I remember your dad didn't want one, but Gramma was insistent, like it was life or death. Just then, Grampa had shown up with a 'snoot full' – that's the way Gramma put it. The color choices were ridiculous. Mine was bright yellow, like parking lot stripes. It did feel cool. But your dad kept shaking his head and ducking. Gramma was chasing him with an orange one; Grampa snatched it from her."

"'What the hell is this?' he said."

"When Gramma told him, he plopped it on his own head. 'Pretty snazzy,' he said. Grampa pulled the lid down over one eye and winked. 'En Garde,' he added, stabbing the air. That's all it took for your dad to want one, but it had to be orange, just like Grampa's."

A quietness settled over us as Olcott shrunk in the distance. An hour later, we sailed close to the twin piers of Wilson harbor before coming about. The wind direction was shifting, from the west to northwest. All three of us were surprised to see the tall spire of the CN Tower in Toronto from almost thirty miles north across the lake, shaking translucently like an apparition. The distance afforded a broad seascape – above, to the west of the vague city silhouettes, there was an advancing cloud formation. We had spent a long day under the hot breath of a feeble wind and a complacent lake. It was tiring. Perhaps an hour left. I could feel a tension developing as the northwest sky thickened in gray among golden streaks of a descending sun.

I stepped down below to make dinner. It was a no-brainer – I keyed open a can of *Spam*, a longtime family favorite. In the cabin, through the opened portholes and forward hatch, the breeze seemed inspired. A slight chop. Modest white caps. The cabin floor picking up the rhythm. I spread my feet and rested a hip against the galley top and built sandwiches. Uncle Clay and Lee brought *Aphrodite* about. I passed up the sandwiches and beers (Uncle Clay told me not to tell Mom) and I climbed back into the cockpit.

"Damn good dinner," Uncle Clay said.

We were suddenly making headway with the wind more behind us.

"Four knots," Uncle Clay said, smiling.

Lee pulled the Greek fisherman cap tight to his ears. We raised our beers. Ahead, off the port bow were the battlements of Fort Niagara. As we sailed closer, the white building of the coast guard station appeared. After we passed the fort, *Aphrodite* was into the mouth of the Niagara River; the water looked like a problem being solved and the wind lessened. Uncle Clay brought her about and told me to take the helm. He pointed northward and went below. Tears escaped under his sunglasses when he appeared in the companionway. His hands were shaking as he carried the jar. He climbed into the cockpit and grasped the wheel.

"I think we should drop him in under sail."

Lee and I nodded. The air was a few degrees warmer, gently lying onto us.

"The blanket?" Lee said, with his arms stretched.

"Yeah," Uncle Clay said. "Who wants to do the honors?"

I knew the answer. I squeezed Lee's elbow. He turned and hugged me. Uncle Clay handed him the vase. As the sailboat came about, Lee moved to the stern. He turned the vase and shook it. A wisp of dust drifted above. The ashes settled into the trail of the setting sun.

Out of Season

The hunting had been a total failure and their moods plummeted by the afternoon of the second day. Rain riddled the metal roof, a constant and annoying reminder that Mother Nature could be a heartless bitch. Glenn Cudzil repeated the condemnation with a variety of additional modifiers throughout the afternoon. During one tirade he compared her to his wife and wondered if there might be a conspiracy in the works. Jim and Dave Duncan, brothers who worked with Glenn, had grown tired of his onslaught of complaints.

"Shut the fuck up," they told him in unison.

Mark Dominic, a new member of the company, shook his head and looked out the window. This wasn't quite the picture they painted a couple weeks ago when they had planned the long weekend and talked him into joining them. Mark was later to find out that they usually went with Jeff Sweeney, the purchasing agent. Jeff recently had been suffering from painful bouts of diverticulitis, swearing off red meat and adhering to a strict diet the others wanted no part of – an almost superstitious distancing, as if the simple knowledge of the condition and its remedies could jeopardize their stolid lifestyles. Every year they made a great ceremony out of purchasing monstrous steaks from Glenn's buddy's restaurant. The glistening marbleized slabs were shipped in from Argentina and rubbed with a secret spicy blend.

Mark told them he wasn't a hunter, had never held a firearm. They received this news with baffled silence until he mentioned being an amateur photographer. He mimicked the act of snapping a picture that vaguely resembled pulling the trigger.

"I've always wanted to *shoot* in the big woods," he added and they were reasonably hooked and relieved to be paying a quarter share each rather than a third for the cabin.

The plan was to drive up on Thursday night, the first week in December. The company, a building supply distributor in Syracuse, annually closed that week for inventory, a decision deemed sensible due to the majority of hunters in its employ. It was a compromise as the hunters had to give up the much heralded *opening day*, but in return they received a paid holiday.

They finished the tedious process late on Thursday afternoon and spent an hour in the break room while a management team spot-checked the inventory. Norbert Greener, the assistant manager finally came in and stood before them, tapping the clipboard with his fingertips. The men became quiet and Norbert seemed to delight in their anticipation, notably Glenn who constantly harassed him and called him Nerfy. His eyes traveled to each of them and settled on Glenn and began bouncing back and forth between his face and the clipboard.

"Come on Nerfy, let us go," Glenn said. "We got a two-hour drive."

"Yeah, give us a break," Jim Duncan said.

Norbert regarded Jim, a friend, at least at work. They sometimes played chess at lunch. He hated to give up this rare opportunity to possess the upper hand over Glenn, but he knew it wasn't fair to the others and it was difficult to find capable chess opponents. Norbert presented the thumbs up and the men scrambled out like elementary school children.

Outside it was raining. The recent stretch of warm weather (records spanning many decades were in jeopardy) had reduced the snow to small dingy mounds at the edges of the parking lot.

They climbed into Glenn's SUV, the back packed with their gear. Soon they were on the east-bound Thruway.

"Do you think it's raining up there?" Jim said.

"Fuck no," Glenn replied. "It's prid'near a hundred miles north."

Dave and Jim groaned when Glenn turned off at the Verona exit and headed east on Route 365. Glenn had wanted to take this route for years, but Dave and Jim had been opposed, arguing it was longer than staying on the Thruway until Utica. They had driven in years past, but Glenn recently purchased the SUV and he was determined to have his way. The debate prompted a map a few days before and Glenn spread his thumb and forefinger over each route.

"See," he said. "It's definitely shorter and you get the feeling of being in the country quicker."

"You lose time going through all those towns," Jim said.

"I think Mark would enjoy seeing them."

"It's going to be dark."

The darkness was compounded by the added concealment of solid curtains of rain. This didn't deter Glenn from announcing each hamlet that snuck by over the rolling countryside – Floyd, Holland Patent and the slightly panicky descent (drama that Glenn enhanced with brake tapping and shoulders squeezing) into Barneveld with the STOP sign at the very bottom.

"You should see this in daylight," he said, bringing the SUV to a head bobbing halt.

"I see a new career for you," Dave said. "A tour guide for the blind."

A few miles before entering the Adirondack Park, Glenn pulled into the parking lot of the Parkside Grill. Inside was the welcoming smell from the wood stove, the few turned heads and the promise from the regiment of lined bottles. A woman smiled behind the bar. Her blonde hair was gray rooted, her furrowed face the result of many years' exposure to North Country weather.

"Boys?" she offered.

The Duncans ordered bourbon and Coke and Glenn requested a Manhattan. Mark considered a soft drink, wondering if he should prepare himself as the designated driver. He could feel the collective intensity – bottles lowered and tilted, the contents cascading generously and pushing the tingling ice cubes. They watched the barmaid's performance in silence. Opportunistic eyes stretched into the open V of her blouse. Mark ordered a beer when she gave him the nod. This plan was quickly diffused as Glenn watched the beer being delivered, in his estimation, with a little less pomp than the mixed drinks.

"That beer needs a lively companion," he said. "Give him a shot."

"I don't think I need it," Mark said.

"Nonsense," Glenn said. "There'll be no timid dogs in this pack."

Jim and Dave hoisted their drinks.

"Here's how."

It had been a three-drink stay. There was a general bitching about the unusually warm weather. The negative impact on business. Then they settled into hunting and fishing stories. Mark cautiously sipped the shot until he felt his elbow being raised by Glenn's hand.

"Now that's a good boy," he said, his eyes rising in feigned suspense.

As they left, Mark casually asked Glenn, "Mind if I drive?" and he tossed him the keys. He was relieved that Glenn had become engrossed in telling stories and stopped surveying his alcohol consumption which stopped at a conservative beer and shot. The hard rain continued with sudden inspired gusts, dancing like twisted spirits across the pavement. The forest leaned in, tall and close against the shoulder of the road. The beam of headlights seemed to dissolve, offering little more than a sense of wet and ragged texture. The openings overlooking White Lake and farther on, Otter Lake, were barely perceived; the signs suddenly solid, as if shouting them.

In Old Forge, Glenn told Mark to park across from the Tow Bar. The bar was full and they sat at a table by the pool table. They played teams – Mark and Glenn against the Duncans, gambling rounds of drinks. After winning four games, Mark was relieved when Glenn scratched while making a nicely banked shot on the eight ball. Dave and Jim were challenged by two locals. Mark dismally eyed a half full beer and three chips awaiting him.

"Looks like you got your work cut out for you," Glenn said.

At two, the tavern closed. Mark returned the keys to Glenn. The air was still warm and the ground smelled like a freshly turned garden. Glenn stood on the sidewalk and lifted his face to the dark sky. Raindrops pelted his tongue.

"I love the water up here," he said. "It's so pure."

"Dumb shit," Dave said. "It's probably evaporated piss drifting over from Milwaukee."

Glenn waved away the remark and slid into the driver's seat. There were about six more miles on South Shore Road to the cabin. Rain was beating hard and the men were silent as the headlights swept the dense woods. At one very tight curve the outline of a deer stood. Eyes flashed like marbles in the splattered light. Glenn for a split second thought the animal was standing on the road. He swerved sharply to the left. Mark pushed one hand against the dashboard and the other pawed across the front seat and grasped the console. As Glenn gained control he threw him a quick glance.

"You looking for change or do you have something else in mind?"

The cabin was a quarter mile off the road along a two-track heading east and away from Third Lake. It was a bouncy, greasy ride until the headlights fell upon the structure, sitting on a small rise about fifty yards from where the two-track ended.

"I don't understand why they put it so far from here," Jim said.

"So you can bitch about it every year," Glenn said.

"I think it's up there so it doesn't get flooded," Dave said.

"I guess we'll find out," Glenn replied.

The path leading to the cabin was creased down the middle. Water ran from the higher ground beyond, elevated in excess of two thousand feet. The area included the little known Fernow Mountain and a variety of scattered ponds. The four men put on ponchos and in two trips trudged up to the cabin and left their gear in the mudroom. In a typical winter (quite frequently with temperatures below zero and a blanket of measurable snow), they would simply stamp the snow off their boots and enter the main of the cabin. They were momentarily perplexed – crowded with their gear piled against the wall in the mudroom. Glenn told Mark and Jim to step outside so Dave and he had room to bend over and take off their boots. Outside in the pouring rain, Jim was resentful, citing that he was the oldest and he held the most responsible position in the company.

"What gives him the right?" he said. "He just gets his way because he's Glenn."

Mark said nothing, holding to a conservative attitude of the *new guy* with opinions best held in reserve. He knew the reason they were out there had nothing to do with seniority or status, but everything to do with Glenn's penchant for positioning himself in the prime spot. It was as if some of the superficialities of adolescence had been prolonged and favored

Glenn and his obvious gifts – matinee idol handsomeness, boundless athletic talent (he was the captain of both the company sponsored bowling and softball teams) and a manic, unquenchable taste for revelry. Glenn had a knack for feeling the pulse of the moment; he stayed ahead with the deftness of a politician. During the couple months he had been with the company, Mark witnessed many instances of his opportunistic abilities. Glenn had a way of worming himself into easier, less involved projects. He was a certified forklift operator, almost never leaving his seat, pointing like a field general for the removal of some troublesome object or to pass on paperwork. He'd nonchalantly take chips or cookies from your lunch. If you were sitting in a particular chair and had gotten up, you'd return to find him on it, sporting a squatter's entitled smile. It was the same expression when he showed up, uninvited at a gathering. One time Glenn took Jim's New York Yankee cap left on a chair in the break room while he was on vacation. He wore it all week. Jim couldn't believe it when he saw Glenn the following Monday morning; the hat was sweat-stained and squashed on his head. He was nonplussed when Jim confronted him.

"I dunno," he said. "It was there awhile. I figured it was just left. You want it back?"

Jim was a starchy fellow and regarded the demise from its original condition. He shook his head and walked away.

A floodlight came on and the door of the mudroom opened. Glenn handed out a stack of four empty five gallon buckets.

"You guys might as well get water since you're already out there."

"Like hell," Jim said as the door closed.

"What're these for?" Mark said.

"Washing and crapping."

"There's no running water?"

"Not in the winter," Jim said. "They add windshield wash to keep the pipes from freezing. You pour water in, you know, all at once to flush it. To bathe, you heat some on the stove and mix it with cold."

"Where do you get the water?"

"There's a well down that path," Jim said. He pointed into thick darkness.

"Doesn't it freeze?"

"Not really," Jim replied. "Just a little surface crust."

After the buckets were filled and passed inside, Mark and Jim entered the main of the cabin. A fire was licking behind the glass of the wood stove.

"That path is deadly in this rain," Jim said.

"Aw, quit your bitching," Glenn said. "You forget how hard it is, lifting those buckets up to your armpits with three feet of snow on each side."

The men finished distributing their gear and Glenn presented a deck of cards. Mark attempted to go to bed, but he shook his head.

"You can sleep at home."

They played euchre, a game Mark had never played, a factor Glenn, as his partner, continued to forget.

"Watch what the fuck you're doing," he said as Mark repeatedly trumped his ace.

Around four they finished. The Duncan brothers had swept them. They "euchred" them during the last hand.

"I can't believe you ordered me up," Glenn said. "You didn't have shit."

"Sorry," Mark said. "I had two trump and two aces..."

"All shit," Glenn said. "I had nothing besides the left, that was showing. If I wanted it, I would've picked it up myself."

"I said I was sorry."

Jim and Dave smiled.

"It ain't official," Glenn said. "If Sweeney'd been here we'd a beat your asses, as usual."

Mark was relieved it was over. He thought the game tedious and drinking had dissolved his focus. He looked forward to crawling onto his bunk, even if it was above Glenn.

- - -

The morning air was stagnant, feculent in the sealed up structure. The four men moved around each other in clumsy, stubborn silence. Strong coffee slowly brought them back. Windows were opened. Dave made bacon and eggs and afterward Mark cleaned the kitchen while the others washed and dressed. This was a time consuming process. Each of them had to boil water and mix with cold in a bucket to take to the shower stall for the "camp bath." Afterward, Mark witnessed a strange transformation – a round to square sharpening of their personalities as they unsheathed their firearms. Even Jim's eyes narrowed as he ran his hand along the barrel and caressed the stock.

Black clouds were looming above a warm breeze as the three hunters entered the woods. Mark watched them disappear and hurried to the shower, knowing his solitude would be brief. He was toweling off when he heard the rain splatter the roof. A few moments later Glenn emerged from the mudroom, followed by Jim and Dave. They discussed lunch and a heated debate ensued when Jim offered his split pea soup in opposition to Glenn's suggestion of *Dinty Moore's* canned beef stew. Glenn based his choice on Jim's offering the previous year – a soup made from canned pumpkin and sausage with a heavy dose of nutmeg.

"Tasted like candy flavored dog shit," Glenn said.

"If I remember right," Jim said. "You ate two bowls."

"Wasn't so pleasant coming out the other end," Glenn said. "It took me a week to recover."

"Probably didn't have anything to do with all the schnapps and whiskey you drank?" Jim said.

Glenn slowly shook his head and smiled as he opened the cans of stew.

After lunch, the rain continued and they played more euchre. Late in the afternoon, darkness filled the windows. The lights had been turned on without much effect. A low simmer of humidity. The wind driven rain beat incessantly for hours and drummed a low hanging branch against the roof. All their spirits seemed to suffer, especially Glenn who became more intoxicated.

"It's been a year since I fired my weapon," he said. "Come all the way up here – and for what – to sit around with *you* assholes?"

The three alleged assholes looked at each other and shrugged their shoulders. Glenn slapped his cards on the table and pushed his chair back. He went to his bedroom and came back with his shotgun. Glenn fed in two shells. He pushed open the door and walked out. They heard the mudroom door swing open, then the two rounds.

The next day Mark was the only one to leave the cabin in the morning although the others had talked about, "catching first light." He pulled on his poncho. His camera hung from a strap around his neck. Sunlight filtered dimly through the trees, but the sky was heavy with thickening clouds. Mark found the muted quality of light enticing and followed a path down to a creek. Three deer were drinking on the other side. He crouched and snapped pictures. Rain came suddenly. The fierce shower scattered the deer. Mark scrambled up the hill, carrying his camera under the poncho. Inside the others were up, drinking coffee and looking dismally out the window. He thought better of mentioning the deer. It rained throughout the morning and into the afternoon. They tired of Euchre. Glenn suggested

Poker. After two hours he had won almost every hand and close to a hundred dollars.

"Like taking candy from babies," he said.

Jim and Dave pulled away from the table. They moved to the couch and played Scrabble on the coffee table. Mark retreated to a corner chair and read. Glenn paced and complained. A couple times he wandered behind Dave and Jim. He offered word suggestions from their exposed letters.

"Shut the fuck up," they said.

"I can't take this," he said. "Do you guys want to get out for a while?"

The Duncans shook their heads. Mark shrugged his shoulders that Glenn took as affirmative and he grabbed the SUV keys.

Glenn drove through Old Forge. He pulled in front of a tavern called The Notch. There were a few vehicles in the puddled lot, mostly SUVs and pickups.

"Fucking rain," Glenn said. "This should be filled with snowmobiles."

As they climbed the stairs to the front porch, a woman was waving in the window.

"Rosey," Glenn said.

Inside, Glenn surveyed the table. Rosey sat with a woman and two men. She made a slight motion with her head, squeezed her lips and rolled her eyes. Glenn went to the bar and ordered four beers. He snatched up two and Mark picked up the others and followed him to the table.

"Sorry we're late," Glenn said. "Would you gentlemen excuse us?"

The closest one to Glenn craned his neck to look up at him. His expression made it clear he wasn't used to being ordered around. He gazed across the table at Rosey who shrugged her shoulders.

"Thanks for the drinks, Mason," she said. "I'll stop by sometime. I'd love to see your new gate."

Rosey explained Mason recently had a new stone entrance built on his property overlooking Fourth Lake.

"Really?" Glenn said. "Are people having a hard time finding the place?"

Mason fired him a quick look as he stood up.

"Pretty slick way of getting rid of them," Rosey said.

"So tell me, Rosey," Glenn said, after watching them descend the porch steps and climb into Mason's Escalade. "Does his dick tastes richer?"

"Maybe bigger," Rosey said.

They both laughed. Mark's jaw dropped. His face pivoted between them. He looked to the other woman who appeared equally stunned.

"My God, Rosey, what a surprise," Glenn said. "What's it been, five, six years?"

"At least," she said. "What're you doing up here?"

"Came up hunting," Glenn said. "But this fucking beach weather's terrible. What about you?"

"Moved up here about three years ago," she said.

"Me and Rosey worked together," Glenn said. "Some corner watering hole back in Solvay. What would you call it, Rosey, during our formative years?"

"Formative. That's a good one," Rosey said. "Yes, we worked pretty well together – wouldn't you say, sailor?"

"Aye, aye," Glenn said.

Rosey introduced her friend, Joan. Glenn's introduction of Mark was more of a presentation, directed to Joan.

"We call him, Big Shooter," Glenn said. "I'll let you find out why."

Mark gripped his beer and attempted a suitable expression on his reddening face.

"You're embarrassing him," Rosey said. "Really, Big Shooter?"

Glenn shrugged his shoulders.

"Come on, sailor," Rosey said. "Let's get on board."

She stood and pulled him to a small area near the bar. They embraced into a slow dance. At the table, Mark and Joan watched. The song ended. Rosey pushed Glenn toward the juke box. She reached into his front pocket. He smiled broadly as the pocket pulled inside out. Coins spun and shone in the dim light and scattered on the floor. Rosey, hysterical on her hands and knees, picking and offering to him – he drew her up. She rolled quarters into the old machine and pushed buttons. The first chords of the song drew each other's eyes.

"Yeah, they've got some history," Joan said.

"I guess," Mark said.

"Come on," she said. "Let's make some of our own."

They ate and drank. Glenn bought. Later, barely moving on the dance floor, Rosey whispered to Glenn, "Let's go to my place."

"What about them?"

"They look pretty cozy to me," she said. "Bring 'em along. Besides, he might come in handy. You've been knocking down those Manhattans pretty steady."

"Don't you worry about me," Glenn said.

Mark drove Joan in Glenn's vehicle, following Rosey and Glenn. It was dark and Old Forge was quiet. Rosey lived in a small ranch overlooking the water. The rain had stopped and the air was riding a soft, Spring-like breeze.

"God it's warm," Glenn said. "I'm still sweating."

Inside they were greeted by Rosey's dog, a Black Labrador that jumped excitedly around the four of them.

"Hey Babe," Rosey said.

She knelt and embraced the dog.

"That's the dog's name?" Mark said. "Babe?"

"Yes, Babe," Rosey said. "You are my sweet little baby, aren't you?"

Babe yelped appreciatively and Rosey poured dry dog food into a bowl and added water. Glenn walked into the living room.

"Looks like a jailhouse," he said.

The inner walls were stripped to bare studs.

"Remodeling," Rosey said. "The contractor is slower than hell."

"I'll show you around," Joan said to Mark.

She led him down the hallway. A sheet was spread and pinned to the studs. Their silhouettes dropped out of sight onto the bed. Glenn smiled. Rosey raised an eyebrow. Her tongue swept her lips. He pulled her down on the couch. From the bedroom came light laughter, then a long train of moaning. Rosey pushed him away.

"What?" Glenn said.

"This is no good," she said. "I can't do this with them right there. It feels like high school."

"Well, what the fuck?" Glenn said.

"Come on," she said. "The boat house."

"Are you nuts? It's freezing out there."

"It's not that bad," Rosey said. "Look. The lake hasn't even froze over yet."

In the kitchen Rosey switched on the floodlight that illuminated the backyard. Babe barked and she slid open the door. The dog scampered out, away from the light, into the shrouded darkness. Rosey picked up Glenn's hand and led him down the soggy lawn. Inside, the boathouse the air was slightly cooler over the water. Rosey turned on a light. On the other side she pulled up the large overhead door. A warm cross breeze rushed through and moonlight tracked in broad wrinkles on the water. In the corner under a work bench she flipped on a space heater; the wavy red elements immediately came to life. Rosey took a blanket from a shelf and spread it on the small area of dock. She sat down and pulled off her shoes and slacks.

"Come 'ere, sailor."

Outside, the dog wandered. Babe had been in the woods, poking her nose into the layers of decaying leaves. She made her way to the lake. The beach stretched about twenty-five feet along the shore and Babe traversed it in a few inches of water. She had been drinking, taking pleasure in the chilled temperature and the mineral flavor when she heard Rosey:

"...Yes, yes, oh... yes, babe, baby, oh... whooo sailor, my sweet baby..."

The dog turned toward the boathouse. The voice tightened as she approached.

"Oh, my God, yes... babe, oh... babe, baby..."

Babe scampered to the golden rectangle of light, over the threshold, into the boathouse. She was confronted by the ivory glow of Glenn's elevated ass. From beyond, the voice that had summoned her, eased to a more contented murmuring. For a second the dog was puzzled by Rosey's languid rendering of her name. The roll of bare buttocks reduced to a pallid tremor. Then the pitch of her voice climbed; more gratitude and encouragement gushed from Rosey's lips. Babe emerged from a paralysis of confusion into the sudden draft of inspiration. She barked. Before Glenn could decipher the sound, his collective senses were shredded as Babe buried her frigid snout into his anus.

- - -

The hospital in Utica didn't have much of a view. That was one of many complaints Glenn repeated to the nurses. After three days they were fed up with him. Initially they had honored the attractive man and the account of his courageous rescue of a drowning woman in the frigid water up north. Since then they avoided his room except mandatory rounds. One of them wondered aloud just how many heroes, celebrated in the news, were also such unbelievable assholes? The swelling had decreased around the gash on his forehead and was slightly uncomfortable. The pain from the stabbing just below his chest was deep and physically poignant as if it was something alive and actively gnawing. The puncture had nicked his liver and he was kept in the hospital as a precaution against possible infection and internal bleeding.

At the end of the second day he cajoled two nurses into giving him sleeping pills along with pain medication. Glenn luxuriated in the result, but he was refused at his next attempt.

"We don't make it a policy to snow our patients under," the nurse said.

Her tone carried the firm and friendly officiousness of a tax auditor. Glenn was undaunted. He reached for her hand.

"I'm having a hard time sleeping," he said. "I miss my wife terribly and, well, I'm scared."

"I understand," she said, eluding his grasp. "But it's against policy."

"They did it yesterday," he said.

"I know," she replied. "It won't happen again."

Glenn watched her inject into the IV. After a few moments he felt the tentative reaching of the drug and shifted his body, crossing and re-crossing his legs. He slid his arms along his sides. It reminded him of being strapped in the stretcher. The ambulance attendants had worked quietly and efficiently under the floodlights, but struggled up the spongy lawn. Inside the ambulance they attended his wounds and comforted him along the winding road.

His scream had terrified Rosey as he hurdled over her. Glenn's head hit the wall and he rolled into the frigid water.

Rosey lowered herself and was able to stand with the water at her waist. Glenn was barely conscious. She managed to pull him outside the opening of the boathouse. There was a splash behind her and Babe's black head emerged, snorting and barking. Rosey was suddenly in deeper water and grasped the collar of Glenn's shirt. She pulled and kicked, rounding the side of the boathouse. Babe followed, pawing at her arm, until Rosey's feet touched and she was able to pull Glenn onto the beach.

Inside, Mark heard Rosey calling for help. He pulled on his clothes and hurried down the lawn, into the glare of floodlights – the spectacle of the half-naked couple and the dog scampering around them. Glenn's head was bleeding, but he gripped both hands over his midsection. Blood oozed out between his fingers.

Mark lifted his shirt.

"There's a stick in there," he said.

Glenn's eyes rounded in horror.

"Just get it out," he said.

"No way," Mark said. "I know that's not the right thing to do."

Glenn raised his head. He turned his palms upward. They were coated in blood. He attempted to sit up, but the pain forced him back. His feet splashed below the shackles of his bunched trousers.

"Get me out of here," he said. "Get me up to the house."

"I don't think so," Mark said. "You shouldn't be moved."

"What's going on?" Joan called from the house.

"Glenn's hurt," Mark replied. "Call nine-one-one"

"Well at least get me out of the water," Glenn said. "Pull my fucking pants up! You think I want to be found like this?"

Mark and Rosey struggled to drag him out of the water and pull up the soaked trousers. Joan came down with a bundle of towels. Rosey ran to the boathouse. She pulled on her slacks and shoes and brought blankets to cover Glenn. In the distance a siren became louder.

"Now listen up," Glenn said. He lifted his bloodied hands, wobbling on elbows. He waved them closer.

The story was really quite simple:

Glenn and Mark happened to be driving by. Joan ran to the road and waved them to stop. Babe had gotten caught on something in the water. Rosey jumped in to free her and also became snagged. Glenn ran from the car and onto the dock, but slipped and fell into shallow water. He hit his head on a rock and was impaled on a branch imbedded in the sandy bottom.

Glenn gathered himself, holding them captive with his dripping hands, eyelids fluttering; he insisted on the ending:

Despite his injuries he had managed to free them before he lost consciousness.

- - -

Vivian drove to Utica, arriving at the hospital around two in the morning. Dave had called her.

"Glenn's been in an accident," he said.

He had mentioned the water, which prompted a flood of questions. Dave became flustered and said he hadn't been there. She found her husband heavily sedated with his head wrapped in layers of gauze. The nurse told her of his heroism and mentioned his friends were in the waiting room. Vivian walked down the hallway and found out they had recently left. She sat down and eventually fell asleep. She awoke a few hours later and returned to the room. A doctor was addressing a group of interns. They were all dressed in green scrubs, some with white coats. Her view of Glenn was blocked, but she heard his voice – weak and muffled as if something heavy was pressing on his chest. The doctor (Vivian suspected she was an attractive woman) mentioned the incredible strength and courage he had mustered to save the woman and her dog.

"I did what any decent man would do," Glenn said. "Besides, it was a nice night for a swim."

There was a small wrinkle of laughter among the group. Vivian recognized the particular timbre of his voice, even in its weakened state – the same as when their daughter brought her high school girlfriends home. A sweet glide. In Vivian's mind it carried an imaginary hand molded to their young, bouncy asses. At that moment Glenn was suddenly visible. Vivian clearly saw his eyes on the doctor as she had pictured it. He managed within a split second to recover when he recognized her, but in that instant she perceived him clearly, within his own fantasy – his pants piled around his ankles.

"Darling," he said. "You're here."

After the medical staff left, Glenn told her the fabricated tale. He was scheduled for tests. Vivian was going to leave after they wheeled him away, but decided to wait for the results. She had coffee in the cafeteria and returned to find Rosey sitting in a chair, watching Glenn sleep.

"Hello," Vivian said.

"Oh, hi," Rosey said. "I'm Rose. You must be – are you his wife?"

"That's right," Vivian replied. She sat in the chair by the window.

"Your husband saved my life," she said.

Vivian knew she had surprised the woman and she instantly presumed she was more than a random damsel in distress. This was confirmed when Glenn awakened and saw Rosey first. He offered a casual "Hey" before her darting eyes signaled they weren't alone.

"Viv, this is Rose," he said. "The woman I saved."

"Yes, I know."

"I thought I was dead and then saved," Rosey said. "And then he fell and I saw he was hurt, but then he just kept coming."

Vivian at that point eased back to a position that resembled complacency, but was really a neutral place where she could gather and sort out, not what the evidence was, but what course of action to take. Within a few years of their marriage she knew he was a man who couldn't be faithful. Vivian had long ago given up on attaining the triumphant moment when all the proof would stack up and topple him. Somewhere hurt had turned to anger and from there had dissolved into a corroded disgust. She let Glenn and Rosey perform their fiction. She almost laughed when Rosey said he had called out her name as he was loaded into the ambulance.

For the next two days Vivian spoke to Glenn on the phone, but didn't visit him. He had complained how lonely and afraid he was, but she told him it was too far for a quick visit and presently her job was too demanding.

On both days Vivian worked until 3:30 pm and was with Dave Duncan in his bed by 4 pm.

After leaving the hospital on Sunday afternoon, she had gone directly to Dave's house. Vivian had been upset the three of them had avoided her in the hospital and bolted home. Dave was surprised when he opened the door. She stood on the porch, railing her version of abandonment until he interjected:

"I think about you every day."

Two years before, at a company picnic, Glenn had left with two other men, "to replenish ice." Vivian knew they were off to a tavern. On a nature trail away from the picnic area, she had walked with Dave and complained bitterly about her husband's short comings. He stopped and kissed her. They were instantly entangled until a branch snapped in the direction of a hidden curve of the trail. They broke apart and rearranged themselves.

Nobody emerged from the trail, but the interruption chilled their momentum. Since then they hadn't spoken, but exchanged long looks at company social functions.

In the kitchen Dave made tea. They sat at the table and he told her all the details Mark had given him. She laughed hysterically about the dog's nose.

"I wish it had been a rhinoceros."

Vivian ran her finger up and down Dave's forearm until he couldn't stand it any longer. They rose and kicked away their chairs. She bent over and swam her arms over the tabletop. Cups and saucers exploded on the floor. They followed-up the frenzy in the kitchen with a long and unhurried evening in his bedroom. The next two days afforded them the same opportunity, but on Thursday afternoon Vivian found it more difficult to fend off the growing dread of Glenn's return the following day. She told Dave her daughter was graduating in June and she would then leave Glenn.

"We need to be careful," she said.

Dave had been overwhelmed by her sexual intensity, but he couldn't believe it when she spoke of a future.

"Maybe you're just going through that rebound thing," he said. "We hardly know each other."

"All I can tell you is life is too damned short," she said. "I say we go and go and go until we can't."

They were sitting in bed with pillows piled behind them, sipping chardonnay and picking from a plate of cheddar cheese, sliced apples and almonds. Dave had prepared the snack after their love making. He had been thrilled to be naked in his kitchen and giddy with the idea of Vivian waiting in the bedroom. She laughed when he returned, aroused.

"Resurrection," she said.

Dave shrugged his shoulders and placed the tray on the dresser.

"Later," he said.

- - -

Within a week of being home, Glenn was miserable. On the drive from the hospital, Vivian told him her job was crazy (a complete computer system overhaul) and she was required to start early and stay late. Glenn's protests mirrored adolescence. She stared through him; her gray eyes were as flat as shale. The idea of spending another six months with him seemed unfathomable. Her hopes remained buoyant because of the time she spent with Dave, but the drive home each day became more foreboding. Glenn was at first bewildered and eventually angered by Vivian's indifference. She reacted by reaching deeper into it. Dinners were less elaborate and less frequent. Her weekly grocery shopping included more time spent in the frozen food section. The only semblance of intimacy between them was the cleaning of the puncture wound that Vivian performed every evening. Glenn reclined on the couch, clutching his hands to his chest. His eyes closed. He winced as she poured saline into the hole and loosely covered it with gauze. Vivian was relieved to see the hole finally close up.

Originally Glenn had planned on milking the injury, but Vivian's indifference left him anxious to get back to work. The following Monday, Glenn arrived at the warehouse fifteen minutes early. In the break room the crew was surprised to see him.

"Well, if it ain't the hero," Jeff Tradnyski said.

"Did the old lady kick you out?" Andy James said.

They were sitting at the table with Jim and Dave. Mark sat at another table with Jeremy Staid and Ralph Falconi. Fresh brewed coffee pervaded a familiar melding of industrial odors. To Glenn, at that moment, they represented the cooperative aromas of belonging.

"That's what I call a hunting trophy," Jeff said.

An article from the *Syracuse Post Standard* was pinned to the wall. There was a photograph of Glenn in the hospital with gauze wrapped around his head. The other picture was of Rosey kneeling down and petting Babe in front of the boathouse. Her smile was inviting. Her sweater was tight.

"Nice rack," Ralph said.

"I'll say," Jeff said.

"I wonder if you would've saved her if she was ugly," Andy said.

"Probably just the dog."

There was a slur of low guttural laughter. Glenn retrieved his coffee cup from the wall cabinet and filled it. The memory of the cold, velvety nose rippled through him. He sat down.

"I bet you thought she was a mermaid," Andy said.

Again, a deep uneven laughter, like digging into gravelly dirt. Glenn snuggled into the erratic network of familiar voices, an indication that Mark, Dave and Jim had not betrayed him. He gazed around the room. Mark nodded and offered a vague smile. Dave a quick glimpse as he turned the page of the newspaper. Jim was staring intently into his coffee cup. Glenn reached across the table and took one of the small powdered doughnuts from Jim's open package. Jim's eyes shot up. His lips parted. Dave cleared his throat. He ruffled the newspaper and lifted it above the table top. He finessed the thin pages together and folded it to quarter size. His eyes were trained on his brother until he returned the gaze. Jim nodded. His face relaxed. He pushed the doughnuts toward Glenn.

"Help yourself."

"Don't mind if I do," Glenn said.

They watched his fingers saunter across the table.

Shoes

Who's putting sponge in the bells I once rung
And taking my gypsy before she's begun
To singing the meaning of what's on my mind...
Neil Young (Nowadays Clancy Can't Even Sing)

He died alone in his bed in the retreating darkness of the morning. He had barely made it up the stairs, the work boots untied and slipping and thudding against each step. His knuckles rubbed along the walls of the hallway in the blackness of night until his legs were against the bed. He had turned and sat on the bed and pulled off his hat. He fell back and was asleep as his head hit the pillow. The snoring had stopped a few hours before his death, had tapered off to a steady rasp from deep in his throat. His last breath was a deflated exhale with a soft airy rattle that startled a bird outside on the windowsill.

At noon, the old woman slowly crept up the stairs. She stopped on the landing by the window, feeling the warm September sunlight wash the side of her face. She turned and looked above the remaining three steps, beyond the slant of dust-speckled light, down the dark hallway. The two empty bedroom doors were closed. At the end of the hallway the remaining door was open. On the bed she saw the worn soles of the work boots leaning against each other. The stench grew stronger as she grasped the handrail and climbed the rest of the stairs and proceeded down the hallway.

"Raymond," she called. "Raymond, what did you do in there?"

A forlorn anger arose as she entered the bedroom. Her son's eyes were wide open, giving her cause to turn and look at the ceiling, but in that small instant she knew there was nothing to see and the prophecy that she had expressed to him daily, had come true.

- - -

People in the village find it ironic that I own a liquor store even though it's never been said to me. I believe this because I too, find it ironic and I know that even the least insightful among us have a natural faculty to recognize irony and a strong desire to express it. An obvious example is John Stetson, our assistant fire chief, who in 1953, at the age of twelve, had burned the front porch off his parents' house. This tidbit of local history rises from time to time in taverns or living rooms. It receives an expression of feigned bafflement, similar to first hearing that Einstein had failed elementary math.

That I know my fellow citizens are aware of the irony of my profession doesn't concern me. The fact that I was once a drunkard lends to history, and when I look at that part of my life, it is as if someone else had lived it. If the information emerges in conversation, I assume it is in context to something in the far past, otherwise it is meaningless, like someone gratuitously pulling a rabbit from his hat. On the other hand, my classmate Roger Strang was a bully and a thief and continued in adulthood as a bully in his capacity as a village cop. He was the first one to tell me of Raymond Sir's death, making the news more disturbing.

"Well, Shoes has finally killed himself," he announced in the doorway of my store.

Roger Strang was tall and very fit. His hair was cut short and his facial features within the squarish parameters were small and restrained, didn't move much when he spoke. The voice came from deep in his chest, had weight and authority. He reminded me of Sterling Hayden and at that moment I could imagine putting a bullet in his forehead like Al Pacino did to Hayden in the *Godfather.*

"His mother found him lying in his own shit and piss."

"How?" I managed to ask.

"How what?" Strang replied. His face was vacant, his gray eyes wide and looking past me as if he couldn't free himself from the vision of the corpse.

"How did he kill himself?"

"Booze," he said. "Dope." His eyes returned to me as he waved his hand toward my vodka selections. "What else?"

"So, he really didn't die by his own hand?"

"Well no, not directly," Strang said. "But you can't tell me he didn't know what he was doing to himself," he quickly added. "In my mind he was hell-bent on killing himself. Imagine that," Strang continued, his voice softened, became reflective: "From the top of the class to worm feed."

I didn't bother reminding Officer Strang that we were all destined to become *worm feed.* With Strang, as well as others whose conversations I find tedious, I've learned to not offer comment and especially not to ask unnecessary questions. Unfortunately, he must have taken my silence as an expression of shock and I guess he's seen quite a bit of that in his line of work. Strang continued at first delicately, recounting Mrs. Sir's futile attempt to clean up her son's body and air out the room before the police arrived. His tone changed and his voice hardened like cheap pulp fiction as he described the condition of Shoes' body and his living quarters. I followed along, nodding until he began introducing his own opinions on Shoes and his life. It sounded like the work of a poorly prepared sports announcer. I picked up a rag and dusted wine bottles. When Officer Strang left, he trailed off with, "What a waste."

In the following days I would hear the same exclamation repeatedly: *"You know, he was at the top of his graduating class...what a waste!"* accompanied by looks of head-shaking disbelief. Some still referred to him as Razor, a high school nickname, although there is confusion as to its origin. Was it based on his razor-sharp intellect, his cutting ability as a halfback, or the slight deviation of his name? I find it strange that this debate emerges every once in a while as it hardly matters; the nickname was replaced in 1984 with Shoes.

- - -

Razor had clomped into the local department store at the plaza on the eastern edge of the village in his old muddy sneakers. A cold October rain saturated the sneakers in a wooded area behind the plaza where he drank a quart of warm beer. The store, a large sprawling structure, part of a regional corporate chain, had opened the week before. There was much heated debate in the village when the store had been proposed, but it passed by a four to three vote by the village board. Razor hated the idea of the store; saw it as the beginning of the end.

Each step oozed bubbly mud through the holes in his sneakers. A clerk named Robby Johnson, standing smartly behind a counter in his black pants, white shirt, and the red vest with the store logo and ROBBY *stenciled on the front, watched as Razor trailed mud over the spotless sheen of the white floor. Robby was a shy boy, seventeen years old. It was his first day at his first job. He thought it odd as Razor sat on the floor and pulled off his sneakers. He watched as Razor struggled to his feet and gripped the edge of a shelf to steady himself. Slowly he made his way down the aisle, one hand on the shelf, his wet socks slapping the floor, leaving a more bestial track than the sneakers. He stopped and pulled a pair of high top work boots off the shelf. As he attempted to lower himself, Razor lost his balance and sat down hard. His long wet hair swung around his face and settled on his shoulders. Robbie Johnson came from around the counter and approached Razor.*

"Can I help you, sir?" he asked.

"Call me Ray."

"Can I help you?"

"Yeah, come here," he said. "Stand right there."

Robby moved to the spot.

"Now brace yourself," Razor said, as he arched his back and swung the open end of the boot over his toes. He pushed the sole against the young man's knee. Robby's knee wobbled and he quickly grabbed the boot with one hand and Razor's leg with the other.

"That's good," Razor said. He extended his arms behind and spread his fingers on the floor. "Give 'er a push."

Robby pushed and felt the resistance of the wet sock. He pushed harder and felt the foot settle with mushy finality. After they put on the other boot Razor slid back against a shelf and laced them up. He extended his arm and Robby grasped it and pulled him to his feet.

"How do they feel?" Robby asked.

"They're okay," Razor replied. He high-stepped in a small circle, looking down at his feet. "Not as good as the ones I got at old Duncan's on Main Street. Those were worth the money."

Robby started to nod, but felt a sudden twinge of guilt. It was his first test of company loyalty.

"I bet these are cheaper," Robby softly blurted out.

"Might be," Razor said. "Have to see how they ride."

He pointed to the wet sneakers in a puddle on the floor.

"You can dispose of those."

Razor walked down the aisle toward the front of the store in solid pronounced steps as if he were crossing a creek on a narrow log. There was a faint squish with every step. Robby picked up the sneakers, hooked them on two bent fingers and carried them behind the counter and dropped them in a trashcan. He watched Razor maneuver past the strategic maze of shelves to the cashier's aisle where he paused, said something to the cashier and continued out the automatic door.

Robby was stunned. He raised his arms and looked around. There were no witnesses. He headed to the front of the store. The cashier was cashing out a customer, doling out change.

"Did that guy pay for his boots?" Robby said as he came behind the cashier.

The cashier, a young woman named Grace was startled, spilling coins on the counter.

"What guy? What boots?" Grace asked as she swept up the coins and dropped them in the customer's hand "Sorry," she said to the customer and turned to Robby.

"The guy with the long stringy hair!"

"That weird guy?"

"Yeah," Robby said. "He had new boots on. I saw him say something to you and walk out. It didn't look like he paid."

"How was I supposed to know he had boots?" She asked. "You think I look at people's feet?"

"I don't know," Robby said. "What did he say to you?"

"It was something like: 'It is a great art to saunter,'" Grace said. "And then he laughed a real strange laugh and walked out.

"Robby went to the front window. The parking lot was busy and there was no sign of Razor. Robby informed the manager who called the police. Within a half an hour Officer Strang had picked him up.

- - -

I was at the Yellow Horse Tavern that evening. It was one of many corner watering holes in the village and was known by the locals as Old Yeller. Happy hour offered half-priced drinks and I was getting my money's worth on that Friday night. I was comfortably situated on a cushioned stool on the curve of the horseshoe shaped bar. Old Yeller was packed, the room loud and smoky and smelling of beer, cigarettes, fried food and rain soaked clothing. A hockey game was on the TV and the Sabres were tied with the Rangers in the first period. Eyes would dart from conversation to the screen, sometimes in mid-sentence at a breakaway or a fight. If you didn't care about the hockey game and cared about what you were saying, the interruptions could be annoying, but the majority of the patrons didn't care. Winning that elusive cup seemed like a legitimate possibility in the early season.

News of Razor's arrest had come over the police scanner behind the bar in the late afternoon. I came in around 3:30 pm. I had finished painting a house on Lawrence Avenue. Luckily all I had to do was touch up some shutters in the garage and refasten them. It was a single story ranch and I didn't mind the rain as I secured the shutters, cleaned up and loaded my van. After a quick shower I went to Old Yeller, paid my tab with a couple crisp one hundred-dollar bills, ordered a burger and sipped on a bourbon and coke. The police scanner said a man had walked out of a local store with a pair of shoes. It didn't become noteworthy until Jimmy Franks from the DPW had come in and said it was Razor.

"You believe that?" Jimmy said. "Just walks in, puts on a pair of brand new shoes and walks out."

It was actually hard for me to believe. Razor and I went back many years. We graduated from high school together in 1968. He was first in our class of one hundred and eighty-nine while I barely made the top third. My family had moved to the village in the summer of 1963 and the guidance counselor convinced my mother that I would meet the right people by joining the eighth grade chorus. I found the counselor's recommendation questionable as I couldn't carry a tune and I felt the same inadequacy as a polio victim would, being placed on the track team. Razor was next to me and he had a beautiful voice and he was often selected to perform solos while I mouthed my way through most songs. What puzzled me was how such a wonderful voice could be so horrifically distorted in laughter. Razor's laugh was hard to describe because it was a strange and energetic convergence of many noises. It was once described as sounding like a pigeon with a bad case of hiccups. I remember a classmate saying it made you think twice before saying something funny in his presence.

I, on the other hand, welcomed the strange arrangement of sounds. Razor was a popular guy – an athlete, a scholar, a leader in student government. As I look back, I realize he was revered for the right reasons and not for the usual superfluous qualities, like being a trendy dresser or an overzealous jokester, that we teenagers seemed to find attractive. He always wore a white shirt, gray flannel pants and white bucks, like Pat Boone. There was nothing flamboyant about him, but he maintained a steady and uplifting manner that had its own appeal. I sensed in him an inherent kindness, and in my frightened status as the new kid, I embraced him, trying to find things from within that deemed me worthy of his attention. I discovered my goofy, self-effacing sense of humor would make him laugh, so I stoked that fire constantly and took the erratic throttling of his laughter as a reward and a form of acceptance.

He had been unusually kind to me, exercising patience not typical in adolescence. I had been nervous and insecure finding my way in the new school and as a result I'd sometimes been silly and immature, looking for the cheap and easy laugh from those who gave it without much discernment. Razor had a way of ignoring the less ripened fruits of my mind, which had resulted in my being more selective in what I offered him. But virtue was not always easy to recognize at that age and for a brief time, mine had taken a dive and impacted our developing friendship.

My parents would divvy out a modest allowance each week and by mid-week the money was usually used up on Royal Crown Cola, ice cream sandwiches, stick candy and baseball cards. There were a couple classmates from my neighborhood that I had unwillingly walked home with after school a couple times. One of them was the before-mentioned Roger Strang who lived a block past our house and the other was Dave Press who lived across the street from Strang. My first encounter with Strang had been on my first day of school. As I made my way down the unfamiliar hallway, he had approached me with a group of other boys.

"Hey look," he said. "A new guy."

He had stuck out his hand and as I offered mine to complete the handshake, he quickly pulled his away and raked back his hair. His buddies all laughed and I smiled nervously and put my hand in my pocket.

"Hey four eyes," he said, moving closer and tilting his head and examining my glasses. "Let me clean those up for you."

Strang licked two fingers and rubbed them on my glasses. There was more laughter and I could sense other students looking at me as they filed by, picking up their pace and moving with a deliberateness so as not to become victims themselves. To this day I can still feel the heat of embarrassment and the isolated shame of my fearful paralysis as I stood there looking through saliva streaked lenses and hearing the dissonance of the mocking laughter. I've found myself in the safety of memory, building an attractive fantasy – rearranging the scene and striking out at Strang, with imagined bravery, knowing I would get my ass kicked and possibly being thrown out of school on my first day. But of course there's no changing what happened, and as far as redemption goes, well, forget that because I was even more cowardly in the following weeks.

I had managed to avoid Roger Strang in school, but one day as I was walking home I heard a distant voice behind me: "Hey four eyes!"

I turned, and half a block away I saw him and David Press waving at me. I waved and turned away, but I heard Strang say, "Hey four eyes, wait up."

Neither of them carried books and their arms swung in a carefree arc, back and forth, the motion rustling the fabric of their open jackets. I noticed this because I was afraid to look into their faces, the one slight glance that I stole at Strang revealing a menacing sneer. My leg started to shake and I cast my eyes downward to see if my baggy chinos were hiding my trepidation. The cuffs rode the tops of my wingtips in slack stillness. I shifted my books from one arm to the other as I watched them approach.

"Where ya headed?" Strang asked me.

"Home," I replied.

"Where's that?"

"Down here, on South Grove across from Griggs Place," I said.

"Eddie Belcham's place?"

"Yeah," I replied. "The Belchams lived there."

For many years after, our house would be referred to as the Belcham place. I found this village quirkiness as interesting as a woman who'd been married for many years, still being addressed by her maiden name. I hadn't met the Belchams, but I remembered my parents saying their name. Strang however, was excited that I lived there.

"Right next door to Jodie Cameron," he said.

"I don't know," I said.

"You live right next door to Jodie Cameron and you don't even know it?" Strang said. He shook his head and rested his hands on his hips. "She's only the hottest chick in high school. Eddie Belcham used to watch her dress from his bedroom window all the time. She never pulls her shade down."

"Nice tits," Press piped in.

"I'll say," Strang said. "Nice everything. I stayed over one night at Eddie's and we saw her come out of the shower. Totally fucking naked!"

I can't say my curiosity wasn't aroused with this information and I have to admit, afterward I did spend some long moments on many evenings in the darkness of my room, with my chin resting on the windowsill, peering across the yard into the golden rectangle of light and the glorious movement of flesh inside. But at that moment on the sidewalk I was struggling for composure. Sudden concerns like Strang asking me to stay overnight entered my mind and fueled my anxiety.

"We're stopping at Riker's," Strang said. "Wanna come?"

Riker's was a delicatessen across the street from the park on our way home.

"I don't have any money," I said. It was Thursday and I'd already spent my allowance.

"Don't worry about it," Strang replied.

I felt the pressure of his hand on my back and I turned with the prodding and walked in front of them. As we continued down the sidewalk I felt uncomfortable. Behind me I heard Strang and Press whispering and intermittent bursts of muffled laughter. I was afraid to turn around, but I did one time when Strang stepped on the back of my shoe.

"Sorry," Strang said, but there was challenge in his face as I bent over and secured the shoe.

I was relieved to reach Riker's. Strang told me offhandedly to leave my books on the newspaper box out front. The bell rang on the door as we entered and old Mr. Riker greeted us from behind the counter. The store was small and dimly lit and there were no other customers. Strang went up to the counter. He pulled some change from his pocket and began making selections of candy from the wall behind Mr. Riker. Press nudged me with his elbow and directed me with a tilt of his head to another counter. Quickly he snatched a handful of baseball cards and stuffed them into his jacket pocket. I was shocked and looked over to the counter. Mr. Riker was bent over, picking candy low on the shelf that Strang had singled out. Press gave me another nudge, his eyes darting urgently toward the baseball cards. I grabbed some and stuck my hands in my pockets.

"Dave," Strang said over his shoulder. "Want cinnamon or butterscotch?"

"Butterscotch'll be good," Press replied.

Mr. Riker put the candy in a small bag and Strang paid him and we thanked the old man and filed out the door. Outside, I picked up my books and followed Strang and Press across the street and into the park, feeling the lightness of relief. We went over a shaded hillock and down the other side to a picnic table.

"Let's see'm," Strang said.

Press pulled a stack of packages from his pocket and dropped them on the table. I added mine. There were thirteen and Strang divided them – five each for Press and himself, and three for me. We sat down at the table and Strang and Press tore off the wrappers and stacked the cards in one pile and the gum in another. I was coming to grips with the fact that I had stolen something, because I had never done it before. I asked if it bothered them and they laughed and Strang said, "Did you see that Cadillac sitting in the driveway next to the store? I'd say old Riker's doing all right. My old man says he oughta be tarred and feathered and ridden outa town on a rail for the prices he charges."

The pilferage had ambushed me and I've wondered if Strang had masterminded it that way when he saw me walking alone on the sidewalk. It was a ballsy improvisation, he not knowing how I would react in the store. Since then I've often reflected on the darkness of Strang's heart and his stealthy arrogance as I see him cruise by in the shiny patrol car. But that day in the park, as the nefarious thrill of the illegal act wore off and we shuffled through the baseball cards and made some trades and I found Tom Tresh of the Yankees in my hand, it was as if a thin soothing veil had settled on us. A passerby would see three boys hunched over at the picnic table, their crackling voices reciting player's batting averages and qualities as they negotiated.

The next day after school we repeated the crime, but I found the whole experience to be deeply troubling. I can understand why lawyers argue the degree of premeditation to a jury – that it has a substantial bearing on a case. An offender who actually plots and carries out a surreptitious and devious act is quite measurably more evil than one who just happens to randomly become involved. I say this with the authority of one who has done both.

Strang and Press had waited for me across the street in front of the school. Neither of them had books again and they both had their hands in their jacket pockets. They greeted me in an easy and friendly manner, but there was no warmth in Strang's eyes. His look gave the impression of calculated appraisal and I felt myself shrinking under his gaze.

"We're stopping at Riker's," Strang said. "You with us?"

I guess I'd thought there was some measure of ambiguity in the question with the naïve hope that we'd make a legitimate purchase, but deep down I knew he was offering me a partnership in another crime.

"Sure," I replied.

I tried to regulate my voice with a tone of natural casualness, but I could feel the movement of dread inside, like the dark cold crawl of a glacier. They turned and walked side-by-side down the sidewalk and I wondered if my new position of trailing behind them was a sign of acceptance. If that was the case, I can't say I reveled in the elevated status, although I preferred it to being out front. I had followed a few steps behind them and each step carried the heavy burden of condemnation. I would have welcomed any excuse to escape, but none came to mind. Even the vague hope of my mother driving by in our Pontiac station wagon, running some errands, gave me cause to scan the road ahead. I followed along, watching congealed blades of hair slither like a wet paintbrush over the upturned collar of Strang's jacket as he strutted along.

Inside the store the scene was re-enacted as if the day before had been a dress rehearsal. Again, there were no customers and Mr. Riker greeted us and Strang had gone up to the counter as Press and I moved to the counter behind him. I watched Press grab a handful of the cards and he looked at me and I did the same. I couldn't believe it when Strang turned his head and asked as he had yesterday:

"Dave you want cinnamon or butterscotch?"

"Butterscotch'll be good," Press said.

"Doesn't the other guy ever get a choice?" Old man Riker asked Strang.

"He's allergic to butterscotch," Strang replied.

The old man nodded and looked my way through the top half of his bifocals that angled forward on his long nose. His forehead was slightly furrowed as if he was expressing concern for my fabricated allergy. I felt the grip tighten on the thick stack of cards in my pocket and I wondered if my face was glowing. I made a mental note to never purchase butterscotch candy in Riker's even though it was one of my favorite flavors. As we exited the store I was the last one and as Mr. Riker bid me a good day my shoes resounded heavily on the old wooden floor and I wished for some fluidity in my gait that had become stiff and teetering as if I was on stilts.

At the picnic table I couldn't shake the deep feeling of remorse. Strang and Press were as unfazed as yesterday. We made a few trades and if there was anything that brightened the moment, it was finding Bobby Richardson in my stack. I already had him in my collection, but I knew that Razor wanted this card badly, as it would complete the full team of the Yankees for him. Press also was looking for Bobby Richardson and he had offered some tempting cards, but I was excited to give it to Razor. Press tried to muscle me, but Strang intervened and overruled him, made it seem like baseball cards were on a sacred level, not to be messed with. Press had backed off. I guess it's true sometimes when they say, "There is honor among thieves."

On Monday at lunch I slid my tray across the table from Razor in the cafeteria and sat down."Hey Ray," I said. "How's it going?

Razor nodded, chewing a bite from his sandwich.

"I got you something," I said. I pulled the card from my shirt pocket and flipped it across the table. We both watched Bobby Richardson's face spin along the surface and stop against Razor's hand. With a flick of his finger he sent it back across the table.

"It's yours," I said. "You can keep it."

"I don't want it," he said.

"What, did you get him?" I asked.

Razor shook his head.

"Ray, it's yours," I said. "It's a gift."

"I don't accept stolen goods," Razor said, looking me squarely in the eyes.

It was the first time I noticed what would become a familiar pose. As his eyes affixed to mine there was an upward shift of his head and a small but pronounced ascension of his chin. His eyes remained straight, focused on mine as he scratched his bottom lip with his teeth. I struggled to hold his gaze and I felt a nervous smile stretch across my face and I averted my eyes downward.

"Dave and Roger were bragging about your robbery in science," Razor said. His face remained in the perched position, his chin riding high. "They're jerks."

That small episode back in 1963 had a huge influence on me. Never again did I steal and my shame was so tortuous that I paid back not only what I had taken, but also the sum of my cohorts. For a succession of weeks, I casually went into Riker's and left part of my allowance next to the lettuce in the produce section, an area I thought safest from other potential thieves. I didn't think of it then, but I've since wondered if old man Riker had discovered my exercise in redemption and knew all along. After school I avoided Strang and Press by leaving the building from the furthest point away from them, and walking many blocks out of the way which took me about twenty extra minutes to get home. The incident never came up again between Razor and me. I told him of my plan to pay back Mr. Riker and he simply nodded.

Over twenty years later I sat in Old Yeller and the news of Razor's theft dribbled in with the gathering crowd of happy hour drinkers and I eased myself into my usual state of inebriation, but without the sense of peace that I habitually sought and seldom found. There always seemed to be some obstacle to nullify the journey. That night my mood was slipping with updates of Razor's crime. Much had changed in

Razor's life since 1963, but one thing I knew was constant – he was not a common thief. I knew this without any doubt and I would stake my life on it. But my fellow villagers (at least the ones in Old Yeller) didn't seem to believe it.

"Doesn't surprise me a bit," Herb Roster said. He owned The Village Diner on the other side of Main Street. "Can't tell you how many times I caught him stealing garbage from my dumpster out back."

"How can you *steal* garbage?" I asked Herb.

"Well it's my property and my food and he didn't have my permission," Herb replied. "He's like some filthy raccoon scrounging around back there in the dark. One time he said he was having a midnight snack and he laughed that stupid laugh of his, like he was in a fancy fuck'n French restaurant."

Herb had conveniently left out the fact that for a long time Razor cleaned for him after hours and one of the perks was leftover, perishable food that would have been thrown out. I don't know how much Herb paid him, but I'm sure it wasn't much. During that period Herb's diner was the cleanest it's ever been. They had a falling out when Razor pointed out some health hazards that Herb found too "cost prohibitive" to remedy.

Rusty Petrowski was sitting on the other side of me, nodding vigorously. I wasn't sure if he was agreeing with Herb or responding to some inner voice from the swampy basin of his washed out brain. He worked in a local factory and the rest of the time he drank himself into oblivion. He usually worked four ten-hour days, from Monday through Thursday and I knew he was still at it from the night before. On my way in I saw his brother passed out in Rusty's car in the parking lot. It was a weekly routine that carried them to all the village and rural taverns and then to Rusty's mobile home until the bars re-opened Friday morning.

"Thou shalt not steal," Rusty announced and pointed a greasy finger toward the ceiling. Suddenly, as if something above had let it go, his arm dropped with a thud on the bar. Rusty picked up his arm and rubbed the elbow until he set it down to pick up his drink. "Razor's been bad," he said to me in a small childish voice.

I noticed Al Pecora inside the doorway. He was the day shift dispatcher at the police station. Al cut through the crowd and I made room between Rusty and myself.

"You still got Razor over there?" I asked him.

"Izz Razor in-car-zer-at-ed?" Rusty asked.

Al looked at Rusty and turned his back on him, facing me. He rolled his eyes and ordered a drink. I paid for his drink and waited while he took a sip.

"The guy's a real piece of work," Al said.

I didn't know if he was referring to Rusty or Razor.

"Did Razor say why he did it?" I asked.

Al shook his head and took another drink. I waited while he looked around the room. Al always spoke carefully. I've often wondered if it was his nature or the result of dealing with emergency calls that he responded to daily.

"All Razor would say was, '*We are all guilty*,'" Al said. "The store manager came down and filed charges. I think if he would've offered an explanation or some remorse, charges would've been dropped. But Razor would only repeat, '*We are all guilty*.'"

"Is he still at the station?" I asked.

"No," Al replied. "The chief had me call his mother and she came in to get him. It was kind of funny because she showed up with an old shopping bag with Razor's work boots. They were almost new. Why in the hell would he steal another pair?"

"I thought he stole some shoes," I said. "That's what the scanner said."

"Boots? Shoes?" Al said. "Who cares?"

I guess I didn't care either, although I found this misinformation to be annoying. I'd gone over the peak, beyond the point where my liquor intake was fueling a smooth upward voyage. I could feel that powerful surge from inside that the threshold of drunkenness offers – distorting vision and making the mind slippery, unable to focus. There are some that can recognize this place beforehand and turn away, but I never could. In retrospect, as a sober person, I can see the milestones of the journey, but then as I lived it, I never really deciphered where I was. I started at one place and simply ended up at the other place – drunk. The rest was like automatic pilot, an unconscious connecting of dots. The afternoon had become the evening and happy hour had ended and Old Yeller remained packed with Friday night drinkers, my dismal self among them.

Sometime later Razor had come in. I was still at the bar. It's remarkable how long you can sit in a place with a drink in your hand, disregarding your state of mind. I heard a few exclamations, some loud greetings and I turned and saw Razor standing there with the old felt hat pulled tightly down to his ears, rainwater dripping from the collapsed brim.

"Shoes," someone yelled. "Shoes!"

And then someone else said it and another said it and heads turned and saw him and joined in until the place thundered with the new chant; "Shoes…Shoes…Shoes…Shoes…"

The name stuck in that mysterious way that nicknames can. And strangely Shoes never felt the need to explain why he had stolen the boots. I knew it was an expression of civil disobedience in a foggy, vague manner, but I'm sure he knew that people perceived it as nothing more than the ridiculous act of a drunk and ridiculous man. I know the dynamics – the pure and naked reality of a drunk's life from the inflated glory of inebriation to the flip side – the dreaded hangover. It arrives with remorse at half-assed recollections that suddenly blossom into focus throughout the day. You stop apologizing, hating the sound of your voice as it exercises the empty gesture. I don't think totally sober people know how much the alcoholic regrets his life on a daily basis – the constant eruptions of trouble from every possible direction and the resolve in the morning to change and the inevitable betrayal that follows.

Within a few days the theft receded behind the upstaging of more recent crimes and scandals – new pages in the fat book that adds color and texture to the seemingly flat drabness of daily life. Shoes paid a fine and performed some community service, spearing wrappers in the village park. Originally he'd been ordered to help out at the local Boys and Girls Club, but a few parents orchestrated an outcry to protect their precious children. Shoes methodically traveled the park in search of litter. He bummed cigarettes from teenagers who didn't frequent the Boys and Girls Club.

Back in the early fifties, my father established the store where I now stand. He had never considered my getting involved in it, knowing my addiction to the product. I understood that and I did well enough with my painting business even with a hangover. I kept it pretty simple and never took on anything too involved. Shoes had worked for me during those years, not in a steady way, but if I had a big job going he was usually available. We weren't fast friends, but we were old friends with a good measure of history and an understanding. Shoes was usually pretty beat up in the mornings and he never charged me for his first hour on the job. "Working out the cobwebs," he said. He would be productive for a few days and then he wouldn't show. I took it in stride, accepted what he had to offer as his best and deep down I was glad he didn't burden me with his worst.

In the winter of 1985 my life began to change. Her name was Rose, a beautiful and soft spoken woman, recently divorced with a four-year-old daughter. They resided a couple doors down from me in the apartment complex I had lived in for three years. There had been passing waves in the parking lot, brief conversations and many times I'd watched attentively from my front window as she bent over, unloading the car. Rose was beautiful from head to toe, coming or going.

The ice had literally been broken on a frigid February night. I had been pacing the meager length of my apartment while watching a hockey game on TV with a glass of bourbon in my hand. I happened to look out the front window. The outside light was subdued with falling snowflakes, but I could see Rose squatting by the rear tire of her car. The waist cut parka rode up her back and I could see a good measure of flesh and below the tight spread of her jeans. Pushing my face against the frosty pane I noticed the trunk open and a tire lying next to her.
Quickly I downed my drink and grabbed my coat. She must have heard me approach, because her hips shifted as she turned and I struggled to look into her face."I can't loosen the nuts," she said.

Her face was flushed in the soft light and I saw her pink, woolen mittens had been blackened by the spare tire. I offered my hand and pulled her up. I knelt down and pushed down on the tire iron. Immediately, the tire iron slipped off the lug nut. The force drove me, full-bodied – striking my hand onto the ground. I had snapped my thumb back to my wrist, a painful but opportune injury. Within a few moments I was sitting in Rose's living room, drinking whiskey while she iced the swollen digit, after having snapped it back into place. Rose was a nurse and she assured me the swelling would subside if I continued to ice it. I called AAA to send someone to attend to Rose's tire. Her daughter, Sadie, had laughed as I feigned cartoonish pain while her mother attended to my thumb. After Sadie had been put to bed, Rose and I had sipped whiskey and talked. To my amazement, we ended up making love on her old but comfortable couch.

Our relationship was launched with an unquenchable carnal passion that consumed us for many months until I suddenly realized, in a cold panic, where I was. An earnest and responsible woman with a child is a scary picture when you're a carefree, alcoholic nitwit and you have somehow evolved within that framework. In the past I had always managed to extract myself, often not too gracefully, from similar scenes, but here I found my heart stubbornly grounded and defiant of my panic-stricken senses. If Rose noticed my strife, she never commented, but continued in her sure-footed daily life, which turned out to be an effective and unassuming power in itself as I was swept into that steady wake. More to her credit we survived the transition from the *Cinderella* stage of our romance to the more contented rhythm of co-existence.

I don't know what Rose saw in me outside of small spurts of boyish charm that were more or less alcohol inspired. Years later, when I brought up the question, she simply said, "I knew you had a good heart." We had talked of marriage and made a decision for me to move into Rose's apartment as it was bigger than mine. We made the move in July with the understanding that we would wed the following March.

And strangely, it was the difference in the layouts of these two apartments that served as the catharsis that ended my drinking.

For the past three years in the small apartment my life was simple and things were kept in the same place. Upstairs, the bathroom was a quick right from my bedroom door. Drunk or sober, I could manage this small journey in the dark. In the new apartment, Sadie's room was the quick right from our bedroom.

A couple weeks after I moved in, after a Friday evening of heavy drinking, I had gotten out of bed and stumbled into Sadie's room in my underpants and pissed into the metal wastepaper basket next to the closet. Apparently she had called out my name, but became afraid when I had turned around.

I awoke in the late morning and went downstairs. Rose was sitting at the kitchen table, cutting out grocery coupons. Through the kitchen window behind her I could see Sadie playing with a friend on the swing set. I offered a half-hearted good morning and received a cold stare.

"Why the mean face?" I mumbled.

Rose told me in the same childish, simplistic manner, what her daughter had witnessed just a few hours earlier.

My first reaction was to laugh, the vision of myself and Sadie's description being so comical, but I could see a slight trembling of Rose's chin and I managed to keep my face deadpan. Rose waited for me to reply, but all I could manage was to shake my head.

"Is that how you'd like her to think of you?" she finally said.

- - -

To enter the realm of sobriety was unnerving. An old drinking buddy, Cider John, used to say of those who consistently practiced the state of sobriety, "They got nothing to look forward to, but feeling the same way all day long." How true that seemed to be and how false it *is*. I was troubled at first as the big face of time stood on my shaky threshold. I felt unequipped to fill the huge gaps of drinking time that I had forsaken. I've always been a little high strung and moody (*"like a high school cheerleader,"* a friend once quipped) and I shuddered at the prospect of facing life without the crutch. I experienced immediate anger in having to give up something that so many seem to enjoy, that is so tightly woven into our culture; I cried helplessly, "why me?"

Rose, true to her sturdy nature, was quietly supportive and extremely patient in dealing with my anxious and fluctuating behavior. We discovered walking – hours and miles of it, a practice we continue today. I also discovered boundless pleasure and companionship in Sadie. I explained to her my drunken antics in her bedroom was a result of sleepwalking, which aroused her curiosity. "What's that like?" She asked, wide-eyed. I fabricated some humorous episodes based on my younger sister's experiences. Sadie and I became instant buddies. Our friendship blossomed and she opened my eyes to the wonders of a more innocent world view.

A month after our wedding my father died. He had complained to my mother about not feeling well, had gone to bed early and had never woken up. My shock was compounded with a deep sense of loss. We had been getting along much better. My sadness wasn't relieved by my mother's revelatory statement, "His work must have been finished here," a point that I'm sure had to do with me finally *coming around.* Would he still be alive if I hadn't given up the bottle? I didn't believe this, but decided against refuting it. She needed something to get her through.

Two weeks after the funeral my mother presented me with the keys to the liquor store.

"I want you to run it," she said.

"You know I can't do that."

"Of course you can," she replied. "You've changed."

"Yeah, I've changed," I replied, "but what if I…"

"You won't go back," she said abruptly.

"Dad never wanted me to."

"Your father wanted it more than you'll ever know," she said.

My mother was right. I didn't go back. Many months of sobriety had afforded me a clear head and a deep well of energy that I channeled into the business. At first the long-standing staff members watched me with guarded suspicion since they knew my history. I could feel them observing me, wondering if I would go awry with so much temptation at such close proximity. Strangely I felt no enticement among the many shelves and racks in the store although I was puzzled by this reaction. Was it the same detachment a male gynecologist felt? I remember the overwhelming consensus among my adolescent friends when we imagined such an auspicious profession. Rose thought my wondering about such a phenomenon as an unnecessary waste of time. "You don't need it," she said. "That's why."

After meeting Rose I didn't see much of Shoes. He had helped me a few times when I still had the painting business, but usually not for more than a day or so. For whatever reason, he never came in the store. After work I would see him at Old Yeller, but by that time of day he was pretty drunk and away from the throng of regulars. I approached him a few times, sat across from him at the small table by the front window, but I found it a risky move.

"Captain," he'd greet me (later, when I took over the liquor store, it was "Commander") and he'd offer a satiric salute. "Seen Ursula lately?" This was in reference to an *Ace* magazine featuring a nude pictorial of Ursula Andress in the early sixties that I had hidden in our basement. I had shown it to him back then and I think it was the first time he had seen a girlie magazine. It seemed to be showcased in his mind since he often brought it up. From that point, the conversation could go anywhere although he generally favored nostalgia if he wasn't too drunk. One of his favorite memories was a party at Jason Dunbar's apartment in the spring of 1970.

Shoes had been a political science major at UB while I studied English at Buffalo State. Our favorite tavern was Anacone's on Bailey Avenue near Amherst Street. From my villager point of view, I thought of it as the archetypal city bar. It was long and narrow, shadowy even in daylight as you moved toward the back, away from the slanted sunlight of the large front windows. The long wooden bar ran along the right side, across from a row of small tables. The pool table was in the back, separated by a wall, but the opening was wide and you could watch the action from a barstool. The owner, Dave Anacone, was a well-known musician and the selections on the jukebox were broadly eclectic, but mostly he favored jazz. Whenever I hear Lionel Hampton's, *Midnight Sun*, I can close my eyes and be transplanted back there.

One Friday in the early evening I met Razor at Anacone's. I hadn't seen him in a while and I wondered how he was since the UB campus had erupted into a chaotic series of anti-Vietnam war demonstrations. The Buffalo police had been called in after a sit-in (allegations of racism in the athletic department) had forced cancellation of a basketball game in late February. Their presence had inflamed an already tense situation and several demonstrations turned violent. The Buffalo police virtually occupied the campus for most of the month of March. Some of it had been shown on national news. I called his apartment a couple times, but there had been no answer. I'd been busy, juggling the demands of school, a part-time retail job and a high maintenance girlfriend. I was thrilled at the prospect of a Friday night off from my job and a night in the city seemed attractive. Finally, I got through to Razor. His voice was weary, but he was interested in getting together.

I arrived late in the day after my classes. The bar was busy with old men drinking their pensions and others stopping for a couple on their way home. There were only two women, strippers from the Capri Art Theater across the street, killing some time at the pool table between shows. They were easy going, friendly women with faces that looked older than their bodies. Naturally their presence drew attention from the regulars. After an hour Razor came in with his roommate, Les Slater. Razor looked tired, his face drawn and dark circles under his eyes. Les on the other hand was jittery and animated, his eyes darting about and he was chewing his lower lip. I figured he was on speed, which I thought unfortunate because he was obnoxious enough on nothing.

"Hey, bro," Les said, grasping my hand. "What's happening?"

Les bellied up to the bar and flagged the bartender.

"How's it going?" I asked Razor.

"I don't know," he replied. "The campus is fucked up. Everybody's tense and the cops are everywhere."

"Fucking pigs!" Les said. He slid a pitcher of beer over, poured foamy glasses for Razor and himself and topped mine off. "The fuckers gassed us."

"Really?" I said. "You got tear gassed?"

"Fucking right we got tear gassed," Les said. "And some of us got beaten."

"It's pretty bad," Razor said. "The cops are attacking anything that moves."

"They got no right to be there," Les said. "Like fucking Nazis. Shooting tear gas right into dorm windows. That shit's horrible – hangs in the air, fucks up your eyes and throat."

"There's no place that's safe," Razor said. "I saw a cop unleash a dog outside of Towers Hall – attacked a woman, bit right into her arm and pulled her to the ground."

Even now, I remember how appalled I was at this news. As much as my sentiments were against racism and the war, I had done little in applying them to action. One afternoon at Buffalo

State I stood on the periphery of a crowd that had assembled in front of the student union. After a few speeches (who were these people and how did they become speakers, I had wondered?) the crowd began chanting, "No more war." I remained for the duration of the rally, aware that I was missing an Economics class that I happened to be unprepared for and I could feel a stirring passion, but I remained silent. That night before dinner, the local news briefly aired the rally. The camera had panned the front and center bulk of the protesters, which of course excluded me. My father had commented something derogatory that ended, "...ungrateful animals," and I told him with inflated pride that I had been there. Months later when I had been put on academic probation, he threw it vehemently back in my face. That was the extent of my insurgence for the most part. In any constructive sense I remained a voiceless part of the crowd who let others echo my feelings.

As Razor told me more details, Les wandered the growing crowd of students that had gradually replaced the day drinkers. Daylight was gone and Anacone's was darker and noisier, a collection of heightened voices, shuffling feet and music that the bartender had strategically turned up. Les had approached a couple young women standing by the front window. His face from a distance appeared malleable as the movement of shadow and light played on it and suddenly it would erupt into laughter. The women seemed to be enjoying him, a circumstance that I begrudged and envied. That time period had been fancifully labeled an era of *free love,* but the benefits came my way only sporadically while Les was constantly getting lucky. Countless times I had stopped at their apartment to find Razor studying or reading while from Les's room I heard the sloshing rhythm of his waterbed.

One Saturday morning he came into the living room in his robe.

"You gotta see this," he said and beckoned me to his bedroom doorway. Inside two naked women lay asleep on the bed.

I found it difficult to turn away from the scene, laboring against the stirring of my desire and not wanting to face Les and acknowledge his good fortune.

"Unfuckingbelievable," he said.

His eyes were wide with open pleasure and he surprised me as he pointed inside saying, "Why don't you crawl in, man? They're game."

The invitation flustered me and I had declined, saying, "I don't take sloppy seconds."

Les merely shrugged his shoulders as if we were youngsters and I had refused a ride on his new bicycle, but for a long time the vision of the two women remained etched in my mind.

In Anacone's, Razor and I had to talk loudly as the crowd thickened. I noticed Les had singled out one of the women and he held her arm as he spoke closely in her ear. She nodded and laughed at what he was saying. He caught my eye and waved. I nodded and Les said something to the girl and he snaked his way through the crowd toward us. At the bar Les refilled his glass from the pitcher and downed half of it.

"There's a party at Dunbar's," he said.

Jason Dunbar was an English major at UB and Les's good friend. He came from the Albany area and he imparted a level of sophistication that you knew was deep-rooted or as my mother would put it, "He came from good stock." Within five minutes of knowing him, you felt he was destined for success, whether he deserved it or not. He was familiar with the Western New York area because he had attended a private boys' boarding school in South Wales, about twenty-five miles from Buffalo and not far from where I grew up. The school specialized in dyslexia, a reading disorder, which at that time seemed to plague only young men from wealthy families. I imagine the condition created quite a challenge in his field of study, although you'd never know it, since Jason possessed a seemingly effortless gift of self-promotion. Unlike Les, he could be engaging without telegraphing his intentions and yet you felt power in his personality. He had traveled some – a train trek throughout Europe (a high school graduation gift from his parents), a summer job working as a ranch hand in Colorado (a friend of his dad's) and during the past summer a short stint on a working barge on the Mississippi River (his uncle owned the company).

For a young man, this is the stuff dreams are made of and I couldn't help envisioning a scene that Les had projected after he picked up Jason at the airport, when he had flown in from New Orleans. Jason had disembarked the plane hefting his backpack and carrying his saxophone, a vision that mushroomed in Les's Kerouac influenced mind. "Can you fucking see it?" Les had said, a few days later. "Picture him on that barge in the dying orange of sunset, blasting notes from the sax across the wide Mississippi!" Les was unabashed in his hero worship, a veritable Sancho Panza. Razor had discharged his strange laugh, cocked his chin up and remarked, "Sounds like Jason's sipping pretty heavy from the silver spoon."

We decided to go to the party. The two women Les had been talking to were going and Les said he was going to ride over with them.

"Here's a little kick for you guys," he said, dropping a couple pills in my hand. "One will keep you rolling awhile."

We washed down the pills with the last of the beer. Outside it was raining and I liked how the wetness reflected the neon signs in bright colored smudges on the city streets. We stopped and bought some beer at a deli on Bailey Avenue. There was a cop car parked by the UB entrance after I turned left on Main

Street. On the campus a few isolated people moved quickly under the scattered lamppost lights. The party was on a side street off Main and I had to park a few blocks away. Jason's apartment was the whole bottom floor of a large weathered house on a street of tightly packed two-and three-story dwellings. A covered porch spanned the front where a few people were hanging out. We traded some greetings and took a couple hits off a passing joint. Normally I would be wary of smoking pot after drinking because it sometimes induced fits of acute paranoia that could leave me on all fours in some hidden corner of the backyard, barfing to exhaustion. That night I felt confident that this was impossible, perhaps because the speed was sending a rippling, like tiny icy - toed feet up my spine and generally brightening my outlook. Music aired out through the open windows. Inside was smoky with tobacco and pot aromas and the music was louder, carried by an expensive sound system with two large speakers in the living room.

Talking was impossible and I stood in there a few moments taking in the scene. Three Dog Night was playing, *Try A Little Tenderness,* the last part, *"...you got to, you got to, you got to, try a little tenderness...",* the repetition building and two guys were across the room, hunched over their air guitars, yelling the lyrics into each other's glistening faces. The song ended and the two young men opened their arms, thus letting the imaginary instruments dangle from imaginary guitar straps. They bowed fiercely and then picked up their guitars and waited for the next song. A couple of the onlookers actually clapped.

The adjacent room would normally be the dining room, but the walls under a high ceiling below a collection of posters, were lined with two sagging couches and a variety of worn chairs. On a long coffee table close to a couch was a bong filled with sherry that bubbled as one of the girls I had seen at Anacone's toked on it. The embers sizzled in the bowl as she drew on it and I was instantly attracted to the green cast of her eyes and the wavy mass of reddish hair that surrounded her face. Impulsively I sat down next to her, a move that even today I view with amazement. I felt the heat of her leg against mine and her eyes narrowed into annoyance. Her face suddenly was wonderfully familiar.

"You look just like Maureen O'Hara," I told her. "You know, from *The Parent Trap.*"

Years earlier my parents forced me to take my two younger sisters to see the movie at a Sunday afternoon matinee. I had protested. There was a John Wayne picture playing at another theater that I wanted to see. They threatened a string of weekend groundings so I had agreed. To my surprise I had enjoyed the movie. I also thought Maureen O'Hara was very sexy.

The girl backed away on the couch, her knees together as bumpers against my leg. The motion afforded me a better look at her and I remember thinking her large free hanging breasts reminded me of Maureen O'Hara's.

"You ever see the movie," I asked her.

"I've seen it," she replied. "You some kind of Disney freak?"

"Can I have a hit on that?" I asked, suddenly feeling foolish.

"Help yourself," she said.

I had expected the draw off the bong with the soft rumble of bubbles to be smooth, but it clawed at my throat and I started a cough which quickly developed into a fit. I felt the sudden absence of her knees and out the side of my watery eye I saw her get up and move away. By the time I had calmed down she was gone. A guy from across the room came over and asked if I was okay. I nodded, but I wondered where Razor had taken the beers. My throat was raw.

There were a lot of people in the kitchen, but it was oddly quiet and everyone standing seemed frozen and focused on the table where Razor, Jason, Les, and the girl he was with earlier were seated. As I stood in the doorway, for a second I wondered if they had been talking about me, but most of them didn't know me. Nobody had even acknowledged my presence. I sensed something serious going on. Jason was shaking his head slightly, an easy smile on his face as he looked across the table at Razor.

"Hey man," Jason said. "There's nothing wrong with it."

"He's right," Les said.

"He's entitled as anyone else."

"Entitled?" Razor said, turning to Les. "What in the fuck does that mean?"

A deep redness had invaded Razor's cheeks. His chin was poised but I noticed a small quivering of his jaw that I first attributed to the speed. However, there was a grave look in his eyes.

"He's got his rights," Les said. "Why in the hell shouldn't he collect?"

"Because he doesn't need it," Razor said.

"What the fuck do you know?" Les said. "What a' you know what he needs?"

"Don't you think you're being a little presumptuous, not to mention self-righteous?" Jason said.

"That your fancy way of saying I'm not being fair?"

"Maybe it is," Jason replied. "Last time I looked it was a free country, equal opportunity for all."

"You're sitting there drinking Heineken, listening to your state of the art sound system and all the while collecting food stamps," Razor said. "You don't see anything wrong with that?"

"Hey, I'm sharing it with my friends," Jason said, smiling and waving his bottle of Heineken.

"You're taking from those that need it," Razor said. "It's criminal!"

The remark had the effect of a face slap. Jason's smile disappeared. He stared up at Razor. A wave of vertigo passed through me and I grasped the door frame. I could feel the music vibrating the wall, but it seemed distant in the kitchen.

"I'm fucking sick of your high 'n mighty bullshit," Jason said. "If you don't like it, then get the fuck out!"

Jason stood up. Razor walked right up to him. Jason raised his fists.

"You would fight," Razor said. "Yeah, that'd be your way."

"Just get the fuck out of here," Jason said, opening his hands and pushing him.

Razor stepped back with the force of the push and turned and stumbled past me. He had this goofy smile as if embracing his sudden loss of dexterity. Jason sat down and picked up his beer. The kitchen had become quiet, everyone looking at the floor. A few seconds later the music had stopped in the living room and abrupt and frantic voices carried from the front of the house followed by a loud crash and then another. There was a collective gasp from the front room and then silence followed by Razor's unique cachinnation.

One of the guys from the earlier duet appeared in the doorway.

"Crazy fuck just eighty-sixed the music," he said.

- - -

Whenever Shoes reminisced about that night his eyes held a distinct luminescence. I think he was simply giddy about his total departure from his typically reserved and composed behavior. But that's how he was if I caught him in the right light, before too many drinks. His memory was uncanny concerning high school and the couple years we both went to college in Buffalo. He could bring back small details – the color of the flowers on Jenny Doel's print dress at a CYO dance in 1965 or the exact yardage a halfback from a rival school had piled up against us in a JV football game. I found this gift extraordinary since my recall had the clarity of dementia. As I get older there are moments of profound fogginess that leave me wondering if I had experienced something or actually heard it from someone else.

Unfortunately if Shoes was very drunk, conversation could be impossible. The last time I sat down with him was a few weeks before I had quit drinking. The greeting had been the usual, but without energy. The conversation that followed was vague and disjointed with sudden grunts and chaotic ramblings. I found I couldn't respond and eventually he fell silent. His eyes seemed detached, looking out the light filled window as if he sought something out there. The long silence gave the impression that if there was something out there, he was unable to reel it in.

I've known Shoes for over two thirds of my life. Like others I've known and have reconnected with in the random flux of our journeys with periodic reunions and separations, there is much of his life that remains a mystery or is stamped with the vague imprint of recollections based on gossip or hearsay. There were huge gaps of time where our paths rarely crossed. I had quit college in the middle of the fall semester of 1971. The reason was a lack of ambition although I fooled myself that I just wanted to experience life rather than read it, probably a result of my dreamy hero worship of Hemingway and Steinbeck. I bought a used typewriter, placed it on a desk by a window in my bedroom at my parents' house and virtually ignored it. Instead of following the creative arc of my favorite authors, I adopted their other passion, drinking.

During those earlier years after I quit school, life still seemed like an eye-opening adventure with promise and the youthful misconception of an infinite future. I could offer milestones, perhaps girlfriends and jobs, that punctuated the stretch of my twenties, but they all amounted to false starts and shameful avoidances. What remained constant was my location, the safe and familiar setting of the village; the only definitive variables were the apartments I inhabited after my parents told me to leave and which tavern I chose to frequent. The few highlights, memorable evenings that I can remember, now seem dry and stale. I still saw Razor when he was home for breaks and sometimes I'd venture into the city, but as time went on we saw each other less frequently. I knew he had started graduate school, but by then I hadn't seen him in a long time and then I heard he'd gone to Florida.

- - -

The dream confused him and riled him awake. Razor thought he had a choice and he closed his eyes and rolled over, grasping the damp pillow as if he could physically draw himself back to sleep. He was in the after spell and desperately clawed after the remnants while the malignancy of panic set in as it slithered away. The image of the woman was vague and he finally recognized her as Trish, but there was something suddenly nonsensical about her that had been reasonable in the dream. His increasing wakefulness was stealing clues. He opened and closed his eyes, squeezing his lids tightly as if this exercise might open a cerebral door and reveal the answer. Razor had all but given up when it popped to the surface.

Ice-skating!

Where did that come from, he wondered? And she was naked; Razor thought he caught a glimpse of this possibility as he rolled over and his erection stabbed the cushion. After settling on his back, it was as if he had entered another room and the dream disappeared and the immediate surroundings crept into his consciousness and began to rouse him.

The distant puttering of a dinghy sent a slight wake that gently rocked the hull. A flimsy breeze strummed a halyard against the mainmast, but Razor felt no benefit in the forward v-berth below the cabin portholes aft of the open hatch of the sailboat. He was reluctant to leave the dream and the attractive woman that had graced it, but the morning air was already sultry and charged with the briny smell of the nearby ocean. A dull pain was wedged in his head – too much rum last night. Razor rose and pulled on a pair of shorts. The low ceiling caused him to duck his head as he dragged the sheet behind him. He licked inside his mouth. The bottle of water in the cooler was almost empty. Solid, searing heat greeted him when he slid open the hatch. Razor climbed into the cockpit under the makeshift canopy tented over the boom. He secured the moist bed sheet high on the backstay with a clothespin.

In the cockpit, under the canopy, Razor sat down. He strapped on his sandals, a recent purchase that he still thought of as exotic. Far out at the edge of the small bay on the eastern side where the channel began and eventually led out to the ocean, seagulls were circling low on the water by the mangroves. They squawked and dove, breaking the stillness of the water, flashing white in the sunshine. An egret flew leisurely in a straight course, apparently unconcerned about the ruckus. Razor watched attentively and felt like a foreigner, wishing he understood all the wildlife around him. He raked his fingers through his long ragged hair and slipped on the faded canvas sun visor. He picked up his towel and the small nylon travel bag and climbed up on the dock. Ahead was the tongue of land and beyond the cluster of whitewashed buildings of Upper Key Campground and Marina. Razor had resided and worked there for the past two months.

At the gas dock in front of the dive shop Chip Foley was gassing up his boat.

"*Morning Chip,*" *Razor said.*

"*Eh Razor,*" *Chip replied..*

"*Got a party today?*" *Razor asked.*

"*I got four,*" *he replied.* "*Steve's fitting them out now.*"

"*How about later?*"

"*Only two on the list right now. Wish I could rise them for this run, but you know how it is.*"

Chip ran scuba diving and snorkeling tours in John Pennekamp Coral Reef State Park which opened up outside of the channel to the east of the marina. During the busy season he usually ran two boats full capacity of ten people each, twice daily. But now in June he could barely fill one boat. The slowness of business in the off-season was expected and Chip's disposition was as easy and friendly as if he had a flotilla of full boats.

"*You off today?*" *he asked Razor.*

"*Yeah,*" *Razor said.* "*It's my birthday.*"

"*Well ain't that convenient,*" *Chip replied.* "*How you gonna celebrate?*"

"*Not sure yet. There's a couple girls I met yesterday at the campground. Nurses from Michigan. Might hang out with them.*"

"*Nurses eh?*" *Chip said.* His eyes brightened with this information. "*Why not bring them out on my boat later? Get 'em to sign on and you can go free.*"

"*I'll see,*" *Razor said.* "*Guess I'll see what's happening in the shop.*"

Chip nodded and Razor walked into the open door of the dive shop. Steve Barber was behind the counter talking to two couples, trying to convince them to rent wet suit tops. It was a hard sell – the store was humid, the two ceiling fans merely shoving around the hot air. Steve's upper lip was dappled with sweat as he explained how the water would eventually draw out *body heat and leave you chilled. The tops cost an extra ten dollars and one of the men finally shook his head and Steve nodded his resignation. Razor worked part-time in the dive shop and he knew this was a normal response, especially from northerners. It took about half an hour for the boat to travel through the channel flanked by the dense mangroves and into the open ocean to one of the dive sites. That left three hours in the water. He knew if they went out again that they'd spend the ten dollars.*

Steve helped the party carry out their gear and came back into the shop.

"Like selling ice cream to Eskimos," he said. "Have you seen Trish today?"

"Nope," Razor replied. "Just got up."

"Well Trish has something for you," Steve said. "By the way, happy birthday."

"Thanks."

"What do you have planned?"

"Not sure," Razor replied. "I met a couple girls down at site thirty six. They were talking about going down to Key West. Chip said we should go on his afternoon trip, but I don't know."

"A couple women should make it interesting, whatever you do."

Razor walked inland across the parking lot toward the main building. The sun beat on his bare back and radiated off the parking lot surface, a concretion of mostly sand and coral rock that was warm and unyielding against his sandals. A long scar of slightly raised ground about a foot wide ran across the lot between the dive shop and the main building. Underneath about a foot deep was a newly installed electrical line. Digging the trench had been Razor's first task when he started working two months ago.

Chet Knudsen, the campground manager, had scratched a rough line across the lot and handed him a pair of work gloves, a pickaxe and a shovel.

"Need 'er pr'd near a foot deep," he told Razor.

A chalky dust covered the surface. Razor had gripped the shaft of the pickaxe loosely and his first full swing stung him on impact – a vibrating pain that traveled from his hands to his shoulder blades. He swung again, his hands tight on the smooth wood and a small piece broke away. Within a few moments Razor was drenched in sweat and his arms and shoulders ached. The hole he dug wouldn't hide a football.

"Hold up there," Chet had yelled from the main building. He carried a gallon thermos and handed it to Razor. "You're from Buf'lo, aren't ya?"

Razor nodded.

"Well, this ain't Buf'lo," Chet said. "And this here," he said, pointing to the ground, "is solid coral rock. They say it goes pr'd near to China. Southerners like taking advantage of you fast moving Yankees, but we ain't like that here. You take that jug and sit in the shade a spell. Then you work some, then break some."

It had taken Razor most of the week to complete the ditch. He had taken breaks on the covered porch outside the office. Chet would sit with him sometimes and tell him stories from his travels. Chet and his wife Myrtis were originally from Minnesota, but Chet had been a merchant seaman and had been everywhere. He told Razor that he had gotten so accustomed to the constant running of the freighters' engines, that after he retired, for a while he had to run a lawn mower outside his bedroom window in order to fall asleep.

Razor went up the stairs to the porch that wrapped around the building, dropped his belongings on a chair and stepped into the campground store. He poured himself a coffee and went over to the counter where Myrtis was dusting. She was a pleasant chubby woman with short silver hair. He reached into his pocket, but Myrtis waved her hand.

"Least we can do on your birthday is buy you a coffee," she said.

"How'd you know?"

"From your application," she replied. "I pencil them in on the calendar."

She handed him an envelope. "**Raymond**" was written in her elegant script.

"Open it."

Razor tore open the envelope. Inside was a card with a slightly religious slant, offering him a "**Blessed Birthday**" and a gift certificate from the campground store for ten dollars.

"Thank you very much."

Myrtis picked up his hand and squeezed it between her plump fingers. She looked deeply into his eyes. Silently she held his hand for what seemed a long time. Myrtis smiled in a way that made Razor feel she was waiting for him to say something. Nothing came to mind and he struggled to maintain eye contact sensing he would hurt her feelings if he looked away.

"Why are you here, Raymond?"

He wanted to say, "For coffee."

"Why are you here?"

"What do you mean?"

"What brought you here, to Key Largo?" She said. "Something brings everyone here."

"Just came this way," Razor said. "Steve said I'd like it and I do."

"Of course you do."

Myrtis nudged forward on the counter and Razor deftly attempted to slide his hand back, remembering a crude joke about chewing off your arm so you could sneak away in the

morning from a sleeping, unattractive lover. Her grip tightened and her smile faded, as if she had read his mind.
"You're different," she said.
"I am?"
"You are," she said. "You're different."
"I don't know what you mean."
"The Barbers," she said. "You're not like them. You must see the way she slips around. The way she looks at other men. The way she looks at you."
"I don't know what you're talking about," Razor said.
"You can't be that blind," she said. "If I see it then you must."
The door opened and Razor freed his hand. Chet came in. Myrtis immediately straightened up and she nervously smoothed the front of her long sundress.
"Chester," she said, her voice a touch shrilled. "You're back already."
"Yes I am," Chet replied.
His eyes darted between Razor and his wife.
"Today's Raymond's birthday," she said. "He's twenty-six today. Can you imagine being twenty-six again, Chester?"
"Can't say that I can," he said, "Seeing that I'm more than twice that right now. See no sense in imagining what I've already been."
"Well," Razor said, picking up the card and his coffee. "Gotta get going."
"So you're off today," Chet said. "What're you planning for your birthday?"
"Not sure," Razor replied, thinking better of mentioning the girls from Michigan. "I might go out with Chip this afternoon."
"Looks like a nice day for it," Chet said.

"Yeah," Razor said. "Thanks again for the card," he said to Myrtis, who gave him a quick, shy glance.

Razor drank his coffee and smoked a cigarette on the deck by the outdoor pool. He thought Myrtis's unusual remark of Trish "slipping around" as strangely revealing. Trish had a way about her – something you felt more than saw, made you watch her closely and kept you wondering what she was up to. Razor recognized it the first night he had disembarked the Greyhound bus on the highway and walked down the road toward the campground. It was almost midnight and the sky was starless, a sheet of black. The road, an eerie lunar stripe cut far into the dark foliage ahead. His legs were stiff from the long bus ride and his steps had sounded loud and crunchy and imposing against an ominous silence. After a while the road curved to the right which had spooked Razor a little because he was losing sight of the few remnants of light on the highway behind him. The air was close with humidity and he stopped to adjust his backpack. He felt the first prickling of sweat as he continued, the shadowy corridor of thick bushes and tall trees drawing closer as he advanced.

He heard a scratch to his right that froze him. A small flame ignited and her face appeared, lighting a cigarette.

"Hey," she had said.

The flame went out with a shake and her face dimly reappeared as she drew on the cigarette. She was sitting on a large, flat rock.

"I'm looking for Steve Barber," Razor said.

"I'll take you to him," she said, turning on a flashlight.

Since October, the Barbers had lived in the campground. Steve and Razor had worked for a builder up north, a job that Razor immersed himself into, after giving up the daily torpor of college life. Four years of undergraduate work and another pursuing a master's degree had drained him of ambition and diminished his original idealism into a growing cynicism. He held a dim view of his peers who journeyed into the political arena or the law profession. To his way of thinking, the means was the end.

He enjoyed the mental and physical accuracy of carpentry and the easy camaraderie of the crew that quite often led into a local tavern after work. Razor started as a laborer, but under Steve's experienced tutelage he had become a framer. Steve, who was the lead man of the outfit, told Razor he had the "knack," a generous appraisal from one who was stingy with compliments. Steve was less than average height, but solidly built with a step-up energy that gave him an unnerving bluntness that kept the crew on track. He liked to drink after work, a binding factor between the two men. Conversations were initially work related. Quite often they threw propitious light on Steve, a third generation carpenter, but occasionally other subjects emerged. Steve had been taking a scuba diving course and had begun talking dreamily of moving south.

Razor was surprised on a Friday afternoon when Steve came into the bar and told him he had just quit the company and was moving to the Florida Keys. He was used to hearing people talking of relocating, but rarely did it materialize. As much as Steve was elaborate when talking of work, he had been vague about his personal life. He rarely mentioned his wife.

"Awhile back, one night I was telling Trish about work," Steve had said, "Suddenly she slapped her hand hard on the table. She glared at me and said, 'Do you know anything else besides shit about hammers and nails?'"

Razor could empathize, but he understood little about the politics of domestic life, having observed the daily existence of his parents as peaceably humdrum. He was amazed that Steve's wife had the raw power to sway the steady course he maintained and drastically change the direction of their lives.

"She's a pisser," Steve had said. "Day to day, I have no idea what I'm coming home to."

Steve and Trish sold the house and most of their belongings and purchased a Volkswagon van and a large army tent. After they settled their debts there was a few thousand dollars left to get them started. Steve's goal was to find a job in a dive shop and he told Razor if anything good came up, he'd let him know.

A few months later he had received a postcard with a photograph of a diver swimming over a mound of brightly colored coral. The other side said, **"Razor – It's paradise here. I'm working in a campground and dive shop. There's a job for you if you want it. Steve."**

"So you're Razor," Trish had said.

"That's right."

"Razor," she said, as if trying out the sound of it. "What kind of name is that?"

"Just a high school nickname."

"Sounds kind of sharp and dangerous," she said. "What's your real name?"

"Raymond Sir."

"I get it," she replied. "But I'll call you Ray. It sounds warmer."

They had followed the beam of the flashlight. The road curved to the left and ahead Razor made out a scattering of lights and the wavering vim of a few campfires. Steve was sitting in a golf cart by the gate.

"Perfect timing," he said, looking at his watch. "We lock up at midnight."

Steve got off the cart and swung the gate closed and locked it. He and Razor embraced and the three of them boarded the golf cart and they drove to their campsite. Trish and Razor got off and Steve drove away.

"He has to plug the cart in at the office," she said. "How about a drink?"

They sat around the fire drinking rum and tonics. At first Razor thought the fire unnecessary, given the sticky heat, but it helped a little to ward off the mosquitoes and no-see-ums. Razor enjoyed the reunion with Steve and a barrage of questions that Trish fired at him.

"Steve tells me you're a pretty smart guy," she said.

Razor didn't normally talk much about himself, having recognized the boredom he felt around those who did it often. However, Trish had been insistent and after a few drinks he had offered some details that seemed to please her. They were both avid readers and traded opinions on writers.

"Steve reads cereal boxes," Trish said.

Steve took the criticism in good humor. "Yeah, I graduated from the University of Hard Knocks," he said. "Trish had a couple years of art school."

"Until he knocked me up," she said.

"You have a child?" Razor had asked.

"No child," she replied.

Her face hardened in the firelight. Razor noticed Steve had thrown a quick glance at her and then his face was lost under the brim of his cap as he watched his hands caress the drink.

"That's why we summoned you here, Ray," she said. "We're thinking of adopting you."

Trish's lips seemed to suck into her mouth, eyes rounded, daffy like a cartoon character. She bobbed her head side-to-side. Razor muttered something about being a good boy and after a few more stodgy remarks the conversation moved to more practical matters. Steve had to get up early to open the dive shop, but he told Razor to sleep-in since he wasn't expected to work until the following day.

"Trish will take you to the office," he said. "She's a waitress at the Howard Johnsons down the road. She doesn't work until four, so she can show you around."

Razor had slept in the back of their van. Trish told him there were screens, but regardless, insects found their way inside. She apologized and handed him a can of insect repellent. He heard the mosquitoes a few inches away during the brief moments he woke up, but they didn't attack him. He awoke in the morning long after Steve had gone to work. Razor crawled out of the van, sweaty and sticky, to find the campsite empty. The campground looked more expansive in the morning light and he noticed there were many empty sites. Trish brought him a coffee from the nearby campground store and Razor couldn't help looking at her – a fresh and natural beauty that hadn't been fully evident in the firelight. After he showered, they went to the campground office where he met Chet and Myrtis.

So far, Razor found the early morning of his birthday and day-off to be unsettling. He wondered if more traps were in store. Steve had mentioned that Trish had something for him, no doubt to acknowledge his birthday, but he sensed the possibility of another emotional pitfall. Their short friendship, nominally based on a mutual love of art and literature, had been encouraged by Steve, but Razor sensed a deeper, troubling undercurrent. Last week on his day-off he had stopped by the dive shop. Steve told him that Trish wanted him to take a coffee to her. At the campsite he had announced his arrival and parted the tent flap. Trish was topless, sitting on a folding stool and brushing her long black hair. She made no effort to cover herself. Razor fumbled the coffee. She had laughed as she jumped up with a towel to soak up the puddle. He was dumbstruck that evening when she had brought it up in front of Steve, who looked at him pointedly and said, "Nice rack, huh."

He wandered down the dusty road to site thirty six, wondering if the girls from Michigan were up. Campers on the few occupied sites he passed were performing a variety of morning rituals. Razor knew that unless you were hopelessly hung-over, the morning heat drove you from the tent much earlier than what was determined by your biological clock.

"Hey, birthday boy," Jill said.

"Morning," Razor said. "How'd you sleep?"

"Like a rock," Jill replied, "Once I got Sandy to quit snoring."

"Hey," a voice came from inside the tent. "You're not supposed to mention that."

"Like a bear," Jill whispered.

She was hanging a towel over a line that extended between two trees. Her short blonde hair was slicked back, still wet from a recent shower. Her pale skin had a pinkish glow from yesterday's sun and Razor couldn't help noticing the dark bumpy texture of her nipples protruding against the light cotton t-shirt as she reached up to the clothesline.

"You look kind of rough," she said. "You feel alright?" "

My head hurts a little," he said. "Nothing a shower won't fix."

The tent began to unzip and Razor saw the vague outline of Sandy's hand and forearm behind the screening. Her long black hair curtained her face as she parted the screen and pushed out bedclothes. She crawled out and stood up – a head taller than Jill and eye-level to him.

"Girls decide what you're doing today?"

"Key West," Sandy said.

"We wanna see Papa's house," Jill said, "And have a drink at Sloppy Joe's."

"Into Hemingway, eh?"

"Jill likes him," Sandy said. *"I think he was kind of an asshole."*

"You're coming with us aren't you?" Jill asked. *"We'll celebrate your birthday in Key West."*

"Sure," Razor replied. *"How soon you leaving?"*

"Pretty quick," Sandy said.

He felt Jill's enthusiasm, but he wasn't so sure about Sandy. She seemed a little standoffish, something he had felt about her the previous night. He had met them in the afternoon as he made the rounds on the golf cart, picking up garbage and making sure campsites had been left presentable by departed campers. It appeared that they were having trouble erecting their tent and Razor asked them if they needed help. Sandy said *"No,"* without turning her head, but Jill had nodded and waved him over. After the tent was up Jill told him they had driven down from Michigan.

"For some fun in the sun," she said, with a wink.

She had inquired about local bars and Razor suggested the Tiki Club over on the west side of the key. That night he had gone there with George, who also worked at the campground. He had been excited at the prospect of the two women. As it turned out, George was disappointed because Sandy refused to dance and barely spoke to him. He had finally left, denouncing her to Razor as *"a fucking dike."* Razor and Jill had danced to almost every song played on the jukebox while Sandy sat at the table and watched.

"Are you sure you want me to go?" Razor said, directing the question toward Sandy

"Why not?" Sandy said.

They made plans to meet in a half an hour at their campsite. Razor went to the shower. As he came out Trish was coming up the path.

"Hey," she said. *"Happy birthday."*

Trish kissed him. She picked up his hand and led him on the path toward her campsite. As they crossed the parking lot, Razor thought he saw Myrtis in the store window.

"I've been waiting for you to come by," Trish said.

Inside the tent, she presented him with a package, wrapped in brown bag paper. Razor peeled off the paper revealing a watercolor painting of the sailboat where he was staying. In the distance the sun was setting, spread out in pale hues of orange and red washes that contrasted a dark silhouette sitting in the cockpit that resembled him.

"Trish, it's beautiful," he said.

He held the picture at arm's length, admiring the languid scene. She smiled shyly and curled her hair around her fingers.

"You're really good," he said. "I can feel it as much as see it."

Razor fought the impulse to put his arms around her. He was overwhelmed with the gift.

"Do you want to go out for breakfast somewhere or maybe just hang out at the pool for a while?" She asked. "I don't have to work until one today."

"I can't," Razor said. "I promised to take a couple campers to Key West."

"I see," Trish said. "Showing the sights you haven't seen?"

"Yeah," Razor laughed.

"The campers wouldn't happen to be those two teenyboppers at thirty six?"

"They're not teenyboppers," he replied. "They're nurses."

"Oh, nurses," she said, her cheeks puffed in mocking seriousness. "Well okay," she added. Her face clouded, but then she seemed to check herself and smiled. "Hey, enjoy your birthday."

Razor had been tempted to change his mind and spend the morning with Trish. He was relieved that he hadn't succumbed to the impulse. Their growing friendship had opened up a familiarity between the three of them that Razor was unaccustomed to. He knew that the attraction between Steve and Trish was strongly physical. He had heard them before he moved to the sailboat. Razor remembered from a sociology course how the Japanese practiced a cultural courtesy of simply ignoring their neighbor's behavior as their walls were paper thin. He found this philosophy difficult in the couple weeks he slept in the van.

Steve often alluded to their lovemaking with blatant vulgarity. Trish appeared unfazed and sometimes openly amused by Steve's remarks. Razor assumed she found her husband's ostentatious display of masculinity as appealing, although at times she could be condescending toward him, and sometimes downright nasty. Steve took his work seriously to the point of deeply ingraining it into his ego. He approached scuba diving with the same zeal as he had carpentry. He had read all the books he could find on the subject and perused the shop magazines from cover to cover. Chip Foley gave him cut rates on dive tours and Steve had made the most of it, diving on all the major sites in Pennekamp Park. Unfortunately, Steve brought an edge of competitiveness that really had no place in the sport. He seemed more poised to top a story than trade information or appreciate the nuances of a shared experience.

Trish had no interest in diving. She feared bodies of water and entered the pool only briefly in the shallow end to refresh herself. Trish only worked a few hours a week, while Steve worked full-time and spent the bulk of his free time diving. It reminded Razor of situations up north where men belonged to two or three bowling or softball teams, their wives or girlfriends left to fend for themselves. He could sense her growing resentment toward her husband, sarcastically calling him, "Diver Dan." Steve took the verbal lumps. To his way of *thinking, he was being single-minded and purposeful, necessary ingredients to succeed.*

"She's got her books and sketchpads," he said to Razor. "She's the one who wanted to chuck it all and reinvent ourselves. She needs to busy herself, work more hours. She needs to quit mooning about everything." He looked away uncomfortably when Steve added with a sweep of his tongue, "Don't worry my friend, I can usually coax her back into the land of happy."

Razor had walked away from the conversation wishing he had minded his own business. He had never gotten involved in anyone's relationship before and he resolved to not do it now. He consciously questioned his credibility, noting his own experiences in high school and college were brief and uncomplicated, due mostly to his innate shyness. There was an uncoiling absurdity that was slapping him like a pinwheel, making him feel like a chameleon in regard to the Barbers. The part that troubled him recently was a festering jealousy whenever Steve mentioned her sexually. At first it had taken him by surprise; he knew it had no right to be there.

It bothered him that this feeling had evolved and furthermore he was perplexed that in the last couple weeks Trish had started to latch onto him. Her reaction to his going to Key West with the young women was the first tangible proof and he thought that it stemmed from her husband's recent preoccupation with diving, although a vague clue came to mind and made him wonder. A couple weeks ago the three of them had gone to a party at Chip's. He lived in a large mobile home and it was packed with a variety of locals and some visiting divers. Razor ended up spending the night with a woman from Costa Rica in Chip's spare room. The next morning he saw Steve and Trish who had ribbed him good-naturedly. Razor had expressed his surprise at the coupling. The woman had aggressively pursued him.

"You're attractive to women," Trish had said. "They feel safe because they can connect to the female part of you."

Steve had looked at her sideways and shook his head.

"Christ Trish," he said. "You make it sound like he's queer."

"Shut up," she said. "This is something you'll never understand,"

"Fine," he said. "I guess I'll leave you two to your woman talk."

In the sailboat Razor placed the painting on a shelf next to the galley. He gave it a long last look, pulled on a t-shirt and hurried down the dock. Jill and Sandy were in the car in the parking lot next to the marina with the windows open and the motor running.

"Why don't you take us out for a sail?" Sandy said as he climbed into the backseat.

"You thought it was mine?"

"Not now," Sandy replied. "You'd call her a 'she' if you were any kind of sailor. But before that, who's to know – you could be some kind of eccentric millionaire asshole, or maybe a dope dealing freak hiding out in your watery Sherwood Forest."

"The boat belongs to the guy who owns the campground," he said. "I don't think he ever uses it, I mean her."

"Don't bother," Sandy laughed. "It's clear you ain't no salty dog."

Sandy drove the car a little too fast out of the parking lot, kicking up a trail of fine yellow dust. Razor scanned the office building to see if anyone was watching, but the windows looked like flat sheet metal from the glaring sunshine. Just outside the parking lot George was riding a golf cart. He shook his head as the dust drifted around him.

"That the dolt you were with last night?" Sandy asked, smiling into the rearview mirror.

"That's him," Razor said.

"Talk about a guy being led around by his pecker," she said." Does his line of shit ever get him laid?"

"I don't know," Razor replied.

"Be nice," Jill said. "He was okay. You just weren't."

"Yeah, yeah," she said. "I'll bet you guys lick your chops and clean your wieners watching us snowbirds come in for vacation."

Sandy swung left onto Highway 1, heading south, tromping on the accelerator that knocked their heads back. Jill turned around and patted Razor's bare knee. The breeze coming in the window pushed her hair forward, the ends dancing on her cheeks, dappled with freckles that he hadn't noticed before.

"Would you pass me a beer?" Sandy said, her eyes lifting in the mirror.

Razor opened the cooler next to him and reached into the packed ice and extracted a beer. He twisted the top off and handed it to her.

She shook two pills from a plastic container to the center of her palm and popped them into her mouth, followed by a swig of beer.

"Let's have one," Jill said.

The beer was very cold, refreshing as hot air blew through the open windows. Jill had turned on a battery-powered tape deck on the floor. The music was instant and loud, somewhere in the middle of the long tune, East-West, by the Paul Butterfield Blues Band. Sandy's head was instantly bobbing while Jill turned the volume down.

"Road music," Sandy announced.

"*The tapes are all mixed,*" *Jill said.* "*We spent the winter making them.*"

"*You made them,*" *Sandy said.* "*I smoked dope, drank and watched and listened.*"

"*You helped,*" *Jill said.* "*You selected this one.*"

"*Yeah,*" *she said.* "*Road music.*"

Razor saw her eyes framed broadly in the mirror, staring at him and then they moved to the road ahead. Razor looked past the dark round of her shoulder, over the sloping visible breast that nosed into the fabric of the black bikini top. Her long brown legs emerged from the frayed ends of cut-off jeans, the right leg taut and the calf bulged from working the accelerator and tapered to a thin ankle and the abrupt, pale pad of her heal. Razor looked up to Sandy's waiting smile.

"*You're all dogs,*" *she said.*

After a few miles all three of them were entering new territory. Razor had pointed out the Waldorf Plaza, specifically the Book Nook, where he'd bought some books. In Tavernier he singled out the side street that led to Chip Foley's place. That was as far south as he had been, but Sandy continued to ask him questions anyway, her face a bemused smirk that rankled him.

"*Sandy, would you cut it out,*" *Jill finally said.* "*He told you he hasn't been this far.*"

"*I thought the bookstore and the side street were just warm ups,*" *she replied.* "*A tantalizing introduction to grander things in store for us.*"

"*I'll find some stuff,*" *Jill said, holding up a guidebook.* "*You hush up now.*"

"*Okay Momma,*" *Sandy said, winking at Razor in the mirror.* *She held up the empty beer bottle.* "*How 'bout a refill?*"

"*This sounds good,*" *Jill said.* "*Long Key State Recreation Area.*"

"Sounds like an amusement park," Sandy said.

"No, no," Jill said. "Listen to this."

Jill read a brief description including a variety of trees that inhabited the area.

"Wow," Sandy said. "Jamaica Dogwood. Gumbo-limbo," she recited. "What kind of fucking fruit grows on those?"

"Let's try it," Jill said. "We've got plenty of time."

Within half an hour they pulled into the empty parking lot.

"Whooo, look at this," Sandy said. "All for us."

She handed Razor another empty. Her eyes were lit up and their focus seemed slanted as if she had pinpointed a particular strand of his hair. The pills she had taken had to be speed, Razor reasoned, remembering his college friend, Les. Her tongue moved in and out of her mouth like a toddler. Long lines of sweat streaked the length of her face. She held her tremulous hand up, waiting for another beer. Razor dug one from the cooler and Sandy snatched it from his hand before he could open it and rolled the chilled brown bottle around her head. She closed her eyes as she rotated the bottle down over her chin and neck and across the rise of her breasts.

"That's nice," she said, then opened her eyes. "Let's explore."

A frail breeze from the west rustled a cluster of tall pines. They walked a worn path between thickets of tangled foliage, the trail at first parallel to the highway but working diagonally toward the ocean. The sun was high and clear of treetops and spread a sparkling glaze over the flat expanse of blue-green water. Sandy carried a small knapsack filled with beer over her shoulder and the bottles clanked solidly together as she led the way. Jill had picked up Razor's hand. They stopped at a weathered picnic table surrounded by hard packed grainy soil that held small patches of scrubby grass. Sandy placed the knapsack on the table. She kicked off her sandals and walked across the thin strip of beach into the water, proceeding until the water was mid-calf and she stumbled.

"Rock," she called back, righting herself and moving away, along the face of the shore, sliding her feet along the bottom past the curve of the beach and out of sight.

Razor and Jill sat next to each other at the picnic table, facing the wide spread of the ocean. He opened two beers and Jill presented a joint.

"Go easy," she said. "This stuff will make you see God."

Razor took only a couple hits and looked eastward to the horizon.

"It's strange knowing that it's so much farther out there in the ocean than where I come from," she said after a while. "The horizon is elusive. It looks the same as in the UP except the lake is darker up there."

"Yeah," Razor said.

He enjoyed the soft dreamy quality of her voice, more than what she was saying.

"I've often thought when I was at the beach on the lake," she said, "that I could be anywhere which made me happy to be right there."

"I know what you mean," he said.

Razor was unable to elaborate, although spinning prisms of thought tumbled through his mind. He remembered during his freshman year at college in the dorm, a student from New Jersey who was astounded that he couldn't see the other side of Lake Erie. He was constantly bragging about the scene at the Jersey Shore – the great surfing and wild nightlife. The kid had looked across the lake and crossed his arms in a pose of distinct superiority and remarked, "There's no way you can surf on it."

"You still here?" Jill asked, squeezing his leg.

Her touch diffused his reverie. Jill's face seemed uncomfortably close. He reared his head and slid back on the bench. She grasped his wrists and pulled slightly toward her.

"You okay?" she asked.

"Fucked up."

"I told you," she replied. "Great shit, huh?"

"Great shit," Razor said.

He stood up and a sudden vertigo tipped him inwardly and caused his upper body to sway. His legs straddled the bench and his hip leaned against the thick edge of the tabletop. Jill's hands were on his shoulders; her face was inches away and Razor closed his eyes and concentrated to steady himself.

"Just roll with it," she said, massaging his shoulders. Her firm, roving hands offered a relief that Razor surrendered into and he smelled her hair and leaned against her warm body.

"Didn't you two get in enough dancing last night?"

Razor opened his eyes. Sandy was out in the water, which was level to her naked pubis, creating the notion in his pliable mind that the water flowed out from inside the dark swatch. She was totally nude with her small bundle of clothing in one hand and the beer in the other. Razor saw this quickly, like a snapshot that he knew should have been appealing, but he closed his eyes, hoping to re-enter the refuge Jill had offered. He heard Sandy's voice, coming closer and felt the shift in Jill's body as her head turned.

"Jesus, Sandy," she said. "The road's right there."

"Fuck 'm. Why come down here if you can't enjoy it?"

Jill disengaged herself from Razor and he gripped the table. Sandy dabbed at her face with her bikini top, making no effort to cover herself.

"What's with him? He's as white as a sheet."

"Got the heebie-jeebies," Jill said, pointing to the half of joint on the table.

"Don't sweat it, Razor," Sandy said. "It'll pass. I've seen bigger boys than you licking the bottoms of their boots from that shit."

Razor sat on the bench, stooped over with his elbows resting on his knees. His hair was wet and hung alongside his face. He hated Sandy's voice. Cars passed on the highway from time to time expelling the sticky sound of rubber on hot pavement. One blasted the horn, male voices yelling out, probably from sighting Sandy in a small opening in the foliage. She was telling Jill about wandering along the shore. He heard her light the joint and caught a whiff.

"I think I saw some of those strange trees," she said, her voice pinched, drawing in the pot. "Are there pictures in your book?"

"Nope," Jill said. "Give me a hit on that."

"Come explore with me," Sandy said. "You okay?" She asked Razor.

Razor nodded, looking up, forgetting that she was nude. He studied water dripping from her pubic hair until she tapped him playfully on the head.

"Jill and I are going to explore," she said. "You just relax; let that shit lift off you."

Sandy insisted that Jill take off her clothes and she finally agreed and stripped off her shorts and t-shirt. He heard them giggling and the splash of water. He looked up and saw their rounded buttocks settling into the water as they plowed forward and held up their beers. Razor stretched out on the table, bunching his shirt for a pillow. He gazed at the empty sky. The women's voices had trailed off, but their presence remained in his consciousness – a scattering of images and words that assaulted him haphazardly and thwarted the empty peace he sought. He held his eyes closed, not too tightly and he could see a film of spotty light behind his eyelids. The hairs on his chest *and arms flickered softly against his skin. He pictured the crimped hairs individually, bending and fluttering in the breeze and he opened his eyes for validation. Systematically he studied singular neighboring hairs on his arm until he had drifted off.*

Razor woke up with the sudden shade of Sandy looming over him, her bare breasts dangling and water dripping on his face.

"Candy, little boy?" she said.

- - -

They stopped at a restaurant in Marathon for lunch. Jill ordered conch chowder that Sandy referred to as rubber duck soup. The bartender thought it was funny, but the Cuban woman who made the chowder was insulted. She swore at her in Spanish. "Touchy bitch," Sandy said afterward in the car.

- - -

They reached Key West in the mid-afternoon. Sandy parked on a side street and they went into Sloppy Joe's.

"Rum for me and my shipmates," Sandy announced to the bartender.

She looked around the crowded circular bar. On the other side two men sat close together, one rubbing the other's neck.

"Thar he blows," she said.

Razor cringed at the remark. He was a little jittery from the pot and beer. Sandy was playful with the bartender, questioning him like an overly astute consumer about their selection of rum drinks. The bartender played along for a while, but he became more apprehensive with Sandy's indecisiveness. He eventually excused himself to wait on other customers.

"Must be another cock sucker," she said as he waited on the gay couple. "Place is swarming with them."

"Sandy," Jill said. "You've got to calm down. This isn't Michigan."

"No shit," she said. "I'm starting to wonder if a woman can get laid around here."

The bartender returned and asked if they had decided.

"Yeah Susie," she said. "A rum and tonic."

The bartender shook his head. He asked her to leave. Sandy stood up, gave him the finger and walked out.

"What's with her?" Razor asked.

"She's just keyed up," Jill said. "She insisted on driving all the way down here, nonstop. She copped a bunch of speeders before we left and now it's like she can't just leave 'm alone. Eats 'm like candy."

"Is she like this at home?"

"Well, not exactly," Jill said. She pulled Razor toward the door. "We better keep an eye on her."

On the sidewalk Sandy was talking to a shirtless man on a bicycle. His long hair was pulled back in a ponytail and his face was lost in a thick unruly beard that wandered unevenly down to his chest. Small braids spiraled from the beard, the ends bound by small colored beads. He was smiling at what Sandy was saying. A gold front tooth sparkled in the sunlight.

"Duane here says we should go to Captain Tony's," Sandy said over her shoulder. "He says they haven't sold out."

"Sold out to what?" Jill asked.

"Tourists," Sandy said.

"That's what we are."

"But they don't give a fuck," Duane said.

Razor couldn't tell if they gave a fuck or not. The barmaid, Nancy, was a transplant from Niagara Falls. She offered them a bright welcoming smile although she told Duane he had to wear a shirt.

"Of course," Duane said, tapping the side of his head. He went outside and quickly returned, pulling on an old sleeveless t-shirt.

Sandy watched Duane, her eyes wide and expecting, as if she was waiting for a gun to go off to start a race. He put his arm over her shoulder and Sandy leaned in and molded herself to his side. Razor watched this development with interest. The atmosphere resembled the worn and lively taverns he had frequented in college. The music from the jukebox was a mix of rock and country. A little reggae. They ordered rum drinks and Sandy and Jill were thrilled when Michigan native, Bob Seeger's cuts from his latest live album filled the air.

"Goddamn," Sandy said. "Road music."

They remained at Captain Tony's all afternoon. Whatever misgivings Razor had originally felt about Duane, slowly dissolved into an easy camaraderie. He seemed to know most people who wandered into the bar. They arrived over the threshold of the wide open doorway, with the bright sunlight behind them like translucent apparitions that suddenly solidified and were transformed into the shadows of the structure – the intermingling of old wooden beams and posts decorated with tourists' leftovers: old license plates, business cards and hanging discarded bras. They greeted each other without ceremony, but Razor felt an intimacy that somehow embodied the tropical setting and added a peculiar grace to their interactions. Tourists that came in reacted differently. Some sensed the scene and blended into it. Others treated the bar and its customers as simple curiosities that they observed over their colorful drinks until the glasses were emptied and they moved on.

Even Sandy seemed to embrace the situation, her demeanor softening and an innocuous smile lifting her face. Duane remained close to her side, rubbing her back and shoulders, running his fingers through her wild hair. He slapped a hundred dollar bill on the bar, waving away Jill and Sandy as they attempted to contribute. Razor had produced a twenty, but he was relieved when Duane told him to put it away.

"Your money's no good here."

They talked and laughed and drank. After a while Duane led them outside, down an alley off Greene Street to his apartment where they snorted lines of cocaine, a first for Razor. Back at Captain Tony's they regained their places at the bar. Duane bought a round for the whole place. They sang "Happy Birthday" to Razor. At times, Jill led him to an open area where they danced to the jukebox music. He felt himself lightening and gaining – a detached and fluid whorl, something he had witnessed in others at weddings and dances but had never experienced. The emotion engulfed him as a new and boundless freedom.

They didn't see Sandy and Duane leave. At the bar their drinks were gone. Duane had left a twenty and there was a note in Sandy's hurried scrawl placed under her car keys, "**Gone fishing. Duane will drop me at the campground tomorrow - Sandy.**"

"I don't know if I like this," Jill said. "She's pretty fucked up and that guy, Duane, well who knows what he's all about."

"He seems okay and we know where he lives," Razor said. "Do you want to go over there?"

"No, no," Jill said. "I guess it's silly to worry. She can take care of herself better than most men I know."

She shrugged and picked up her glass, tilted it toward Razor and drank. "I guess it's just you and me," she said.

- - -

Razor drove back to Key Largo. It was dark and Jill had fallen asleep with her head resting on his leg. Only a few miles from the campground, she stirred and her hand brushed across his lap. She drew it back quickly and sat up. A small panic swept across her face.

"Didn't know where I was for a moment," she said.
The sign advertising the campground came into view.
"There a quiet place in there?" she asked, returning her
hand to his lap. "Where we can have some privacy, maybe take
a swim?"
"Yeah," he said, "On the other side of the marina."
Razor entered the campground and turned off the lights. He
took the first right, a two track that quickly disappeared into
thick foliage and came out the other side to a beach overlooking
the small bay. It was too dark to see much, but the sky was
moving and the clouds shown as dark drapes with the moon
shining behind. Jill pulled off her shirt and shorts. She knelt on
the seat and pulled Razor toward her. Jill reached over him and
pulled the t-shirt over his head and bent over to pull his shorts
down. He felt her mouth around him and then her head climbed
in a hike of small kisses until they were face to face.
"Let's go in the water," she whispered.
They entered the water which was the same temperature as
the air, the sensation both silky and oily. They slid in up to their
chests. The moon was covered and the darkness was strange to
him as it had only two textures – the inky liquid that surrounded
most of his body and the prickly, humid air that seemed to be
actively evaporating. Her body was slippery against him and
she gently pushed his chest and he felt her other hand prying
between his legs and lifting. Razor yielded to her prompting, his
hips rising as she moved them closer to shore, until he floated
on his back in the salt water with his legs spread and she was
between them and able to stand in the shallow water. He moved
his arms outward on the water's surface as she bent over him
and he watched the moon present itself from the last thin veil of
the drifting clouds.
Jill began to choke and lifted her head and Razor righted
himself. He moved his hands under the water and she moaned

and threw her head back. They left the water and he pulled her down on the beach. Her breathing quickened and her face became impressionistic from the limited moonlight behind him. Suddenly her features rounded and swelled in a panic. He felt her body stiffen and her hands pushed against him.

"Stop," she said. "Stop! You've got to stop!"

Razor rolled off to the side. Jill stood up and walked a few feet into the water and turned around and came back. She stood over him and he could see the dark silhouette of her etched against the moon and her elbows spread as she buried her face in her hands and cried.

"I'm sorry," Jill sobbed. "I'm sorry."

"What's wrong?"

"I'm sorry," she said. "I have to go!"

"Why?" he said. "What's wrong?"

"Please Razor," she said. "It's not you, but I really have to go."

Jill walked to the car and he stood and watched her dress. She returned with his clothes.

"I've got to go now," she said. "I'm so sorry."

"But why?"

"I just do."

Jill went to the car and started it. The headlights came on and flooded over him and retreated as the car backed into the foliage and left him to dress in the dark.

After he had patted himself dry with his t-shirt and pulled on his shorts, Razor walked down the road leading to her campsite. Jill's car was parked next to the closed tent. It was dark and quiet. He stood there a few minutes and moved on. Sounds carried from the other side of the campground where the Barbers resided. A heavy bass rumbled and he could hear guitar licks and the thumping of drums. Razor noticed something else carrying in the air – voices that didn't sensibly accompany the music, but still had some of the primal quality. It was Trish's voice, high pitched and wavering, screaming insults:

"You lying bitch," he heard as he approached the campsite. The light was dim around a campfire and shadowy figures cast in an orange glow seemed frozen in a circle. Trish was standing close to the fire, directing her tirade of half-slurred expletives over it, the recipient's back to Razor, the head snapping back, as if absorbing a volley of punches. He didn't know who it was until the head surged forward and the voice uncoiled:

"Slut," Myrtis said. "Sinner! You've tainted the garden!"

"Fuck you!" Trish said.

At that moment she saw him, her reaction uncanny as if an electric shock jolted her body; her legs buckled and her arms struck out to gain some balance.

"Ray?" she said, her voice softening. She stumbled backward and stopped and her face leveled to childlike innocence. "Happy birthday," she said and smiled weakly.

Razor scanned the small group scattered around the fire. Steve and Chip were next to each other in folding chairs and George sat next to an empty chair where Trish apparently was sitting. On the attached bench of the picnic table was a couple from Ohio who had spent the last couple nights in the site next to the Barber's.

The music abruptly stopped.

"What the hell," Chet said, coming up next to Razor with the end of an extension cord in his fist. He threw it on the ground and looked at his wife. "What's all this racket about?"

"Chester, where have you been?" She said.

"Over to the north hook," he said. "Making the rounds."

This was the area where Razor had been with Jill and he turned to Chet and studied his face. Chet gave him a quick glance that revealed nothing and turned back to Myrtis.

"What's - this - all - about?" He asked her in the manner of an adult talking to a child.

"Well, it's her again," Myrtis said, her voice dropping, the drama subtle with understated fatigue. She reached into the pocket of her sundress and pulled out a crumpled piece of tissue and dabbed at her forehead. "She's at it again!"

"What – is – it?"

"Oh Chester," she replied. "You know. We've talked about it."

Chet nodded, but his eyes turned upward, betraying the fact of understanding and giving the impression that he was a man who suffered plenty of conversations that he was not an active participant in.

"I want to know what is going on now, this moment," he said. "Not what we've talked about."

"She's leading another astray," Myrtis said, pointing at Trish. "She's taking another man under her spell, down the dirty, sinful path."

"Oh bullshit," Trish said.

"Wait," Chet said to Trish and turned back to his wife. "How do you know this?"

"Why, are you blind, Chester?" She replied. "She pulls them with her eyes, her body. She touches them, shakes them from their footing, from God's own heavenly grip and seduces them."

"I don't know what you're talking about," Chet said.

"I saw it tonight, just moments ago, from the right over there," she said, pointing to the dirt road in front of the campsite.

"What were you doing out here at this hour?"

"I forgot something in the office," Myrtis said. "...to turn off the coffee pot and I heard all the noise – the evil music and I heard her voice, that laugh that chills my bones and I thought I

should investigate. I saw her fondling young George right there, in front of her husband."

"What?" Steve said. "She's crazy!"

"Wait, wait!" Chet said. "Myrtis, do you know what you're saying?"

"Of course, Chester. I know what I saw," she said. "And I know that he'll lie to protect her because she has him under her spell. I think he helps her get them. She has them all, even Raymond here. He wouldn't listen to me, but I saw that he knew – didn't you, Raymond? You can't deny it –I saw her kiss you and I saw her pull you into her tent. And I saw that day as you left the tent and she came to the opening naked."

"What the fuck," Steve said. "What the fuck's going on?"

"You see, Chester?" She said. "You see how he talks with no regard for decent people, a mind full of filth and corruption and all because of her."

Razor's attention was jarred away from Myrtis's zealous attack, right now her arm pointing and shaking in Trish's direction; it was Steve's eye he caught and it held him as he approached.

"What's this about?" he said.

"Nothing," Razor said. "It's about absolutely nothing."

"What the fuck's she talking about?" Steve said. "Kissing you and coming from the tent naked?"

"Last week," Razor said. "Remember? You gave me the coffee at the shop to take to her. Why, she told you that night and you laughed."

"I laughed about my wife being naked with you?"

"Well, yes," Razor said. He thought about reminding him of his comment about her having a nice rack, but he didn't think it would float, so he continued carefully. "She wasn't naked, not all, just her top off. She was brushing her hair and I walked in on her with the coffee you gave me."

Steve's face was inches away, staring up into his eyes. Razor remembered watching Steve use this tactic with the construction crew up north. It usually caused one to step back, but Razor reasoned it was important right now to hold his ground. He also felt a strain of guilt – the kiss he had received from Trish that morning.

"Leave him alone," she said. "Nothing's happened between us."

"See, Chester," Myrtis said. "Do you see what she's doing? She's lying. I saw them kiss this very morning. They embraced like animals and she led him into her tent!"

"Fuck you, you crazy bitch," Trish said. "I gave him a birthday present. That's all and then he left," she continued to Chet and then turned her head toward Razor. "He had plans."

"Oh my God, oh my God," Myrtis said, turning her eyes upward and wringing her hands together. "She has no shame, no limit to her evil ways. Right George? You know? I saw you just moments ago. Why I came in here to save you from her evil caress. Admit it, George and God will offer redemption!"

"She was working a knot out of my shoulder," George said, "That's all."

"Ah, there!" She said. "Do you see the deceit, how she tricks them with her cleverness, her dirty mind and body and the drugs. Do you see the drugs, Chester, right there on the picnic table?"

All heads turned to the table, behind Paul and Mary, the couple from Ohio. A small plastic baggy sat on the bench. The couple seemed shocked. They looked at each other like it was the first time. Chet reached between them. He held up the baggy and squinted in the firelight.

"What's this?" he said.

The small group looked around, avoiding each other's eyes. Chet sighed and looked at the bag. He knew it really didn't matter who owned it and he also understood it would be foolhardy to condemn them all; he had no intention of kicking anyone out of the campground or firing a member of his limited staff. He was angry with Myrtis for her snooping. The situation was nothing more than a domestic disturbance and the only real issue Chet had to address was the noise and he had to figure out a way to calm his wife down. In dealing with the employed inhabitants of the campground, he understood it wasn't what you'd call a career move, so he generally held to the simple philosophy of live and let live. He figured on letting Myrtis spout off her fire and brimstone to the point of contradiction where she usually painted herself into a corner and it would fizzle out. The discovery of the baggy had created a tougher obstacle and now he saw Donald Hall, the assistant manager of the campground, coming down the road with his long-handled flashlight. The retired Pennsylvania State Trooper carried it like a nightstick, slapping it in the palm of his other hand.

"What's going on?"

"Nothing really, Donald," Chet said. "A little noise is all. I've got it under control."

Donald gave everyone the once over and nodded. He turned to leave. Myrtis, perhaps sensing the wind shifting against her and the possibility of humiliation, reached out and tugged at his arm.

"Drugs," she said. "They've got drugs."

"What's this?" Donald said..

"I'll take care of it," Chet said. "I told you I have it under control."

"I didn't hear you mention drugs."

"It's a small amount," Chet said. "Nothing to get all shook up about."

"I don't understand," Donald said. "What kind of drugs are we talking about?"

Chet handed him the baggy. Donald shined his flashlight on the bag. He questioned the group, his demeanor trimmed and his voice terse, but the reaction was the same – the group quietly obstinate.

"I think we should call this in," he said.

"Not a good idea," Chet said. "You'll have everybody in the campground nosing around here. You want to make a big stink, get all these families all riled up and losing sleep about that little baggy there?"

"The sheriff found a bail floating outside the channel two weeks ago," Donald said. "You see the news. Do you think we should overlook that, Chester?"

"Of course not."

"We're talking about hard drugs here," Donald said, "And I'll tell you something I know. If they're using, chances are they're selling. I'm surprised at your attitude given your position. Makes me wonder how Ralph Jenkins would feel about all this."

Ralph Jenkins was the owner who lived in Miami. Chet enjoyed the fact that he was an absentee owner, his only contact an afore-warned monthly fly-in on his seaplane for a short visit and then off to other holdings in Key West and the Bahamas. It was all business – a look at the books and an inspection of the grounds. He paid Chet well and there were the added perks of living in the double-wide trailer in a quiet corner of the grounds and a slip at the marina for his boat. He and Myrtis had a good life and he wasn't sure if Donald was being opportunistic or righteous, but he knew he was cornered.

"Now, this is your last chance," Donald began. "I want to know who this belongs to. If you don't come forward," he continued, eyeing each of them, "I'm calling it in and we'll let the police sort it out."

The ensuing silence exaggerated the slightest movement among them: the shifting of feet, a dry draw on a cigarette, but their faces remained empty. Nobody spoke.

"Okay," Donald finally said, looking at Chet. "I'm calling it in."

"It's mine," Razor said, stepping forward and raising his arms as if the announcement demanded the posture. "I surrender," he added and he laughed nervously, his voice a twisting somersault that turned all their heads.

— — —

He awoke in the morning, the boat slightly listing as someone boarded. He could tell from the angle of sunlight it was late. Chet's face peered through the open hatch into the shadow of the cabin. Razor kicked off the sheet and swung his legs from the v-berth. He cradled his face in his hands and yawned.

"You alive in there?"

Razor rose and climbed into the cockpit. Chet was seated aft, by the steering wheel. "Thought you'd want this," he said and handed Razor an envelope. "It's cash."

"Appreciate it," Razor said.

"Know where you're going?"

"Key West."

"You know anyone there?"

"Sort of."

"We both know that shit wasn't yours," Chet said. "Why'd you take the fall?"

"I seemed to be the right one," he said. "And thank you for keeping the cops out of it."

"The Barbers pulled out of here early this morning," Chet said. "Steve felt bad about not giving notice, but he said Trish wouldn't stay another minute."

Razor was numbed with the news. He looked out on the bay and tried to digest this information.

"Well, I'm sorry it turned out this way," Chet said. "I'm sorry for Myrtis's part in it. All those years of leaving her alone – I guess they took their toll."

Chet's tone invoked an acceptance of responsibility and the stoic resolve of a condemned man. He stood up and ducked under the boom and moved to the other side of the boat. They shook hands and he stepped onto the dock and walked away.

Razor went below and gathered his gear and stuffed his backpack. He hefted it over his shoulder, tucked the painting under his arm and climbed into the cockpit. He was surprised to see Sandy standing on the dock.

"Well if it ain't Jesse Fuck'n James," she said.

He waved her aboard. She told him she had gone to Miami with Duane.

"He dropped me off late. I think he deals coke," she said. "I heard you're a big user."

"Oh yeah," he replied.

"So, where you off to?"

"I guess Key West."

"Not a bad idea," she said. "Know what you're going to do there?"

"No," he said. "Seems like a good place. I should be able to find something."

"You want a lift?" she asked.

"I don't think Jill would want me along," Razor said. "I think I went a little too far last night. We were pretty fucked up and I guess I took advantage of her. She was pretty upset."

"So you violated the frail, defenseless girl?" she said. "You evil man."

"Come on Sandy, give me a break."

"Well, I'll tell you, Razor," she said. "Jill had this big plan to come down here, a last blast before her wedding next month. She's marrying this fucking anal, dorky doctor for reasons I'll never understand. She's been with him a couple years and, I don't know – she thinks she loves him and they're getting married and she wanted to come down here. Jill had this notion, like a goofy schoolgirl, to have some sort of torrid love affair. And guess what, cowboy? You were it."

Sandy's explanation made him laugh, which startled her. She stepped back and looked at him as if he was a machine on the fritz.

"What the fuck you got in there?" she said. "You eating alive the local bird life?"

"So, she was using me," he said.

"Well, I suppose that sounds pretty cool for a guy. Don't let it go to your head, big boy," she said. "It gets real old after a couple times. It can turn your heart into a rock. I took Jill to the Miami airport early this morning. She wanted to get back to real life, she said. And she wanted me to tell you that she'll always remember you. She said she was sorry and you were very sweet."

Razor ignored the mocking turn of her face. He was overwhelmed that Jill and the Barbers could vanish like a magic trick. Up to this point his life had sat mostly on a level plain with the long view of gradual transitions very clear – the coming and going of people and events expected and seemingly normal. Even the death of a beloved grandfather had been a drawn out erosive battle against cancer. Right now he felt little significance – a pushpin on a map a mere hundred miles north of the "Southernmost point in the United States." Sandy lit a cigarette and the smoke drifted away, carried by a southeasterly breeze.

"I'm not going back," she said. "Duane has a boat on Stock Island. He said I could live there until I was situated. He said there are plenty of jobs down there and you don't need much to live. I don't think he'd mind if you came along."

Razor regarded Sandy for a moment. He reached out and she passed him the lit cigarette. He took a drag and handed it back.

"Why not?"

- - -

It's strange how the message of death comes to you. My first reaction as I watched Strang walk out the door was to hate him. He stopped on the edge of the sidewalk in front of his patrol car and hiked up his dark trousers. I watched him look side to side, his square head hawking in military precision – no doubt his mind onward into his responsibilities, thoughts of Shoes filed or discarded like yesterday's paperwork. Not that I was thrown into an instant state of mourning. My first thoughts were of Strang's vivid description of Shoe's stinky room and his pants loaded with crap. I shuddered at the lack of dignity and wondered if he would be recounting the event to others in the same manner. News of this kind originating from Strang's sour mouth didn't stand much of a chance. Each new voice adds personal flavor – perception as it is, based on prejudice and preconceived ideas. But then even I had thought harshly of Shoes' life in recent years; I'd watched him stumble along our village sidewalks, a bleary and bloated figure, his bloodshot eyes framed by dark and tired circles under the shadow of his dirty hat. His voice had become a scratchy drawl of unfinished sentences and verbose and meaningless fragments, interrupted without provocation by his spasmodic laughter.

"Actions speak," I tell young Sadie when her intentions waver. She nods solemnly, which at that moment feels like I've done my job, but I know full well how difficult it is for all of us to live this way. I wonder how Shoes faced up to this idea, this quickly spoken mantra – the key to a life well lived. The result is obvious, but I can't help wondering what was in his head each day.

A few years ago I saw him in The Station, a tavern that had once been a train station. It was before I had quit drinking and before I thought I should, so I had deceived myself into thinking I was okay and had regarded his lifestyle with disfavor. It was a beautiful spring day. The afternoon light flooded through the high windows behind the bar. Shoes was standing next to Half Lank Ravens. They were drinking shots in tribute to Lank Ravens, Half Lank's older brother who had died of a heart attack a few weeks earlier at the age of forty-eight.

Shoes had seen me walk in and waved me over.

"Hey Captain," he said, "let me buy you one."

"Sure," I said.Shoes had turned to the bar, picking up a handful of crumpled bills and waved Shelly over. She owned the place.

"More of the shit that killed Lank," he said.

Lank only drank Travelers Club Whiskey. I have never been much of a shot drinker, but I didn't want to refuse, feeling I'd disrespect the memory of Lank even though we really hadn't known each other very well. I could see that Half Lank and Shoes were drunk and even Shelly seemed a little unsteady as she poured the shots. Lank and Half Lank (he was tall, but shorter than his towering brother) managed to scrape up a living at odd jobs that usually involved hard and menial labor. Lank had hung around The Station whenever he and his brother weren't working and he would sometimes jump in as a bartender when it was busy. I remembered how ridiculous he looked, hunched over to shorten himself, with a cigarette hanging from his constantly muttering lips, the ash falling around drinks he was mixing. I tried to ignore that vision, seeing the solemnity on their faces as we toasted Lank's life.

"Lank was a good man," Shoes had said, after Half Lank had gone to the men's room. "He wasn't the sharpest nail in the pouch, but he knew enough to ask and he didn't forget."

At that moment Shoes dislodged a strangled laugh. I too, started laughing until I saw tears running down his face. I'll never forget the look he gave me at that moment. It held the same weight as being caught in an outright lie and it immediately brought me back to sitting across from him in the cafeteria many years ago. As drunk as Shoes was, he held his head high and his jaw line swept upward like a hull cresting a wave. His wayward, crimson edged eyes were suddenly focused with a hardness I couldn't ignore. I felt estranged, as if suddenly in a foreign country, bereft of the common language.

"Lank was the real thing," Shoes finally said. "I can see you don't understand."

"Understand what?" I asked.

"He was real," Shoes said. "The real fucking thing. There was nothing false about him. No illusions, no bullshit."

"Okay, fine," I said. "The real thing. Let's drink to that."

I pulled some money out and waved Shelly over.

"More of the shit that killed Lank," I said.

"No, no," Shoes said, shaking his head.

He had placed his hand on my shoulder. I felt his fingers tightening and turning me toward him. His eyes had softened and reflected a weary patience.

"Have you ever been in an audience for a performance or maybe a speech and at the finish a few people stand up – you know a standing ovation and you find yourself standing up although you really had no intention of doing it?"

"Yeah," I replied. "I guess I've done that."

"That's what you're doing right now."

"Come on, Ray," I said. "I'm just here having a drink, like always. You invited me over. You want to drink to Lank, well that's fine by me. I think he was an okay guy. Do I have to love the son-of-a-bitch to drink to his fucking memory?"

At that point Half Lank exited the men's room and was heading toward us. Shoes dismissed the subject with a wave of his hand. I ordered myself a drink, not the shit that killed Lank, but a bourbon and moved down the bar. I fell into conversation with a couple other guys and after a while I shook off the episode. However, I remember feeling a slightly smaller man as a result and I was relieved the conversation had been severed. I knew what Shoes was getting at and I knew, drunk or sober, it was painful for him to tell me. Shoes always traveled with a moral compass and he tried to follow the direction of rightness, regardless of the prevailing social wind. I think he had always liked me even though I had frequently disappointed him. He had never told me this because he simply couldn't, but I knew it was true. What I realized in the bar that day was Shoes wanted everyone to do well. His cynicism came from the fact that as a whole we weren't capable of letting each other. I don't know how much he had cared for Lank Ravens. They had shoveled a lot of dirt together, stacked a lot of stone and shared a multitude of drinks. I can only imagine the many hours of conversation between them. For that moment, I was temporarily small-minded enough to feel a twinge of jealousy that he had experienced a richer relationship with Lank.

- - -

After hearing of Shoes death I found I couldn't think of anything else for very long. It was as if my brain was a carousel that kept highlighting images from different parts of his life. I was upset with the typical reaction I heard over the counter in my store. "He had become a disgrace, an eye sore and public nuisance," a woman who had been in our class said."He had a great heart," I told her."So what?" she replied.

The obituary in the Buffalo paper was sparse, stating that Shoes had died suddenly and that he was survived by his mother, a brother who lived in Connecticut, a sister in Maryland, another in Maine and some nephews and nieces. There was to be no prior visitation, only a Mass at the local Catholic Church and burial right after. The gathering for the service was small. Outside of his family a few locals showed up – mostly patrons from Old Yeller. I was surprised when Craig Dillman slid into the pew next to me. He was a high school classmate and had attended Canisius College in Buffalo after high school. We had hung out some during our college years. He was the last person I expected to see since he lived in California. The priest spoke sparingly of Shoes' life and he had mistakenly called him "Richard." However, he had become annoyed when there was no response when he paused while reciting the *Our Father*. He stepped down from the altar and scanned the group. "You know it, now say it," he said sternly, waiting until he was satisfied with the concerted mumbling. At the cemetery the sendoff was brief and quiet, only Mrs. Sir's whimpering accompanied the priest's farewell words. The family had dispersed quickly as if they were embarrassed to be there.

Afterward I went to Old Yeller with Craig and some of the locals. It was strange to be in a bar, especially so early in the day. I noticed the regulars were friendly, but cautious and reserved with me. They carried on with each other in the same familiar way as always. Craig and I moved from the bar to a table. I sipped a ginger ale and talked with Craig who happened to be visiting his parents when he heard of Shoes' death.

"They said he drank himself to death," Craig said. "They said he was the town drunk."

"Well, I suppose so," I replied. "But as you can see, there's others here competing for the position."

"You used to hit it pretty hard yourself," he said. "What was it you used to like? What made you give it up?"

"Bourbon," I said. "I guess I realized it was getting in the way of things."

"Do you miss it?" He asked. "What do you do instead?"

Craig had always asked questions in tandem. I remembered how annoying he could be and I was momentarily amused that he still carried on with this strange habit. I guess the combination of him being an old friend and yet unfamiliar with my recent life and simply the sudden need to talk had opened me up. I told him about my journey to sobriety, probably in more detail than I normally would due to his frequent and insistent questions.

Old Yeller had filled up for lunch and afterward the bar remained crowded as the weather had changed from a sunny morning to a rainy afternoon. I mentioned to Craig how easy it was for Shoes and me to not go back to our painting on a day like this.

"It seems like it never changed here," Craig said.

"True," I said. "The faces might change, but the scene really doesn't. That could be us playing pool thirty years ago," I said, nodding toward four young men surrounding the pool table.

They were suntanned and they all wore empty hammer holsters on belts looped through their baggy cargo shorts.

"You know, we probably never would've gotten into that mess out in Littleburg if you'd had pants like those guys are wearing," Craig said.

"What do you mean?"

"Those big stupid looking pants with big pockets that close with velcro," Craig said.

"Yeah," I replied.

"The night from hell," Craig said.

The thought of that night dredged up a feeling of shame that I had long since buried. Of course there are other moments in my life I'm not especially proud of, but this one stands out as an ugly spot that won't wash away or even fade a little. I resented Craig bringing it up and at that moment I chose to ignore his comment. I didn't want to relive it with him, but my mind wandered back to that night in late May of 1971.

- - -

Craig, Razor and I had finished our junior year in college and were home for the summer. I remember that it was an unusually rainy spring. The tree branches were fully laden with vibrant green leaves that rustled against each other in the early evening breeze. I was enthralled with this beauty as I drove in my parent's station wagon east on Route 20A, trying to visually capture all that I could as we passed farms among the rolling hills.

"Watch the fucking road," Craig yelled from the back seat as the right side of the car dropped off onto the shoulder, throwing up a cloud of gravelly dust. "Let someone else drive if you want to take in the sights."

All the windows were open and the radio was turned up and we had bottles of cold beer in our hands. Our moods were high pitched with the new freedom of the coming summer and the broad horizon of possibilities it could offer. We were headed to a campout near a village called Littleburg, in Wyoming County. Friends of Craig's roommate organized this event, now the third annual and Craig had touted it as a "mini Woodstock" although he had never gone to either event. The back of the station wagon was packed with our gear and we planned on stopping at a restaurant in Sheldon called the Pepperwood Grill for a fish fry. Earlier we had stopped at Old Yeller for a couple to get primed, but back then it was never very comfortable as the regulars didn't like long hairs.

The parking lot at the Pepperwood was full and we had to wait at the bar for an available table. A plumpish, smiley waitress aptly called Bubbles knew Craig.

"What are you young lions up to," she asked, playfully pushing Craig's hair off his forehead.

"A little camping trip out near Littleburg," Craig said.

"You with that hippie outfit?" she asked.

"Yeah," Craig replied. "They come by here?"

"Sure did," Bubbles said. "Beads and all."

"When did they come through?" Craig asked. "How many were there?"

"Around noon or so," she said. "They stayed into the late afternoon until the dinner crowd started coming in. They were having quite a time, playing the jukebox and dancing – like they owned the place. I'll bet there was about thirty or so. Never saw so much hair in one place," she laughed. "Nice bunch though, friendly and they spent lots of money. That made the boss happy," she chuckled. "He was a little nervous when they first came in. Turned a few heads of these good old boys at the bar, but it turned out as sweet as Thanksgiving. I think old Fred Dugan got himself dusted off by one of the women," she said, pointing to a man wearing a John Deere hat sitting at the end of the bar. "She got old Freddy dancing and then they went outside to see her van. It was a pretty long tour if you know what I mean. You send women like that out here with all their goods showing and shaking and acting like it's there for the asking, why it rattles these farm boys out of their cages."

Bubbles told us this with her roundish face beaming and her eyes frisky and moving among us. I would guess she was about thirty-five back then, a real woman in my callow and dreamy estimation. As much as I was making a mental note regarding free women with the camping group, at that moment I would have given it up without hesitation to spend the weekend with Bubbles. Naively, I felt all my receiving senses pushed forward and alert, hoping to detect any form of attraction focused in my direction. But as luck would have it, she seemed more responsive to Craig and his double whammy questions.

"How's the fish tonight?" he asked. "Is the potato salad homemade?"

"The fish is great. I recommend the perch," she replied and added coyly, "The potato salad was made here this morning by yours truly and it's as fresh as you, sweet prince."

It killed me that he could get such a response by merely asking about the menu. I wanted desperately to say something, but my mind reacted like a stubborn child and hid itself. Razor was no better, crossing his arms and clawing at his elbows with a grin that seemed to be painted on his face. He had always been a little shy and at that moment I could empathize, but I felt more irritation as I pictured us as two dolts with our ankles chained to the floor and our mouths zipped shut. Craig was oblivious as always, just talking and laughing for the simple joy of it which in a strange way, made me feel better as I knew he had no romantic interest in Bubbles.

We had a couple beers at the bar while waiting for a table. I was beginning to feel a little drunk and I couldn't help eyeing Bubbles as she navigated between the tables. Her round and ample rump tightly bound in her short waitress uniform was indeed an appealing sight, made more delicious by the swishing sound of each step. I felt myself blush when she caught me staring and gave me a wink. I took a fair amount of ribbing for it at the table. Razor had laughed and I saw heads turning to decipher the strange sound. From the windows I could see the change outside, the solid glare of twilight, low and with little angle. Bubble's description of the group partying in the bar in the afternoon had fired our imaginations and created some anxiety that we were missing a great happening in progress. We ate quickly in determined silence and finished off the beer in long hungry gulps that frothed our lips and watered our eyes.

"Be good lads," Bubbles told us on the way out.

"Hope not," Craig had said.

Outside, the sun was dropping into the treetops to the west and the air felt cooler. Craig lit a joint. I only took a couple hits. As I drove down hills, the small margin of light would suddenly disappear in the rear view mirror and then return as I ascended. The new flash of light chased a line of shade up the hill. The creeping darkness was drawing in the interior of the car, a spatial shrinkage that cast my companions as more magnified, animated and shadowy. The view of the road ahead became vague in the waning light. I put on the headlights and the dashboard lights added a mysterious highlight to their features. Craig's forehead and cheekbones in the rearview mirror seemed to jump from his face.

"Come on, Razor," he complained. "Get that rinky-dink shit off."

Richard Harris was singing, *Macarthur Park*. I had been oblivious to the radio playing as my focus was single-minded on driving. Razor had turned up the radio and Craig suddenly reached over my shoulder to turn the station. Razor swatted his hand away and Craig flopped back in his seat.

"What the fuck, Razor," he said. "'Someone left the cake out in the rain...' - what kind of wimpy crap is that?"

"It's a metaphor," Razor said.

"I know it's a fucking metaphor," he said. "But it's shit."

"I like it," Razor replied. "It's nice."

"Nice?" Craig said. "I'm wasting a good buzz on nice."

"Just let it play," Razor said. "It'll end soon."

"Like hell," Craig said. "It's one of the longest songs ever made. '…and I'll never find that recipe again…' my God!"

I knew that Razor was buzzed because he was stubborn about hearing his song. Normally he might've yielded to Craig's request, given his generous nature, but I could sense his obstinacy as he turned up the volume when Craig began singing, *I Can't Get No Satisfaction.* All this noise ran wild in my mind.

"Cut the shit, you guys," I yelled.

Razor turned down the radio and Craig gripped my shoulder.

"Easy man," he said. "What's wrong?"

"I'm just fucked up and you guys aren't helping," I said.

"You want me to drive?" Craig asked. "I'd love to pilot this big 'ole boat over these tall sodden waves."

My first impulse was to turn over the wheel to him, but his attitude was too casual and I considered the possibility of accompanying carelessness. Also, I interpreted challenge in his offer and I gathered myself with renewed determination.

"Just keep it down," I said.

"I think we're almost there," Craig said. "We should be able to see their campfires before we get to the village. That's what I was told."

Within a few moments we were descending the hill that led into Littleburg. In the distance there was a small twinkling of lights where the road narrowed into the village, but the surrounding countryside was vague and drained of color. The setting sun was out of sight behind us, offering a reddish smear in the settling darkness.

"Pull over there," Craig said, his arm reaching past my head and pointing across the road to the opposite shoulder by an open field. I pulled over and turned off the station wagon. The air had turned cooler and I shivered as I got out. Razor put on his denim jacket and Craig put on the army jacket he recently purchased at Goodwill. I walked through the grass to take a piss. The field sloped downward, wide and expansive until it seemed to disappear in a dark fuzzy crease that was probably foliage bordering a creek. Beyond, the landscape was thickly wooded; a broad valley stretched away and upward toward dark, rolling hills.

"You see anything?" I heard Craig ask.

"Not really," Razor said.

I was enjoying the momentary freedom from the responsibility of driving, hoping the cool air would smack some clarity into my head. In the distance I could see small points of light, but nothing that resembled campfires. I headed back to the car where Craig and Razor were smoking cigarettes.

"Don't see any fires," Razor said. "What'll we do now?"

"Go down to the hotel," Craig said. "My buddy, Brian said it might be hard to find, but we could get directions there."

"Alright," I said, fishing in my pockets for the car keys. I checked my two front pockets and then the back.

I checked again.

"Are they in the ignition?" I asked Craig who had gotten in.

"Nope," he said.

I opened the door and looked on the floor and felt under the seat.

"Must've dropped them when you took a leak," Craig said.

Razor pulled a flashlight from his pack and handed it to me. I switched it on and followed the beam a few feet in front of me toward the area where I had relieved myself. I moved the light around and shuffled my feet in the tall grass. After a while Craig and Razor walked out, but our search was fruitless.

"I don't fucking believe this," Craig said.

He raised his hand in my direction, palm up, as if offering me to an imaginary buyer as damaged goods. I felt around my person again.

"Guess we better get down to the hotel," Razor said. "If we can find out where the campsite is, we can get someone to pick up our gear. Come back in the morning to find the keys."

"Yeah," Craig said.

"I'll stay here with our stuff," I said. "Really be dumb to lock the doors."

"You mean dumber," Craig said.

"Forget it," Razor said. "Let's go, Craig."

I sat on the hood smoking as I watched them disappear into the darkness of the wooded road that led into the village. Then I saw them under streetlights before they crossed the road and entered the hotel. At first I felt some relief in their absence, a reprieve from feeling foolish, but there was little comfort as paranoia began slinking into my frail and warped consciousness. I slid off the hood and got in the station wagon behind the steering wheel with the intent of starting the engine to turn on the heater and the radio. My only consolation was this stupid idea hadn't been shared. I stretched out on the front seat to await my friends' return.

- - -

"Looks like a hopping place," Razor said as he and Craig crossed the road in front of the Littleburg Hotel.

"Yeah," Craig said. "I've never seen so many pickup trucks in one place."

"You sure we'll be okay in here," Razor said.

"Shit yes," Craig said. "Brian said they always came in here. He said the owner was a good guy and let them use the bathroom and gave them free ice for their coolers."

Razor followed Craig up the stairs across the wide front porch and inside the open door. Craig stopped and looked around the large room, his head bobbing to the jukebox music, *Charley Pride singing,* Kiss an Angel Good Morning. *To their immediate right was a pool table with a few men scattered around it. A lamp hanging from the high ceiling cast a green haze over the smoky area above the table where a man was crouched to shoot, now stopping to look at them. He straightened up and the other men followed his gaze. Craig was oblivious as he took in the rest of the room.*

"C'mon," he said to Razor, heading to the bar where two women were smiling at him.

"Hey," he said. "What's happening?"

"You're seeing it," the closest woman said.

Craig nodded and pushed the long drape of his hair over his ear.

"Who does your hair?" she said.

"Mother Nature," Craig said.

"She treats you better than me," she said, tilting her head to one side, causing the, bleached blonde hair to shift behind her neck. "I get a little help from the salon down the street."

"I'd say a perfect collaboration."

The compliment brought her mouth open, an authentic smile that displayed her bad teeth. Razor stood quietly next to Craig, thinking it was poor timing for Craig to be turning on the charm. The men around the pool table had stopped playing. He felt their eyes on them. Razor pulled lightly on Craig's sleeve and Craig stepped back and placed his arm over his shoulder.

"This is my buddy, Razor," he said. "I'm Craig."

"Mary Sue," she said. "And this is Darlene."

Razor nodded. Darlene offered a small wave. Her hair was dark and pulled back in a ponytail.

"Getcha' beer?" Craig said. "Wanta' refill?"

Mary Sue turned to her friend who shrugged her shoulders and turned back to Craig.

"Sure," she said.

Craig waved to the bartender, a large man with a full beard and a crew cut. He turned slowly and his sour expression didn't change as he approached.

"Yeah?" he said.

"Can we have a round here?" Craig said.

"Got I.D.?"

Craig pulled out his wallet and opened it and presented it to the bartender.

"Take it out."

Craig slid out his driver's license and handed it to him. He looked at the card and at Craig.

"Hard to tell with all that hair," he said. "Got anything else?"

Craig handed him his college I.D. and draft card. The bartender examined them and eyed Craig, shaking his head. He threw the cards on the bar and took Razor's and regarded him with the same scrutiny and contempt.

"Drinking?" He said flatly.

"Same as the girls," Craig said.

"Jesus," Craig said, after the beers arrived, "Feel like I'm from Mars."

"You college guys?" Mary Sue said.

"Yeah, in Buffalo" he said. "How about you?"

"We're from around here," she said. "What brings you out here?"

"Came out to do some camping," he said. "We ran into some car trouble up the hill. You know of a group camping around here? Might've come in here earlier."

"Nope," she said. "We just came in before you guys."

"That guy the owner?" Craig said, pointing toward the bartender.

"Yeah," she said.

"Strange," he said, remembering what his friend, Brian had told him. "What's his name?"

"Sam."

"Hey Sammy," Craig called out.

Sam was sitting on a stool by the cash register. When he recognized who was calling him, his bottom lip puckered out over his beard as if he was remembering a terrible meal.

"What?"

"Would you come here?" Craig said, beckoning with his hand.

Razor was feeling an increased uneasiness as he watched Sam lift himself off the stool and lumber toward them. The beer in his hand was warm and he didn't think it was an oversight. Craig seemed heedless as he took a long swig and waited with a big smile for Sam. Razor wished he'd been more prudent with his appetite. Craig had talked him into this trip as "the perfect medicine to shake off the cobwebs" – illustrating a pastoral scene, "all natural, no hassles" he remembered him saying. Regret was the useless emotion he now felt as he regarded Craig who was clueless that he might be working against the wind.

"What?" Sam said, his beefy hand stretched on the bar.

"You know Brian?"

"Brian who?"

"Brian, the guy with the group that's camping around here. They come every year, camp in the woods."

"Those assholes," Sam said. "So you're with them."

"Well, kinda," he said. "We were coming up to meet them, but we had some car trouble up the road. Brian said that if we couldn't find them, to come in here, ask you. He said you were a

pretty good guy, that you let them use the restrooms and gave them ice."

"Tell you what," Sam said, flexing his fingers and moving his face close to Craig's. "I don't know any Brian, but if I did I wouldn't piss in his mouth if his tonsils were on fire. That bunch came in here today and we turned them away."

Sam pointed in the direction of the pool table to emphasize "we" and Craig turned his head, took a look at them, too long for Razor's comfort and turned back to Sam.

"What'd they do?"

"What'd they do?" Sam mimicked. "They didn't get a chance to do noth'n. Fuck'n fairy assholes ain't welcome here and you ain't either."

"Easy," Craig said. "I'm only... "

"Don't easy me," Sam said and pointed his thick finger at Craig's forehead. "I said, git."

"Okay," Craig said, raising his hands and stepping back. He gave a little nod to Mary Sue and Darlene and turned toward Razor who had started to move. The group from around the pool table followed them out the door, stopping on the porch as Razor and Craig retreated down the stairs and crossed the road. Craig stopped on the opposite shoulder and lit a cigarette, a move that baffled Razor who was in full stride and actually skidded to a stop in the loose gravel.

"What?" He said incredulously.

"You think they scared them off?" Craig said. "You think they might still be out there?"

"Do you?" Razor said. "And if they are, how're we going to find them?"

"Fuck," Craig said and stared across the street.

"Who you looking at, pretty boy," one of them said.

"Come on," Razor said, pulling on Craig's elbow.

Craig started walking. He heard something said about holding hands and laughter from the porch as he widened his gait to keep up with Razor.

"I hate taking shit from these fuck'n hillbillies," he said.

"I know," Razor said.

They were in a full stride, halfway up the hill when they heard the same voice from the group, "You look like you shit out of trees."

Craig stopped and turned.

"You look like you'd stand under me."

Razor pulled Craig by the sleeve. They heard the intense shuffle of feet down the stairs of the porch, the opening and slamming of truck doors, engines igniting and the sincere and joyful delivery of physical threats from drunken mouths. Tires skinned the pavement, screeches that pierced the cool, night air. They continued trudging up the hill, neither one looking back, but hearing their approach with headlights running past them that threw wavy shadows of themselves, stretching up the road.

- - -

I have no idea how long I was out, but I remember how terribly rude the awakening had seemed in the dark station wagon – flashes of light splashing the ceiling like fireworks and sounds of revved engines, horns and loud voices. I had been flat out on my back and I sat up and peeked over the dashboard. I could see the dark figures of my friends coming up the hill, their bodies haloed from headlights behind them. The air seemed to vibrate with noise and I could tell by the gruff bark of voices that they were in trouble. There were at least three vehicles lined up behind them and a pickup truck was suddenly passing them and skidded to a stop next to them. I saw figures climbing out of the bed before I ducked down under the steering wheel.

- - -

265

When the pickup truck pulled up next to them and they heard feet hitting the road, they stopped. The first man from the truck punched Craig with a wide right that landed above his left ear. Craig spun with the impact and cart wheeled awkwardly to the ground. Another man stepped in and kicked him in the head. Craig covered his head and was then kicked in the stomach.

"What a yah say now, pretty boy?"

Razor had moved to pull the man off Craig, his effort thwarted by two men grabbing each of his arms. The walked him backwards and pinned him roughly against the cab of the pickup truck. He was slapped hard across the face one way and backhanded the other

"You want what he's get'n?" one of them said.

"You have to make them stop," Razor said. "This is insane."

"You should of thought of that before you come traipsing into our place, trying to steal our women."

The man's voice seemed too high-pitched for his size. He was fat, with rings of jowl shifting below his chin. The comment about stealing women was too absurd for Razor and he impulsively laughed.

"What the fuck?" the fat man said, surprised at the strange sound and finally recognizing it as laughter. "You think this is funny, asshole?"

"I don't accept that salutation as a form of criticism," Razor said.

"Fuck'n dipshit," he said, grabbing Razor's jacket by the lapels and pulling him within inches of his face.

"I don't accept that either," Razor said, his chin up and his eyes trained on the other man's eyes.

"Ya don't huh," he said, bringing up his knee into Razor's crotch. "How do ya accept that?"

The fat man let go and Razor bent over and fell on all fours and vomited.

"Messy, messy," the fat man said.

He moved around to Razor's side in a mocking, tiptoeing gait, seized a handful of Razor's hair and flung him against the side of the truck. Razor felt something in his shoulder release as he slid down and rolled on the ground, settling on his back. The fat man rested a heavy boot on his chest and looked down at him.

"You accepting now?"

Razor retched to his side and looked over at Craig whose back was to him in the fetal position. Between them was a small forest of denim clad legs and worn boots.

"Get up you fuckers," the fat man said.

Craig managed to wheel his head over and looked at Razor.

"Git up," the fat man said, "or we'll boot ya some more."

Razor rolled onto his stomach and pushed up on his hands and knees, the one arm painful and useless. The fat man again grabbed his hair, pulling his head back, forcing him to stand up. Craig was trying to get up, but balked on his knees and the fat man nodded to two of the group and they yanked him to his feet. He struggled to free himself and the fat man motioned another man to attend to Razor as he went over to Craig and grabbed him around his chin and squeezed.

"You don't stop this shit, we're gonna bust ya into pieces."

"Craig," Razor said. "Ease up."

Craig twisted his head, shaking off the fat man's grip and looked over at Razor.

"You gotta stop," Razor said.

The fat man re-gripped Craig's face and bent his head back.

"You should listen to your friend," he said.

He must have felt the release of tension in Craig's face, because he let go and wiped his hands on his pants.

267

"What you want to do with 'em now, Steiny?" one of them asked the fat man.

"Send them on their way," Steiny said, tugging his pants up close to his hanging belly. "You turn that car around and go back where you came from."

"We lost the keys," Razor said. "That's why we're here."

"Then get walking," Steiny said. He pointed at Craig. "But first, take off that jacket. Ain't got no right wearing military eh' tire."

"It's my brother's," Craig lied. He looked into Steiny's eyes.

"That so?" Steiny said. "Where'd he serve?"

"He was in the National Guard," Craig said.

"Oh, I see," Steiny said. "Some dangerous place like Niagara Falls? He hung stateside, prob'ly fuck'n our women while we was get'n our asses shot at."

Razor knew all this had nothing to do with anything, but the entertainment of a bunch of bored and ignorant men.

"Leave the jacket," he said. "Just leave the fucking jacket."

Craig regarded Razor who shook his head and looked to the ground. He slipped off the jacket and flung it on the road and peered into Steiny's eyes.

"Don't you eyeball me," he said, throwing an open palm against Craig's chest. "You turn away right now and start walking."

Craig shot a glance at Razor and turned and started walking away. Razor followed, his right arm across his chest and squeezing his left shoulder to alleviate the pain.

"Night ladies," he heard from the group behind.

Razor caught Craig's eye, a warning that shit was the only thing on the menu right now.

"What about him?" Craig whispered as they approached the station wagon.

"Just keep walking," he said. "Let him be."
They walked past the car, their eyes trained on the ground ahead of them.

- - -

I saw their heads move the length of the car. I heard laughter; the townies reliving the scuffle like teammates in a bar after a ballgame. Then doors opened and closed. I waited while the headlights that were pooled on the ceiling of the car turned away and I heard the vehicles go back down the hill into the village. When I finally sat up, all was quiet and very dark. I exited the car, foolishly forgetting the flashlight and jogged up the hill. I was immediately winded and slowed. My chest and throat were raw. The beating of my heart resonating throughout my body, which made it impossible for me to hear anything around me. I could feel the shoulder of the road become level and then downward, my gait changing to a braking lope that jarred my legs. The sky was black and I felt the damp wispiness of fog, giving me a sensation of moving inside a closed closet.

I wasn't sure how long I had waited, so it was hard for me to judge how far ahead they were. I continued as fast as possible and struggled to diffuse the vexing panic marking my concealed progress. Ahead was the sound of moving water and I remembered the creek that was slung in a hollow between two long hills. I saw the metal structure of the bridge seconds before I embarked on it, but I stopped as another sound intermingled with the voluble rush of water. I lowered myself to one knee, gripping the rail of the bridge, straining my eyes and ears to determine the sound that was sharp and intermittent. It was Craig cursing and throwing up. I advanced quickly, calling out to them.

"We were going to get back to you," Razor quickly said. "The townies railroaded us out, beat us up. We thought it best to keep you out of it."

So, what was I going to say at that point? Razor looked at me in earnest, seeking forgiveness that I thought they had forsaken me. But Craig turned his head from over the bridge railing and regarded me. His face was swollen on one side.

"You must've been pretty out of it," he said.

I nodded and returned his gaze, but I was relieved when another spasm of nausea turned him over the rail of the bridge. Razor filled me in on the details of the confrontation, but we all fell silent as Craig waved us on and we followed him up the next hill. About a half hour later we saw the headlights coming down behind us. We were next to a stretch of woods and I was tempted to run and hide among the trees, but Craig and Razor kept on without turning their heads. The car passed us, but suddenly the brake lights flashed and it came to a skidding halt. The back-up lights shown white as the car, a small Fiat, backed toward us.

"Guys want a lift?"

Razor climbed carefully into the backseat, angling his injured shoulder first and sliding to the other side behind the driver. I followed him and Craig eased himself into the front. The driver was a young man and looked directly at me in the back seat.

"Who are you?" he said. "You weren't there."

"What the fuck," Craig said. "You were with those assholes?"

"Wait a minute," the young man said, raising his hands. "No, I wasn't with them, but I was there."

"Well, thanks for the help," Craig said, opening the door and stepping out.

"Whoa, wait a minute," the young man said. "Sorry I'm not such a stupid shit as you."

Craig stopped half way out the door. I saw his eyes go wild under the ceiling light of the car.

"Craig!" Razor said, through grimaced teeth.

"Alright," Craig said.

He shifted himself back into the seat and pulled the door closed.

"I was in the bar," the young man said. "Next to the chicks you were talking to. I stayed there when they all came after you. Sorry, but I ain't no fool. I've seen Sam and his brother in action before. They're mean motherfuckers."

"Wouldn't have been much without his gang," Craig said.

"I wouldn't be too interested in testing that theory," he said. "Those guys like breaking bones and kicking ass. I'm surprised you look as good as you do."

The young man shifted gears quickly as the car sped up the hill, the velocity a little much for the limited vision, I thought. He told us his name was Jerry and he had recently moved to Littleburg, but his mother lived in our hometown. He was going to visit her, which I thought odd given that it was so late, but he said his stepfather, whom he hated, worked third shift. He told us his mother was taking care of his daughter, a two year old. He didn't mention the child's mother, but he made it clear that the arrangement was temporary, "until I get my feet planted," he said. Jerry asked about the abandoned station wagon and Craig told him how I had lost the keys.

"Where were you during all the action?"

"Passed out in the car," Craig said and I saw Jerry lift his eyes in the mirror.

I asked him when he was heading back to Littleburg. He said after a short visit to his mother's apartment. I told him I'd give him some gas money if he would take me back after I retrieved the spare keys from my parents' house.

"I'll do it for a ten-spot and a full tank of gas," he said.

I agreed, a little irritated at the opportunistic price, but I settled back in the seat, relieved that there was an end in sight. It took almost an hour through the dark and winding, fog laden road to get back. Jerry talked the whole time, about a variety of subjects that neither Craig nor Razor responded to. I listened quietly, answering only when necessary. The only information I found interesting was Jerry's discussion of Sam and his brother, Steiny. They were actually twins (not identical) and had served together in Vietnam. They were natives of Littleburg and after discharge from the army, a little less than a year ago, Sam had purchased the hotel. Of course I hadn't seen either of them, a fact that Jerry must have forgotten, because he continued as if we were talking about family members at a reunion.

"Steiny's the real sicky one," Jerry said. "He's got color pictures from Nam, lots of them, of dead gooks, like hunting trophy pictures. He carries them in his pocket and shows them around."

"You've seen these pictures?" I had to ask.

"Sure I've seen them," Jerry said. "You think I'd refuse look'n at 'em?"

"Guess not," I responded, wondering what I'd do.

I remember reading an article in *TIME* about similar situations; the article called these atrocities "casual brutality" and showed a photograph of a soldier holding the severed head of a Vietcong by the hair. He was smiling as if he was hefting his bowling ball bag and it was league night. The memory and this new and nearer account gave me a chill. That my friends had been victims of such a man was horrifying and I wondered naively how close they'd come to serious injury or even death. I was sure there must be a point of no return, but couldn't begin to comprehend where that was or what exactly led up to it. My experience with violence was exclusively from the safety of TV. Even on this particular night I had again been spared. I must've drifted off with this thought, because soon we were pulling into Mullen's gas station.

Jerry pulled up to the pump and turned off the motor.

"Glad we made it," he said. "Been riding on empty the last few miles."

Craig opened the door and slowly got out. He pushed the seat forward and I climbed out and helped Razor.

"You got the money," Jerry asked me.

"Yeah."

As I slid my hand in to locate my cash, my thumb grazed across something solid above the pocket opening. To this day I don't know what it's called although I've been told it's a pocket watch pocket or a change pocket. It's that three inch by three inch square pocket between the right front pocket and waist band of a pair of Levis. It's the reason they're called five pocket jeans. As it turned out, this pocket that I've never paid any attention to, ignored as if being superfluous, snugly housed the keys to my parents' station wagon.

"What the hell," Craig said as I pulled them out.

There was nothing funny about it. You'd have to be a moron to think it was funny. I guess I rest my case, as Jerry started to laugh, pointing at me and looking around, I guess to have some sort of an audience to witness such an idiotic affair.

"I don't believe it," he said. "Those guys got their asses kicked because your keys got lost in that little pocket? I don't believe it!"

Razor had simply shaken his head. He and Craig walked across Main Street and down South Willow toward Craig's parents' house. I handed Jerry some cash and sat in the car while he fueled it up. I could hear him chuckling and when he got back in the car he looked at me and exploded in laughter.

"Too much, man," he said. "Your buddies didn't look too happy."

I guess there was a fair measure of justice in the next few hours I had to endure with Jerry. We drove to the other side of the village, an upper flat where his mother sat at the kitchen table under the garish blaze of an overhead light. She was smoking a cigarette and drinking whiskey in a pink, plastic glass. By the end of the night I was to fully understand why Jerry was such a stupid shit even though I finally fell asleep amid a miscellany of arguing, accusing, cursing and crying.

He woke me at the seeping light of dawn by kicking my foot, I guess a sensible way to rouse someone if you don't know his name. Silently in his car we shared the gray-tinged morning light as the sun slid up behind the hills before us, heading east on 20A.

- - -

That was my recollection as I looked across the table at Craig. In deeper and quieter moments as I drilled down into the history of my life, this episode always comes up muddy with a stench of decay – the pale yellow dreariness and the slow pulse of shame that is difficult to expel. Actually, it struck me as remarkable how little I had brought it up for review all these years. I had somehow insulated myself by continually pushing it deeper as if the denseness and distance of time could eventually render the episode as fiction. Well, here it was again as vivid as a moment ago. I was thankful Craig had merely commented on it, because I might've been tempted to confess my cowardice.

The rain continued throughout the afternoon and basically everyone in the place became drunk while I remained sober. Craig finally left after we exchanged promises to keep in touch. The old regulars, who had been awkward and nervous at the church and cemetery, were leaning against the bar – neckties loosened, collars open and jackets piled over vacant chairs. Now their eyes were alive and there were bottles and upside down shot glasses lined in front of them. Crumpled bills and scattered change lay on the bar; cigarettes were left smoldering in ashtrays as smoke rose and clouded under the high ceiling.

Their voices rose in varying cadence, perhaps a strange example of the flaws of natural selection as the loudest and deepest voices drowned out the weaker ones although they were not always the wisest. Many stories of Shoes' life had been recalled and rebuffed – faces puckered with righteous authority, fingers emphatically stabbing the air. There was much of the local stuff that was common knowledge, but so much was simply conjecture and it made me realize he was not quite the local fixture we had perceived. It also made me realize how little we actually knew about him.

I know for certain he had lived in Florida for a while and from there he'd gone to Texas and Colorado. I remember he'd been gone a long time. And sometime afterward California and then Alaska for varied periods of time, but I couldn't recall exactly when or why he went. He would be gone and then he'd just be back and he seemed to blend into the flow of life here. I'd run into him in the earlier years when I had the painting business. Sometimes he'd work for me and then he wouldn't and I'd see him on the street or a local tavern. If anything, the inability for me to pinpoint his whereabouts at any specific time reflects how mundane and self-centered my life was. I guess it's simply convenient for me to picture Shoes sitting on a local bar stool, his chin high and his old felt hat tight over his ears, engaged in drunken conversation. So why should I expect it to be any different from others that knew him?

I became perplexed with the idea that I had never seen him arrive or leave anywhere with a companion. This was a strange and troubling vision; as if, for some reason I was trying to paint him as lonely. I knew it was false and yet it tormented me into coming up with a concrete example to negate it. It brought to mind the idea that even our memories are tarnished by our attitudes and these attitudes are unconsciously contaminated by our quick assessments and conclusions based on little information. And yet we feel the confidence of an expert in measuring another's life. Such arrogance, I thought, remembering the condescending remarks I'd heard the last few days. Would all these people somehow benefit the death of this man with their self-righteous comparisons?

Finally, I settled on the memory, not of Shoes and another, but rather him and me walking out of Jason Dunbar's apartment the rainy night of his party, after he had toppled the sound system. His face was lit up by the streetlights as we hurried over the wet sidewalk to my car. He was breathing loudly and kept looking back toward the house. At first I thought he was afraid of being followed, but he slowed down and then stopped.

"I can't believe I did that," he said.

"Me neither."

"It felt wonderful," he said.

"I bet," I said, but I didn't have a clue.